OCTOBER FIRE

OCTOBER
FIRE

ELEANOR
MAYO

REBEL SATORI PRESS
Bar Harbor • New Orleans

Originally published by
Thomas Y. Crowell Company

ISBN: 978-1-60864-048-5

Rebel Satori Press
P.O. Box 363
Hulls Cove, ME 04644

OCTOBER FIRE

CONDITION 1. LOW FIRE DANGER

CONDITION 2. WOODS DRY—BE CAREFUL

CONDITION 3. WOODS VERY DRY—BE
CAREFUL

CONDITION 4. DANGER

CONDITION 5. EXPLOSIVE—EXTREME—
TINDER DRY

THE SPRING was a wet one—rain every day—great downpours lasting twenty-four hours at a stretch, until the earth trickled like a stepped-on sponge. The day that dawned fair as the inside of a mussel shell at four o'clock was deluged and inundated by eleven.

On July nineteenth it rained for half a day, hard, then cleared. Then nothing. There was no more rain.

People all over the Peninsula were glad to see the sun. The season was an ideal one for the summer visitors. From the middle of July there was never a day when they had to stay indoors. The wind boxed the compass as it usually did, but any direction meant fair. The land was as lovely and as lost and as unbelievable as a Maxfield Parrish picture.

The bulletin board at the Frenchville firehouse, behind the village green, officially registered the inevitable approach of the dry season. In August the red warning figure changed from normal 2 to warning 3.

By September fifteenth leaves started to drop, rustling dryly across parched lawns. An early fire season was on the countryside.

There had been fires in the fall before. Tiz Arey, resentfully examining her thirsty garden, smelled woods' smoke and thought little of it. One year there had been a fire back of Hio Lake that burned underground from August until the November rains took care of it. She remembered the year well, less because of the fire than because that was the year her nephew Mike had left town instead of settling down and getting married as she had been expecting him to do. Wondering again what had ever happened between him and Ginny Hanscom, Tiz forgot the smoke.

The red figure on the board at the firehouse changed from 3 to horrifying 4.

In October, after the first cold snap, Indian summer settled in—an Indian summer such as nobody could ever remember. Mike Arey came home to a month of misty, warm, gentle weather with soft winds and nights as mild as mid-August. And everywhere there was the smell of smoke.

Some of it came from a stubborn, little smudge fire that started on the first of October near the Sanger town dump and traveled from there into what was, in a decent season, a low, marshy area well behind the town. It was dry and springy underfoot this year, and fire struck deep into a substance like peat. When it burned deep there was little to do but watch it and take care of the occasional outbreaks.

Driving up the Barrett's Harbor road, Jay Stone, Frenchville's first selectman, would think of it uneasily, seeing a faint veil of something too thin for smoke, too thick for mist, drifting sullenly westward before the wind. But there were twelve safe miles between Frenchville and Sanger.

On October twelfth Allen Carter, the fire chief, came slowly across the crackling brown grass of the village green. It was a warm morning, but he felt cold as he took down

2

the red 4 and put up a number he had never used before. Grim faced, he stood back to look at it. There it was, irrevocable and disastrous.

CONDITION 5—EXPLOSIVE—EXTREME— TINDER DRY

PART ONE

Fair today and tomorrow. Winds gentle easterly, shifting to increasing onshore twenty to twenty-five miles per hour late tomorrow afternoon.

MIKE AREY'S forehead came down with a star-raising thud against the big steering wheel to which he was clinging with both hands. At the shock he jerked awake with a wry grin slitting wearily across his face.

"Good thing I wasn't going anywhere," he said aloud, trying with the sound of his voice to shut away the encircling sleep. Its dark, lovely shadow advanced and retreated behind his squinted eyes and he would have liked nothing better than to put his abused forehead down on that hard wheel and sleep forever.

Three days of struggling against that ever-advancing wall of flames—flames that rushed through the tops of the spruces flashing a mile in five minutes, then, as the wind's force lessened, surged through the underbrush or drove deceitfully underground—had left him more exhausted than he had ever been in his life.

He stared into the night along the ribbony, pale concrete, finding it difficult to focus his eyes on anything. Once he had begun to concentrate, he could make out the bull-like rear of the next fire truck a hundred yards to the north.

4

The pumper Mike sat in was unfamiliar to him. It belonged to the Barrett's Harbor Volunteer Fire Department and it had been down here on the fire line since the fire had blown up. If the wind had shifted to the south, this long, straight stretch of road backed by fields would have been the one place where they might have stopped the rolling wall of fire that would have come up out of the heart of the Peninsula. There were more men and two more trucks on the line tonight, though Mike could see no signs of them. Weary quiet lay uneasily over the road that had been the lifeline of the Peninsula. Far to the west the water was darkly luminous beyond the black stretch of cleared land.

A rustle in the dry weeds at the road shoulder and Powder Tilton's thin, anxious voice preceded his shadowy figure out of the darkness.

"You see anything, Arey?"

"Not a thing, Powder." Glad even of such company, Mike leaned out. "I can't see anything you can't."

"God knows, that's enough." Powder's voice didn't change and, in spite of darkness, it made Mike see the habitual, colorless anxiety of the man. "I thought I heard you say something."

"You probably did," Mike conceded. "I'm having one hell of a time staying awake."

"*I* don't feel's if *I* could ever go to sleep again and sleep sound," Powder said virtuously.

"Well, I don't know. I feel kind of relaxed. I guess no matter how bad anything is and how hard you work to keep it from happening, when it finally does you can't help being relieved. Stands to reason it can't happen again— for a while anyway. Touch wood."

Powder's face came into range of the dim parking lights.

5

Mike saw the small, squinting eyes, looking red instead of pink, and the tight, lower face with the jaws narrowing into a beak.

"Depends, kind of, on what you've lost, don't it?" Powder said shortly and moved away.

Guess that puts me in my place, Mike thought. He sat watching Powder's stooped shadow move up the road. Powder's large head was heavy for the thin neck. Like a melon grown too big for its vine, it hung forward, hauling him along at a quick, uncertain jog.

Thoughtfully Mike dug a cigaret from the crumpled pack in the pocket of his blue shirt. At the flare of the match, Powder stopped and turned deliberately to stare. As deliberately Mike held the match to his cigaret and let it burn down in his fingers until Powder moved slowly away.

The flickering match flame surrounded Mike in the cab of the truck with twinkling points of light reflected from every polished knob and surface. His glance found the rear-view mirror and his own black eyes. He stared with dreamily interested vanity at his reflection. The eyes looking back at him out of deep, bony sockets were feverishly bright. The straight, too-long, too-thin nose had sharpened. The heavy-lipped mouth, the underlip as red as a girl's, was thinned with tension and he could see the little ball of muscle come and go at the point of his jaw. His jutting chin, accentuated by the four-days' growth of black beard, looked jowly. Impatiently he flicked with his free hand at the thick forelock of rough hair that hung over his low forehead.

The heat of the match flame grew unbearable on his fingers. He tossed the burned stub in his cupped hand until he could hold its head with ease and flipped it out the window.

The acrid, windless night flowed back in on him and he looked with habitual care at the place where the horizon would be a little later.

For a long time he would not look to the east without seeing the red death pouring down the hills, as liquid as water, in a great curtain of flame so high it might have come downward from the hostile sky rather than up from the once friendly earth.

He would hear for a long time the sirens shrieking in the little, lost towns in the night. He could hear, at this moment, through the hushed, waiting darkness, the steady thud of pumpers to the east and south. It was nearly dawn and there should have been a chill in the quiet air; but it was as warm as midsummer.

Mike closed his eyes and could see behind the lids the thick, block figures on the bank calendar that hung under the clock shelf in his Aunt Tiz's kitchen. October 16.

Three days ago, at three o'clock in the afternoon, he had stood there in the familiar room staring at the clock above that calendar, unable to make up his mind whether to take it or leave it there.

Outside the window a northeast wind had snarled at the branches of the old Spy tree and the twigs were like thin, bony fingers tearing helplessly at the glass.

Everything in that room was in its proper place and the things had the worn, polished look of neat self-possession Tiz had given to her life. But the clock meant time and Mike felt it should go with her.

"Mike," she'd said quietly from the door. "You better come, I think. The smoke's getting awfully strong."

"The clock, Tiz!"

"Not one thing goes out of this house. Everything that's here belongs, and here it'll stay. If I ever come back into it again, I want to find it just the way it is right now."

She stood, lean and tall, contained and nervous, in the door, and when he went out through the wind-flattened grass, Mike heard her close and lock it behind him. She brought nothing but the big, ventilated cat-carrier, through the holes in which Satan kept poking a huge, offended forepaw.

The road he drove that afternoon had once been so familiar to him he could have driven it with his eyes closed and with his car steady as a good horse on the way home to stable. This trip robbed it of all familiarity. Everything that was known and customary to his entire life was exploding in wind and horror behind him.

He was tired with a week of unavailing fire fighting and two climactic days of completely hopeless struggling, and his foot was uncertain on the accelerator. The Chevy's nose kept creeping up on the rattling tailgate of the wood truck ahead of him; then he would stab for the brake, slowing so quickly he could hear the screech from the brakes of the Ford sedan behind.

The cavalcade of cars slowed and stopped at the road block. Bill Woodstock got out of the Ford and came up to Mike.

"Mike," he said tautly. "Look, for God sake, will you please take it a little steadier? I've nearly piled up on your rear end four or five times now. Please, Mike—"

"Sorry. I get watching that in the mirror."

"Yeah, I know. But you'll get a close view of it soon enough."

Bill went quickly back to his car as the line started along. When the lead car rounded the turn toward Barrett's Harbor, Mike felt his breath get tight in his throat.

"I thought we were going over to Sanger," he said blankly.

"The way this wind's acting—" Tiz's voice was flat—"I guess they figure that's no better than Frenchville. It would be a waste of time, having to go through this twice."

They must be evacuating the whole Peninsula. Mike thought of the great tongue of land, two hundred and fifty square miles of it, emptied of people, the places men had worked out of the wilderness abandoned. The howling wilderness, his mind said. It was not what the original phrase had meant, but a howling wilderness just the same.

Mike fastened his eyes on the faces of the three children in the truck body ahead of him. They sat side by side on top of a heap of hard to identify belongings thrown in one after the other without a thought for what they were or how they'd ride. Round eyed as young owls, scared expressionless, the kids stared backward down the Peninsula with a blankness more revealing than any look of dismay would have been.

Once the long line of cars turned the corner by the traffic light in Barrett's Harbor, Mike had no more memory of what had happened. He knew he must have left Tiz at the auditorium and that he himself had gone back. Most of the men had.

He hadn't seen Frenchville since. He had been shoved off into the backlands and, when the fire had quieted there, he was among those hauled out to sit on that ridiculously inadequate fire line and wait. So he had nothing but hearsay to tell him what had happened in the little town on the shoulder of the point.

At first the reports that came up out of the Peninsula were fragmentary like the tapping responses of men imprisoned in a drowned submarine. Terrified and weary, men said the first things that entered their heads:

"Oh, it's all gone—"

"Wiped right off the face of the earth!"

"There ain't a thing left. Not a house standing."

Mike thought of the town as it had been and, he could see it in his mind more clearly than he ever had with his eyes. Safe and secure and tidy, lying along the ledge between the forest and the sea with the whale-backed hills behind it; land coming up from the water to the solid-rooted hills in a flowing curve.

Aghast he had listened to the reports, hardly able to make himself believe this had happened to him and to people he knew. It was like the impersonal vengeance of a God with an anger so large it could not be confined to a single sinner and so He punished the innocent too with the same force.

Hours later, when the fire was dying a writhing death and the men fighting it down there to the south really knew what had happened, the detailed truth came up to those who waited along the Barrett's Harbor road.

Mike's whole body, tense with his effort to let not so much as a syllable escape him, stung and throbbed as if living blood were flowing back into veins where water had been.

Life here would have been impossible if he could never again have come in through the channel in the darkening fall afternoons to see that row of white gables as clear and sharp and clean as a Greek frieze against the looming hills.

Mike opened his eyes hastily, surprised to find himself sitting there in the truck, aware that if he sat there a moment more with them shut, he would be asleep. This time he actually *saw* the hills, and the sight took a jump out of him before he recognized the light behind them as the coming of morning. The long, western slope of the fields

10

went down to the quiet water, shining faintly silver between him and the still dark islands. The gray bulk of the destroyer escort rode peacefully upon the breathless water, making pygmies of the lobster boats around her.

"The shooting's over," Mike said softly. "You boys can go home. We aren't going to need you after all."

He craned his neck to look down to the south. A low-lying pall of smoke over the trees was as quiet as mist. The griping sensation in his stomach meant there was something to be done and every nerve in his body pulled away from doing it. Perhaps if he went in the uncertain light of early morning, realization would come on him gradually with the daylight.

The heavy engine responded to his foot on the starter and its roar shattered the simulated peace that hung over the blue-gray morning. All up and down the length of concrete, men leaned and peered back at the articulate truck, apprehensively.

He rolled down to the largest pumper. Jay Stone, who was sitting behind its wheel, leaned forward to peer over at him. Jay's eyes, usually gray, looked as if they had been dipped into red ink.

"Hoy," Jay said. "Where you going, Paul Revere?"

"Looks pretty quiet down the line," Mike's grin was mechanical. "Thought I'd take a run down. See what it's really like."

"Well—" Jay hesitated and Mike saw the simplest decision was almost impossible for Jay, too. Immediately Mike felt better, knowing his own dismay was shared.

He edged the truck away slowly.

"Hey, wait." Jay tumbled out of the pumper's cab. "Wait. I'm coming, too."

After Jay climbed up beside him, Mike swung across

11

the road shoulder to turn in the field where the cars of the fire fighters were parked.

The road swerved sharply eastward and up into the first rolling slope of the hills. From it they could see only the woods against the paling sky and the long funnel of gray smoke. The truck slid into the shadow of the woods and it might have been midnight again. Mike leaned to switch on the powerful lights. Their glare picked the shambling figure out of the darkness ahead.

"Hey, there's Powder," Jay said unnecessarily. "I wondered where he went to. Better stop for him, I guess."

"Who's that driving?" Powder climbed into the seat. "Oh, it's *him*."

Unanswered, he sank into the corner. In a constrictive silence the three men rode toward whatever had happened to their lives through the silent, undamaged, explosive, October woods.

At first they might have been alone in a world drained of people and emotion; but as they neared the crest of the ridge above the last, long slope, the lights began to pick out slack-jointed walkers who stopped to stare as the engine passed them. Light flashed back whitely from distended eyes and stonily from the blades of axes and saws polished with recent hard use.

The trees thinned out and when the truck ground to a stop at the peak of the hill, daylight was stronger than it had been when they'd left the fire line. They sat staring unbelievingly down to the shining sea that had never before been so widely visible from here.

The thick, furry pelt of the land was gone. The hills lay like blackened porcupines behind the slopes, and the small patches of green that remained were brilliant as finished jewels stuck in a granite ledge.

12

From the rise where they sat—halfway down the big vertebrae of the hills—the country rolled steadily away to the south and west. South into a blue distance over ten miles of undamaged spruces to the invisible point where blue distance turned to blue water. West across the maimed town to closer, greener water. In the east, behind the spine that split the Peninsula from north to south, invisible to them, lay more wide miles of what had once been spruces. There, for nearly a week, like a wave gathering strength, fire had washed from the ocean to the bases of the hills, turned back on itself, and turned a third time with a gathering roar that carried it up over the dry mountains and across the narrow, bulldozed firebreaks with heartrending ease.

Half of Frenchville still lay on the last shoulder of ground above the water. It had always had a clinging look, as if the slightest shudder of the earth could have sent the houses sliding off over the edge.

To Mike the newly revealed roads looked like the fingers of a hand. The palm was the unburned village green. From it the fingers sprawled toward the water, some dotted with roofs, others marked too clearly by the space where roofs had been.

Looking down on it, he could see where the two-mile front of fire had come raging into the north end of town. It wasn't so easy to understand—if one couldn't remember how the wind had slammed from northeast to due east—why the fire had turned and sent licking tongues of destruction diagonally behind the green, past the brilliant steeple of the Congregational Church, in some places right to the water.

Jay took a deep, shaky breath.

"Hell, it ain't so bad—" he began heartily, but his voice broke. "Oh, God, what a mess!"

The heaving in Mike's stomach reached a pitch of regularity that told him what was going to happen. Blinded and staggering, he got out of the cab and around to the back. Clutching helplessly at the warm metal stanchions and gasping for breath, he was sick on the road.

The retching stopped finally and he wobbled uncertainly over to the shoulder to pull a handful of grass. When he bent to wipe off the toes of his shoes, he thought he wasn't going to be able to straighten up.

"Mike." Jay's steadying voice came across the spinning dark. "You all right, boy?"

"Oh, sure."

"Well, take it easy."

Too emptied out and weak to be ashamed of weakness, Mike came back to the cab.

"I don't know where it came from," he said wonderingly. "I haven't put that much into me in two days."

He wiped his streaming eyes while Jay stared steadily ahead.

"I don't see what *he's* got to be upset about!" Powder's snappish voice reminded them both that he was still there. "*He* never lost anything. Is *he* all right? Hanh! Better ask about somebody who's ruined. Better ask about me!"

Mike and Jay exchanged a thoughtful glance. Without noticing what he did, Mike lit a cigaret and drew the normal tasting smoke into his bitter throat.

"Put that damn thing out," Powder said softly.

Mike dropped the cigaret and rubbed it out on the floor-boards. He turned on the ignition and, shoving the truck into second, let her coast until the engine turned over. Beside them, like a Greek chorus, Powder's slow chant went on:

"Everything I ever had—gone—wiped out. I'm a ruined

14

man. And with nine kids. Winter coming on. Might's well be dead."

"Oh, shut up," Mike growled. "You aren't the only one."

He guided the truck into the north end of town, between rows of empty cellars. If there had been more than one way to come home, he wouldn't have been sure where he was.

"Was either one of you down here the night it went?" Jay said.

Mike shook his head and Powder was silent.

"I better warn you then. It's gone, right down to the Church. The wind changed there and the fire got freaky. Took a house, left another right next to it, and maybe burned one across the road. It come so fast they couldn't do a thing. They tried to blast a firebreak through by that parking space north of Bob Collier's. Put a couple of charges in his cellar and let them off. But the house was burning before they could set off the dynamite and they had to stop. It just spread the fire around more."

They idled past the Congregational Church, its white spire clean as snow, its golden weather vane gleaming.

"Don't know what saved that." Jay indicated the burned grass around the granite-block foundation and the brown blisters on the lowest clapboards.

The church door flew open and a black-clad figure, as incongruous as a crow, came flapping down across the browned lawn.

"There's the Reverend!" Jay said. "My gosh, he must have been here all through it. I don't remember seeing him go out."

The three of them sat looking seriously down at the small, unimpressive man who clutched the big spotlight and stared back at them. Usually he wore a pair of steel-

15

rimmed glasses, behind which his eyes were vague and spiritless; but the glasses were gone and the eyes, instead of losing presence, were as fanatical as the muzzle of a double-barreled shotgun.

"You shouldn't have stayed here, Mr. Perry," Jay said gently. "You might have gotten into real bad trouble."

"I stayed and I saw the working of a miracle." The minister's face was transfigured and his voice was the voice of a man who believes firmly in what he is saying.

"There!" He pointed a shaking finger at the sharp line beyond which the grass was black. "It stopped there! I was in the church praying when the fire came down across that field and no man's hand was turned to stop it; but it stopped. The Lord Himself worked a miracle to save this place for His children to worship Him."

"The wind changed," Mike said sharply, a little ashamed of himself in the face of such completely honest belief.

"Even the Lord," Perry said with gentle reproof, "needs some means to work His Wonders. I think He saw that even I might come to doubt Him and chose this way to let me see His Presence in the midst of the holocaust. He set His hand upon the whirlwind."

"When He did," Jay said, out of embarrassment and with no intention of being irreverent, "He had His hands full."

Powder was staring at the minister intently, his own face blank and his mouth slightly open in concentration.

Mike let the truck slide away, leaving the minister to look after them a moment before he turned back to his unburned church.

They passed the green with its still-standing buildings, the firehouse, the post office, the drugstore. Beyond the drugstore, Mike took the familiar right turn that led to the sea.

Since they had passed by the first ruined cellars, Mike hadn't raised his eyes beyond the immediate foreground to glance at the place where the ridge of Tiz's square, gray house broke the pallid sky. He couldn't make himself do it with Powder there watching him. He really couldn't believe it would be there if Powder's place, two houses away, was gone.

"Pardon me." Powder leaned across Jay's determinedly peaceable bulk. "You can let me out here if you will be so damned kind. In case it's escaped you, that cellar over there is all I've got left. I'd kind of like to go gloat over my possessions."

Jay watched him wade across the blackened field as if he waded through mud.

"I don't know but I better go with him," he said finally.

"I'll come, too."

"No, no!" Powder yelled, seeing them climb out of the truck. He started to run and so did Jay. Puffs of black, burned grass shot glittering into the air from under their pounding feet. More slowly Mike crossed the field and came up with them as they stood looking down into the cinder-filled cellar.

"Really, you shouldn't have come," Powder said. "I can't ask you in. The last company I had was careless with his cigarets and you can probably see the parlor's gone."

He glanced around and his eyes were visibly arrested by the only upright walls left. His woodshed, built at a distance from the barn, still stood, its silver shingles singed to a light tan.

"There's the guest house," he said. "I was really worried about it."

He started for the small pond where his white Pekins had grubbed for roots. One of them still floated on the cindery

17

surface with its white breast up and its yellow legs helplessly in the air.

"It's a relief to me to see the swimming pool's still here; but the swan seems to be a little worse for wear."

At the pond's edge he kept on going, lifting his feet almost clear of the shallow, riled water. When he reached the center where the water came only to his hips, he turned and faced the two men who were standing goggle eyed on the cracked, baked mud of the shore.

"Won't you join me?" he inquired carefully. "I think I'll stay here."

The strengthening sunlight unkindly revealed his white, peeled-looking, albino head. He made them a jerky, little bow and lay down in the muddy water. He sank at first and floated up again, flaccidly.

"*Do* something," Jay yelled. "The damn fool's drowning himself."

"I'll do it," Mike said grimly.

He reached Powder in four strides, grabbed him by the slack of his shirt and the seat of his pants, and lifted the slight body out of water. Powder didn't stir. Furiously Mike slacked up and sozzled him vigorously up and down. Powder went along limp as a sheet being given a thorough laundering.

"Drown, will you?" Mike's breath was short. "*I'll* give you drowning! *I'll* see you get water enough!"

On the fourth time up, Powder got back enough wind to yell.

"Let me up, you cussed fool! Whatta you trying to do, drown me?"

Mike's jaw dropped in surprise and he let go.

Powder scrabbled to his feet, streaming mud and water and yelling at Jay.

18

"Fine town official *you* are! Standing there and letting this crazy man drown me right in front of your face and eyes. By the holy old jumped-up judas, if I was the size of either one of you, I'd tear you apart. Now get out of here!" He turned on Mike and spit at him like a cat.

Mike came out of the pond and started across the field. He heard an enraged scream from Powder and then Jay's hurrying step. Involuntarily both men glanced back. Powder was still standing in the middle of the pond shaking his fists.

"Don't come back," he roared.

"Is he all right to leave?" Jay asked soberly. "He won't try it again, will he?"

"He meant right along for us to pull him out. I'd have been for waiting a little longer." Mike grinned sheepishly. "I must say, I seldom enjoyed anything the way I did that ducking."

"It seemed to me you were putting your soul into it." Jay's answering smile was fleeting. "I hope he's all right. If he does it again and we ain't around to pull him out, I'll hold it against myself the rest of my days."

"Depend on it, he won't," Mike said firmly. As they drove away, Powder was wading out of the water with the big duck's white body limp in his hands.

Next door to Powder's empty cellar, Jasper Hanscom's stand of buildings was only half of itself, as if somebody with a gigantic dull knife had sliced it in two and removed the detached barn like a piece of cake.

"That goes to show you what them asbestos shingles'll do," Jay said as if it proved a favorite argument. "Jasper got them on the house a month or so ago, before his wife died. When she got real bad, he didn't get around to shingling the barn."

Mike wasn't thinking about Jasper Hanscom. He was trying to make himself look to see if the last house above the sea still stood. His brain said yes; but everything else in him asked: How could it?

When he turned his head to look past the neat fence, he blinked once, as if he tried to clear dust out of his eyes. The house was there. Three hundred yards behind it the burned trees marked the stopping of the fire. The field was not burned at all.

"It's still there. *Look*, Jay!"

"But you knew that." Jay's face was patient but uncomprehending. "*I* knew it. You must have."

"I guess I never really believed it could be." Mike felt slackness flow over him like water, loosening all the tight muscles that had held him upright like a man.

He glanced across the field to see Eddie Hanscom come stepping airily through the back of his father's shed. Eddie was making wide, brushing movements with both arms as if there were cobwebs strung across the opening. But he was still doing it as he came slowly over to the truck.

"Glad to see you boys back again." His pleasant, young voice slurred over the syllables. "Come right in. *I'm* still here."

"*Oh*-oh!" When Mike hit the ground, muddy water squelched out through the cracks in his broken shoes.

Eddie's eyes widened. "Mike, you're all wet. Been wading?"

"More water than *you've* seen lately, I should judge."

"Let's not be like that," Eddie said peaceably. "Let's just all be happy here together. I'm so tired! I guess I'll just lie down here and have a nap. I'll feel better after that."

He took off his denim jacket, spread it carefully on the brown grass, and lay down.

20

"He's really done in," Jay said. "Did you see him stagger?"

"I saw him." Mike restrained a desire to give that lank, young rump a good kick. "He's not tired, though."

"I be blessed! Drunker than a hoot owl!" Jay pointed out the obvious with surprise.

"He'll sleep it off." Mike shook his head wearily. "Guess I'll go get Tiz. It'll be fairly safe here tonight. We got as good a firebreak as we could ever have, with the wind to the east."

Jay drove back to the fire line. Once or twice his head nodded and the truck swerved under his hands. Sitting there with his own head snapping back and forth to every jolt like a cattail in a stiff wind, Mike was beyond noticing further danger. After the last two years spent horsing the big refrigerator trucks up and down Route 1 from Portland to Boston three times a week, the resistance of these springs was like the rocking of a cradle.

Mike let out a snort of laughter at his own thoughts and Jay jumped nervously.

"I was just thinking." Mike answered the unspoken question. "When I came back here, I was worried for fear there wouldn't be enough going on. Not enough excitement."

"Well, we got this up specially for you. Wanted you to have a warm welcome."

The truck stopped at the parking field and Mike climbed out for the last time.

"I'm glad you didn't make it any warmer."

Jay's concession to kidding was over when he leaned forward.

"I think we better start riding patrols while the condition's still five," he said. "If there was another fire and we

21

could catch it young. Gorry, I get to feeling I could start one just rubbing two sticks together."

"All right with me," Mike agreed. "I'll ride any shift. What I'm scared of, a bunch of kids parking out in the field. They get drinking beer and throwing butts around."

As Mike started his car he was thinking with amazement how well he knew Jay Stone. It didn't take much of the stuff they had faced together this last week to make friends of men who, a week ago, were nothing but hello acquaintances.

Mike knew how Jay behaved when he was too tired to see; how his competent, slow mind worked; how he could drag a dogged, unexpected humor from behind his weariness. He knew that Jay possessed a solid, slow-burning courage that was sending up a strong flame when the quick-flaring heroics of other men had burned down to flaky ash.

At the road block, two soldiers with their rifles at rest waved Mike through casually. On the far side of the barrier a long string of cars stood waiting to be let down the lonely road to the burned country. A good many of them had out-of-state licenses, he noticed resentfully. Sight-seers!

Impulsively he stopped opposite one gleaming roadster with a Nebraska plate. Leaning out, he brought a sooty grin to bear on the four, smiling, chattering people. The driver stopped talking in the middle of a word.

"Quite a picnic down that way, bud." Mike nodded judiciously. "I sure hope you folks brought your cameras with you. You'll get some dandy pictures. Be careful, though. It's pretty black and you might get soot on that nice jacket."

The driver brought up one hand and self-consciously spread it over the lapel of his beige, gabardine jacket, the fingers starred out and brown against the clean fabric.

22

"I—I—"

"That's all right." Mike waved airily. "Don't think of apologizing. You're our living. We like to put on a good show for you every now and then. Have a good time."

Driving on, he noticed with satisfaction that they had quieted down. No wonder, either. He must look like nothing on earth, uncombed, unshaven, and filthy.

He turned left under the light at Barrett's Harbor and coasted down toward the faded, brick block of the Eden Auditorium. Twisting the car to the right along the traffic circle, he pulled up to one side of the porticoed entrance, disregarding the parking lines painted on the macadam.

At the door he met a group of four women coming out of the auditorium. Their high, excited voices, active as the clucking of hens, stopped short. Their faces were familiar; but he couldn't put a name to one of them. They knew him, though, and what was more important, knew where he had been. He could see it in the pitying glances.

Their pity was personal and hard to bear because it was underlaid with the fear that what had happened to him might happen to them.

Unreasonably Mike couldn't meet their eyes when he pushed past into the hall. After the hazy, dazzling October sunlight, the auditorium was dim. He could see only the slanting columns of dusty light from the clerestory windows.

He hesitated in the doorway, hoping his eyes would get used to the fusty room before he had to talk to anyone. He wanted to see nobody but Tiz and he couldn't find her. Hastily he stepped out of the frame of doorway, finding with despair that he was one of very few men in a milling sea of anxious women, squalling children, and vociferous animals.

A large part of the commotion came from a sort of grumbling dog-conversation. One Great Dane, leashed in a corner, had been reduced to a bass mutter of protest by the continuous, interested contemplation of two, well-mannered French poodles. A small boy swerved nimbly past Mike, clutching a squalling, half-grown, White Leghorn rooster.

Mike took a hasty, backward step and stirred up a spitting, screaming fury. The familiar, agonizing claws went through the thin khaki of his trousers into his leg, and kept on coming until the huge, black cat clung to his shirt front and the yellow-eyed mask stared him accusingly in the face. As relieved as anyone would be on seeing a supposedly lost friend, Mike and Satan regarded each other with mutually respectful relief.

"You black devil, you," Mike said. "I thought I'd never see your gaudy, old mug again."

He freed his ankles from the fine leash and pushed the collared cat onto his shoulder, hearing the rumbling purr start just behind his ear.

"I know she's around somewhere, if you are," he said.

"Poor old Satan." Tiz's controlled voice spoke behind him. "His tail was just getting back to normal and you come along and step on it again. Clumsy baster!"

Mike spun to face her.

"Oh, my judast, Tiz, I'm so glad to see you I could yell!"

In the second when they were oblivious to the crowd, their faces were nearly identical. Strain had taken away from hers some of the small, feminine things about it and had added to his a few softnesses it did not ordinarily have. Mike saw her speechless, and there was a look about her that made him think hastily: Is she going to kiss me?

She never had within his memory and he realized instantly she had no intention of embarrassing either one of them by such an unusual display. She reached up and scratched Satan's ears and Mike felt the light, apparently accidental pressure of her hand on his shoulder.

"Can we go home, Mike? What's happened? What's left?"

"It's pretty bad."

"I heard the Portland radio. That's all we had to go by. That, and talk."

"Yeah," Mike said disgustedly. "I was standing right beside that guy when he was sending in his report night before last. I set out to let him have it with a spade. Why, he wasn't anywhere near the real front of the fire and he was describing it like he was looking right at it."

"I figured that's how it was when he put the church next door to the town hall. Can we go home?" She repeated her important question with no sense of having asked it before.

"Sure can."

"Well, I'll check out. We're all on some list and if you go running off without letting them know, everyone comes to find you."

He turned to watch her pick a way through the bickering, wailing women. Her long, dungaree-clad legs carried her jauntily through the press of thick-hipped matrons, many of whom were years younger than she, none of whom looked as young. It was only at detached moments that Mike ever thought of her in terms of years, as an aunt. In his romantic mind, the word aunt implied age, knitting needles, lavender shawls. The only thing he'd ever seen Tiz throw over her square shoulders in the coldest winter was a checked mackinaw.

He lost her and his glance, carrying on across the room, found another familiar face. It wasn't the first time he'd seen Virginia Hanscom since he'd come home; but it would be the first time he'd spoken to her if he followed his in-

25

stantaneous impulse. It was the first time he'd looked at her and thought: What a cussed fool I was, saying I didn't care whether I ever saw her again!

Ginny was sitting in a bright yellow, folding chair against the far wall, not looking directly at anything, her hands clasped in her lap.

Before Mike's conscious mind had decided that he wanted nothing more than to be closer to her, he had started across the hall. He thought afterward he must have looked like Beelzebub himself, crossing that room with the black cat riding his shoulder.

Ginny was not immediately conscious of him and he had a second to look at her, taking in the detail of her dark, arched brows, as surprising as they had been the first time he'd noticed them, beneath the light, upward-springing crest of hair.

There was a blank, strained, unnatural look about her which he put down to nervousness any woman would have felt during the fire. It canceled every trace of normal change and left him knowing as little as he ever had.

It occurred to him that it might have been easier for him, going back down into the Peninsula, than it had been for those who waited here with nothing but rumor for company.

Ginny looked up and her glance left Mike feeling as if somebody had poured a bucket of ice water over his head.

"Fancy meeting you here," he said brashly against his discomfort. "I felt like Eliza crossing the ice, coming across that floor."

"I don't remember that Eliza carried the bloodhounds on her shoulder."

Her voice was light; but there was a betraying nervousness in the speed with which she stood up, bringing their eyes more nearly on a level. By rights it should have been a voice he hadn't heard for seven years; but it was a voice he had never heard.

As soon as she stood up, Mike remembered what else had happened to her to account for that new look of loss. When it was too late and he had already greeted her with the flipness she had always detested, he knew there had been something else he should have said. The death of one person had been unimportant enough for him to forget while a whole countryside was dying.

"Ginny," he began helplessly. "I don't know what I can say. About your mother—"

"There never *is* anything to say." She shrugged.

There wasn't, either. He fumbled hopelessly with the "I was so sorry—"

"It's funny," Ginny said on a quick breath, her voice holding importance for him through its lack of inflection. "I used to think what it would be like if Pa died. I remember thinking it would be like God Himself dying. I never thought she *could*. It was Pa."

"She—was she sick long?"

"Four years." Ginny summoned up those four, lost years for him as clearly as she did for herself. Puzzled, he stood listening. The thing that had happened to her happened to everyone; but with her it went beyond understandable sorrow to the betraying and bitter edges of fear.

"I can't remember the funeral. The fire was getting away and everyone was scared. Only when it was all over and they came to look at the departed." She had always been able to say to him the things most people never find anyone to hear and that had not changed.

"I had my head sort of down. I could look past the end of the pew and see those feet, shuffling. They were all so

27

old. You can tell, the way they're too old and tired to bend and they hit the floor all at once with every ounce of weight right there, spreading them out. The shoes are different. I didn't realize till then how old she was. Pa was always old; but she didn't seem—"

Her voice cracked without warning and she looked desperately away from Mike's face.

"I shouldn't be able to talk to you like this, Mike."

"I guess it's because you're supposed to."

"No." She shook her head decisively. "No more. I always used to cry on your shoulder. Seems I'm still doing it."

"No need to stop."

"What puzzles me is I can *say* to you the things I only think with other people." She looked thoughtfully at him. "Do me a favor and forget it, will you? I would have spilled over to anyone who came along."

"But you *have* changed."

"I'm older," Ginny said with a friendly smile. "It would be dreadful if anyone got older without changing, wouldn't it?"

"Prettier, too," Mike said daringly.

Instead of bristling, Ginny looked pleased.

"Thank you."

"Ginny, for the Lord sake!" he exploded. "I've got to see you. I've got to know about you. When can we—"

"I'm sorry." She retreated irrevocably. "My time's pretty well taken up, Mike."

"You aren't—? Are you? I would have heard if you were married."

"I'm not. But I will be on December first."

"Oh." Mike wondered if he had ever had any bottom to his stomach. "Who?"

28

"Byron Sawyer."

"Oh," Mike said again. "Well—well, I—"

But he didn't wish her happiness and he couldn't say he did.

"Is it out yet?" Ginny asked suddenly and had to repeat it before he heard her. "The fire. Is it out?"

"No, of course it's not out! And won't be till we've had a week's solid rain. But I doubt it'll do much more harm."

There were more reassuring things he could have said to her; but she was a stranger again and he wanted her to realize as clearly as he did that nothing was over.

"*Your* house is still there," he said harshly.

Ginny's face went blank and wary and she moved impatiently away, leaving him to be assailed by the unavoidable smell of masses of women and the sour, underlying odor of many children too small for anything but diapers. His nose wrinkled.

"I've got to get out of here. It's so— It's too—"

"You get used to it after a while," she told him pleasantly.

"Do you want to ride home with me—us?" Mike made the offer, feeling as if he'd swallowed a nutmeg grater on a string and somebody had pulled it up again.

"Thank you, no." Her flicking glance passed over his face and stung as if it touched a place where the skin was gone.

Mike swallowed hard against the obstruction in his throat and grabbed her hands clumsily in both of his, staring down at her face.

"Look, Ginny," he began and his own weariness stopped him. It would be better to wait until he knew what he was saying. He turned away, having seen the startled, denying look in her eyes, knowing there would be another and a better time to say all the things he had discovered he was going to have to say to her.

29

Clasping the big cat, he stumbled out into the sunlight. Tiz was waiting stiffly in the Chevy.

"I was hoping you wouldn't forget Satan," she said tartly.

"How could I?"

"Stop at the Green Front, will you, and get a fifth," Tiz said.

"But you never—I thought you were death on it." Incautiously he jerked around to stare.

"I need it now."

When he came out of the liquor store, Tiz said:

"One more stop. Polly Hanna's up to her aunt's and I told her she could come back with us when we went."

Mike groaned.

"All right," she told him firmly. "You can stand it."

"I don't know whether I can or not."

With an exaggerated sigh he stopped in front of the big, drab Boynton house. Polly, looking taller, thinner and paler than ever, came out the door so fast he knew Tiz must have taken time to call and tell her to expect them.

After Polly's first frightened look at Mike, she behaved as if he weren't there.

"Tiz, it *was* good of you— I'm afraid I'm being— I hope it wasn't too much of a nuisance."

"It's all right, Polly." Tiz soothed her as she would have quieted a fractious mare. "Just relax."

Having Polly along was like having nobody when the first flurry was over. She crouched in the corner trying to make herself invisible and Mike, glancing at her, wasn't sure she had not succeeded.

Pounding down the long road home with the two women beside him as silent and impersonal as shadows, Mike could feel his mind turn irresistibly to the third one who was almost as materially present as Tiz and Polly.

30

He still felt the echo of that quick, betraying tingle that had attacked him when he looked up and saw her an hour ago. Weariness had scraped his mind down to essentials and he recognized the moving force behind his singular intention for these last years since he'd been out of the service. He'd taken his time and it was nearly too late.

Remembering the way they had said good-by seven years ago, Mike's face got as hot as if somebody had picked him up like a lobster and shoved him into a vat of boiling water. He wondered how he had ever had the nerve to cross that wide floor to her that afternoon.

No girl had ever looked at him since, the way she had that early evening, her eyes living and light as sunlight. There had never been a night like it since; never another dimly enchanted, moon-drunk field above such a silver sea.

He had reached out and found her waiting for him. Silently they'd got out of the car and crossed the field to where the grass grew high and thick above the slope.

He had been so cynically sure of himself and aware that every girl was like every other girl. The signs had been there to tell him he was wrong and he hadn't noticed them until later when he'd stood waiting for her to get up and she hadn't moved.

"Ginny?" he'd said uncertainly, sensing at last that something was wrong.

"You make me feel cheap." Her voice was muffled and she stared blankly at the water, deliberately refusing to look at him.

Mike's complacent triumph had been uncertain and young. It shattered easily and he said: "Well, you asked for it. Girl acts the way you did, gets just what you—"

"All right, Mike. Then give me my two dollars and just go away. I— Please go away."

He had plunged furiously across the field to the car, blind with hurt pride, not stopping to wonder how she would get home. And he had left Frenchville the next day.

Now he would like to wipe that night out of time. He wondered what his life would have been like if he had never touched her that night, because he had never intended to.

The first letter he'd written Tiz had been from Los Angeles. By the time she got around to answering it, he was gone. The letter followed him up the coast to Seattle and back to Berkeley. Only three letters marked the two years he'd spent there, slinging hash in an all-night diner and scraping through four semesters of university work. He was on the verge of moving on when the world settled his problem for him. In the next few years MoMM 1/c Mike Arey got his fill of traveling free.

After he'd got out, he'd been smart. He had worked hard to be able to come home and start out on top instead of from scratch the way a sucker would have done. But it had nearly taken him too long.

Byron Sawyer, he was saying violently to himself. She can't marry him! And he felt betrayed because he could think of no reason why she shouldn't.

"Hold it, Mike," Tiz said sharply. He hadn't noticed the road block. The two uniformed guards were standing restively in the middle of the road with a state police car parked behind them.

"Sorry, bud," the younger soldier said. "Nobody goes down this road today."

"Look. Remember me? You let me out."

"Never said anything about you coming back in."

At the signs of argument, one soldier brought his carbine up into the crook of his elbow and the other stepped over

32

to the car. Polly let out a smothered squeak as the state trooper, burly in his tight-calved uniform, climbed out of his sedan.

"You having trouble?"

"Naw. We can manage this bird."

"Look—" Mike began again, resenting the "bird."

"No 'look' to it, brother." The soldier was only a kid and Mike could see the soft growth of young beard shadowing his rounded jaw. "Nobody goes down in there. The folks that live there've got enough to do without all you fellers coming in to see the fun."

"I want to talk to that cop." Tiz got out of the car, pushing a protesting Polly before her and bore down menacingly on the big man, her eyes flashing. She let her voice out full and they all, including Mike who had been expecting it, jumped nervously.

"Amory!" she shouted. "You come over here and tell these young cowboys I want to get home."

The officer turned red under his powder-blue cap.

"Lord, Tiz, I didn't see who it was."

Sheepishly, but still retaining his innate dignity, Amory came over to the barrier.

"There now, Tiz," he said peaceably. "Nobody's trying to abrogate your rights as a citizen." He glanced at the soldier who had lowered his rifle. "You can let these folks by, son."

"Friends of yours?"

"They live on the point." Amory's answer was indirect. "They are also lucky enough to have a house left to go to."

Tiz was silent until they reached the high hill from which Mike had seen the full sweep of the ravaged country a few hours before. Then, in a voice that made him look anywhere but at her, she said:

33

"Stop here a minute, Mike."

He heard Tiz tearing at the paper-wrapped bottle and when she handed it to him, he was astonished to see how much she had lowered its level.

The sting of whiskey in his own tired throat nearly choked him. He glanced at Tiz as he passed the bottle back and stayed frozen, staring at the tears running down her controlled and stony face.

"Damn you, Mike," she said. "Look the other way! Now let's go home."

The October night, warm and with little wind, settled in over the burned hills. The savage smell of wild fire lay like a blanket over the Peninsula. Sometimes, far back in the charred valleys, fire still burning underground would shoot up a freakishly unburned tree. But there in the backlands, surrounded by acre after acre burned to its bone, fire could do no more damage, and the men who patrolled the boundaries of the lost land gave its minor outbursts no notice.

The moon, barely past full, rose almost with the sunset. Its light was no relief from darkness. Brutally it brought out the empty cellars and the black snags of unnaturally dead spruces and pines. The cold, deceiving light fingered down across the hills to the western slope where what remained of the town of Frenchville lay facing the impersonal and lovely sea.

The first thing Tiz had done when she came back into the house was to push the coffeepot onto the front of the stove and start a good strong brew. After that she went stolidly over to the calendar under the clock shelf and tore off the top sheets. October 20, it said. There was nothing in her manner to show she had ever left her house with the fear that she might never come back into it.

In the kitchen, dimmed by the unaccustomed lamplight, Polly and Mike were eating mechanically. The food had no taste for Tiz. She got up, went over to the window, and stood staring out into the moonlit night. The light from the kerosene lamp, reflected on the shining windowpane, gave their reflections back to her like a mirror. She seldom had such a chance to examine these two, familiar faces. Seeing them unaware, she saw them as strangers. Mike's dark, young face, brooding and sulky with weariness, devoted with an intent beyond reason to the food on his plate— Polly's as expressionless and pale and expectant as a white, china dish.

For a minute Tiz considered turning on them, saying, What are you waiting for? I haven't got anything to give either one of you.   .

But she knew without asking. They wanted the reassurance of her presence; they waited for her words. And she stood here, emptily unwilling to say anything to them.

I'm not even here myself yet, she thought angrily. If I could have come back alone, I would have come in one piece and there wouldn't be just a part of me here now like a shadow and half its body.

Outside her own place she was no longer whole, either. Up there in the auditorium, she had felt as tenuous and wispy as fog. Knowing that people looked at her with curiosity even through their terror and despair, talked about her, she had felt her soul stretch like a catgut string. Good sense said that those women had something more to talk about than Tiz Arey; but that didn't help.

For God sake, she thought, I'm no different. What is there about *me?*

When you tnought the battle was over and won, you found it had to be refought in miniature every day of your life just to retain insecure victory. All her life emotion had been a thing she'd found safer to avoid. If it couldn't be avoided, then shove it down under the straight, impersonal stare, behind the shell of self-possession. But the stare was weakened and betraying tears had breached the shell.

Sharply clear in Tiz's memory was another time when she had come into the house after a battle to hold it. When Aunt Mattie Arey had been here like a fat, white spider in the center of its comfortable web, Tiz had always avoided the place. Nothing went on Mattie didn't know about. If she could find out in no other way, she asked direct questions and Tiz had shrunk under them all through her adolescence.

Aunt Mattie had died quickly and alone. Her death made little impression on her family because it came just after Mike's father had married his lovely Kentucky wife and all attention had been centered on them.

Shortly after Mattie's death, Lawyer Backer had called Tiz into his office.

"The old girl left that house to you, Tiz," he said. "Made me write it down properly. Says: 'To my niece Elizabeth, who needs it most.' Don't know what she meant. Maybe you do. I suppose you'll sell it. You young ones don't have much feeling for property."

Tiz wasn't listening. Behind her eyes two syllables had exploded in a shower of sparks: Freedom.

It was hers. That compact, weathered house with its wide, old front door long unused, going under in a rising tangle of lilacs and white rugosas. It was the last house above the sea. Jasper Hanscom's comparatively new buildings were between Mattie's and old man Tilton's. The three

36

houses stood far apart, their frontages taking all the land between the main road and the shore.

Humbled and ashamed, Tiz had gone home thinking of that forsaken, old woman, locked inside her rooms by ponderous flesh, yet seeing so much.

Her news had created an explosion through which she passed like a tall tree in a wind, bending with it and not giving an inch.

Jack had leaned forward, his handsome face smiling and sure.

"Give it to me, Tiz. Nita and I could use it right now."

"No," Tiz said stiffly. "I want it."

"Oh, look!" he protested. "What d'*you* want with a house? A woman alone. Why, you'll be getting married, too, and it'll just sit there and rot. Here I am with a wife and all ready to start out. I could *use* it."

He was the one person in the world whom Tiz loved without question; but he was also the one reason why she would not be getting married for a long time. Not until she had been away from him long enough to forget the complete, abject service he demanded from his bride as he had all his life from his mother and sister.

The battle had not stopped there; but it had been won there.

If the way others lived offered you nothing, she thought, you should be permitted to grow a shell of resistance. It didn't work that way. You chose to do as you pleased; but the core of your difference left you undefended against the thing from which it should have protected you.

There was always Polly or somebody to mistake your surface for the truth and to envy and try to share something you didn't have to give even to yourself.

37

Sometimes—and tonight was one—Tiz felt older than anyone had a right to feel who had to be a rebel.

I'm forty-five and rebellion is for the very young or the very old: the young because morning comes with its twenty-four hours of possibility; the old because morning has come again. But Polly helps me keep up the illusion because I'm her idea of a rebel and I suppose that's why I need her.

Mike, caught by the quality of her long silence, looked up and felt that she had left her body standing empty, and gone, leaving him alone with Polly. Not even seeing that he demanded reassurance of her as definitely as Polly did, he said:

"Tiz, what d'you see?"

"Nothing." Her return was instantaneous. "It just looks so funny to see this town dark. It must look now the way it did a hundred years ago, before people ever had electricity or cars."

"I suppose." Mike heaved his bone-weary body out of the chair and went to look. Before the house the deserted road lay silverly flat. The big elm at the corner threw a patch of utter nothingness across it and he felt that if a car should turn the corner and try to drive down past these cut-off, shadow-isolated houses, under the elm it would go whirling downward forever with its astonished driver clinging to his useless wheel and wondering what had happened to him and why it didn't stop.

"Makes you feel—" Tiz said intently—"as if everything had ended. Everything else but what you can see has just stopped going on and there's nothing else left in the world."

"Tiz. For God sake!" Mike switched on the radio, forgetting that its response to the battery would be so quick. He jumped as the authoritative, tired voice instantly filled the room.

"Citizens of the state," the voice began slowly. "Our weather forecast tonight gives us no hope of rain for at least five days. Our woodlands are becoming dryer every moment and extreme caution must be exercised. There are things we can all do. Particularly if you live on outlying farms, please stay at home. Keep supplies of water where they can be easily reached. Report to your local fire chief at the first sign of smoke. Patrol your back roads regularly. Be careful. People all over the nation are with you in their thoughts tonight. With those of you especially who have lost their homes in the last week. All I can say is: We are doing everything we can."

"My Lord," Mike said into the silence after the governor's voice had stopped. "I thought I could find something that would cheer us up a little."

"That did it!" Tiz laughed bleakly.

The commentator went on with the roll of the lost towns, the dead lands: "East Brownsfield—Goose Rocks Beach—Bar Harbor—Centerville—York—Washington—Hancock—"

"Turn it off," Tiz said abruptly.

"I'm tired but I don't feel like going to bed." Mike wandered toward the door. "Guess I'll take a run uptown, see what's going on."

Looking back from the door, he found new gentleness in Tiz's face under the lamplight.

"Tiz, will you be all right?" he asked hesitantly.

"Go on, go on." She made a shooing motion at him. "I promise faithfully if the bogy man comes, Polly and Satan and I will put up the fight of our lives."

39

"I'll leave the car here," Mike said carelessly, and went shambling into the inimical night.

He supposed Polly must be going to stay. They had stopped at Job Hanna's house on the way home to find it still locked and silent.

Mike waded through the elm shadow feeling as if he wanted to walk with his arms outstretched so he might touch and be warned against whatever was waiting there. Unconsciously moving faster, he came out into the empty main street.

When he passed the drugstore, he saw far back in its darkly cavernous interior, two candles burning like lightning bugs in a bottle. Between them, suspended neckless in dark space, hung the bald, ginger-fringed head of Jonesy Dawes, the druggist.

Jonesy Dawes, in his old Model T, had come through the road block five minutes behind Mike that afternoon. Jonesy drove in a state of constant amazement at the speed he attained. It was only on the upgrade he had to get out and chock the wheel while the Ford rested. Once let her get over the crest and Jonesy had to give vent to his astonishment in a constant string of self-addressed comment: "My judast priest, don't she want to go! Look at her pull! Holy old wind-swept Hannah, I can't hardly hold the bitch back."

As he roared down the road, his mother sat in the back seat, as erect, thin, and rigid as an old bird.

Jonesy came up with Mike parked on the last hilltop and the Ford was attaining such a paean of speed, he couldn't take his eyes off the road for more than a second. His mother leaned forward and rapped him smartly on the shoulder with her cane.

40

"Them Areys are sitting there drinking liquor, Jones."

With surprise Jonesy caught a glimpse of Tiz lifting the revealing bottle. He also saw the woman sitting beside her and averted his eyes quickly, thinking with relief: Then *that's* all right.

The old lady let him have another belt with the cane.

"Don't, Marm, when I'm driving. You'll have me up a tree, the way this car pulls."

"Well, Jones, what're you going to do about it? They're sitting right out in broad daylight, putting down the rum. And that was Polly Hanna with them and certainly not what I'd expect of her."

"My Lord, Mama, I can't go back and tell them not to." He was frantic. "What do you expect me to do?"

"I never expect you to do anything, Jones," she said bitingly. "Only turn around and take me back and I will tell them what any decent, law-abiding citizen should. They're a scandal, a byword, and a hissing."

"I can't stop while I'm going downhill, Mama. You know that."

She didn't answer and he saw thankfully that she had sunk suddenly into some private cave of thought. With deep relief, he stopped before the house at last and helped her out. Her old bones felt like sticks. She leaned heavily on his arm and moved at a dependent, insistent creep, across the yard and into the house.

He established her in her chair and went into the kitchen to get her something to eat. He wanted to open the store for a while and it would be simpler to leave if he could get her fed and happy.

When he stepped silently through her door with the tray, his nostrils were assailed by the musty, faintly corrupt, faintly sweet smell of age. His mother was asleep, sit-

41

ting there bolt upright in her rocker, her thin hands clasped loosely in her lap.

The unquestioning way she had settled back into her life, refusing to see the charred hills and empty cellars, made Jonesy feel they existed only in his mind. He saw she had been writing at her little lap desk since he'd left her and he went over and sprung the secret drawer he was not supposed to know about. Inside was a stiff, yellow curl of paper. Holding it easily so it would not rattle, he read the few words in his mother's steady Spencerian:

"You are a meaching, little mouse."

Jonesy put the paper back as if it had turned unbearably hot in his fingers and started to tiptoe from the room, his ears burning.

"Meach, little Mousie," her deep organ voice said bitterly.

"Mama," Jonesy protested weakly, "are you asleep?"

"Yes, Mousie."

"Mama, why do you lie so?"

Her eyes were still shut and her ivory-stick fingers moved restlessly across the stiff, black fabric of her skirt. Suddenly her hand flicked out, grasped a small, leather-bound book, and flung it accurately at his head.

Jonesy ducked out the door and hovered hopelessly out of sight. Presently her voice softer, she said: "Jonesy, dear, are you there?"

"Yes, Mother."

"Well, come back, son." Jonesy appeared, breathing hard. "I forgive you. The Lord says: 'Do unto others.' If I didn't I'd get so mad I'd have to kill you and have that on my black soul, too."

"I'm sorry, Mother."

"You are so meek, Jones. You'll inherit your share of the

42

earth and mine, too. But sometimes just to look at you, son, is so cussed aggravating I don't see how I can stand it. No. It's too much!"

Her hand moved idly toward the laden table.

"Mama!"

"Poor Mousie," she said. "You're enough to make anyone forget she's a lady. What you'll do when I'm dead, I don't know."

Her eyes lit on the tray of food. Greedily she hitched her chair forward and bent over it.

"It's good," she mumbled.

She didn't glance up when Jonesy left and he had nearly forgotten she sat there waiting for him until Mike pushed open the door and came into the dim store. Seeing him, Jonesy was reminded of injustice all over again and he thought bitterly: *You* never have to put up with anything like that!

Mike had gone in solely for the sake of speaking to somebody.

"Just me, Jonesy," he said. "Mike Arey."

"Walk into my parlor," Jay Stone said comfortably. Startled, Mike turned to find the first and second selectmen sitting at one of the small, wrought-iron tables where Jonesy's summer clientele of big-hatted ladies drank its afternoon sodas.

"You're the fifth one we've caught tonight." Jay sounded complacent. "I thought most of you boys would be in after cigarets or something."

"You set up a new office?" Mike grinned stiffly.

The big, blond, young man who sat beside Jay didn't even look up. His tremendous shoulders were bent and he concentrated intently on the paper he was marking into neat squares. Mike had the chance and good reason to look him over carefully.

Byron Sawyer's hands were big and the pencil he clutched was too small for his fingers. Standing over him, Mike looked down thoughtfully at the tight-curled, crisp-looking hair; the long, handsome, freshly-shaven face; the self-confident quirk at the corner of his wide mouth. He had to admit almost any girl would think By was good looking.

Mike had never looked at him before with anything but indifference. Tonight that had changed to active dislike. Byron glanced up, his yellow eyes silvered by lamplight, and met that look with astonishment.

"Hello, By," Mike said, coolly intent. "I didn't know but we'd managed to lose you somewhere the last few days."

"Hey?" Byron's surprise made him a little slow. "How's that?"

"Well, I don't remember seeing you around. What'd you do, spend your time in Barrett's Harbor taking care of things on that end?"

"Whatta you— How— What—" Completely taken aback and thunderously angry, Byron began to splutter like a wet firecracker.

"That's what I mean." Delighted with the success of his gibing, Mike added, "What did you do in the Great War, Daddy?"

Behind them Jonesy began to make an excited, twittering. Mike found himself looking up at the towering figure that moved toward him across the table with the slow inevitability of a turgid avalanche. Jay simply put his hand on Byron's arm. Mike took a breath and found he hadn't been breathing at all. Byron's eyes were cold and watchful when he sat down.

44

"What in hell's name ails you, Mike?" Jay said furiously. "You can take my word for it, there's nobody here didn't do his part and don't you forget it."

Mike was already ashamed of his unwarranted attack, but he still wanted something to fight about. His gaze tangled with Jay's before he looked unapologetically away.

"Here, take a look at this," Jay said quickly. He twitched the ruled sheet of paper from under Byron's hand. "This is a kind of schedule we've made out for riding fire patrol."

"You really think this is necessary, Jay?" Byron was still watching Mike with surprised fury; but his voice was concealing and undisturbed.

"Yes, I do." Jay's glance was as impersonal as a microscope. "I don't like to waste my time any more than you do, and I don't consider this a waste. Matter of four hours a day maybe twice a week."

Pausing, Jay could see in his mind's eye the big, white house on Bolling's Head where By lived. Water on two sides of it, open field on the other two.

"It depends on your point of view, of course." Even as he said it, Jay felt he was hitting below the belt. "You take some of these fellows living back in the woods, they feel considerably different."

Byron didn't look as abashed as Mike would have in his place.

"I knew when I said that it could be misunderstood. *I* don't mean anything personal. I'm a big taxpayer, Jay, and I stand to lose more than most; but my position's pretty good, I know. Of course, you can't count on being safe. *My* place would burn as easy as yours would."

At the slight emphasis on that possessive pronoun, Mike, too, remembered the big house on the Head. He didn't know anyone who had got so much for so little as Byron.

45

He'd fallen into possession of that house by a process of elimination, just as he had fallen into a going business. When Mike had gone away, Byron had been working by the week on Chet Ballard's wharf. Chet was dead now and By had taken over and when Mike went out to haul his traps, he saw By's sign which was larger than Chet's had been. BYRON U. SAWYER, it screamed across the harbor, LOBSTERS—WHOLESALE—RETAIL.

"I was thinking of the town." Byron was still at it. "A lot of people when you ask them to ride patrol will feel like the town ought to pay them for their time. You don't want to forget we've lost a lot of taxable property. A man isn't going to feel much like paying his regular tax on an empty cellar hole. And you know what kind of shape that fire left the overlay in."

"Look." Jay didn't let his impatience get through. He had no idea why Mike had jumped By; but he saw that By's insistence on importance was more for Mike's benefit than to disagree with him. "This is entirely volunteer."

"I just think it ought to be made clear from the beginning." Byron seemed impervious to impatience. Watching him, Mike saw it wasn't obtuseness. That ability to drive other men to madness while he himself appeared completely unmoved by emotion was part of Byron's stock in trade. He knew, too, that if By hadn't been worn thin tonight, he would never have got such a satisfactory rise out of him.

"Haven't got nobody yet for the four to eight shift in the morning." Jay followed down the list of hours with a cracked, blackened fingernail.

"Put me down for that," Mike said. "I'll do it for nothing."

"I thought it would be a good idea to go in pairs." Jay

46

wrote busily. "Could you find someone hasn't got a car to go?"

"Sure," Mike said heartily. "I'll get Eddie Hanscom."

Meeting Byron's inviting stare, recognizing his own absurdity, he told himself firmly he'd never trust a man with yellow eyes. Before he got out the door, he noticed vaguely that even inside the building the stale air was made potentially dangerous by the added smell of smoke.

Eddie was kind of a weak reed; but he would do for the time being and he should be pretty sober by four in the morning, after a night's sleep.

Sleep, Mike thought. Bed! He was sighing with weariness when he reached the shadow of the Spy tree. He found Tiz sitting beside the table as if she hadn't moved; but Polly was nowhere in sight. Tiz looked up at him and before his tired mind remembered that Tiz always looked at you as if you were going to say something important, he wondered if something more had happened and he hadn't heard about it.

Lord, he thought, if she waits like that all the time, she must be terribly disappointed in most of us. Black and so deep he couldn't find bottom in them, Tiz's eyes met his.

"What on earth are you staring at, Mike?"

"I don't know." He collapsed on the handiest chair. "It's the damndest thing. I seem to be seeing everything like—well, for the first time. Or the last."

He could feel laughter bubbling up in his chest and he stared at her heavily, knowing if he once let it get away, he would sit there laughing like a maniac for the rest of his life. In the lamplight he looked white and drawn and young.

"Tell me what you did uptown," Tiz said sharply. "And then, for the Lord sake, go to bed."

47

"Oh, yes. Oh, yes. Oh, yes."

"Mike!"

His head jerked and his eyes flew open.

"I saw By Sawyer."

"You've seen him before, I don't doubt." Tiz was uncomprehending.

"Oh, yes," Mike said again, agreeably. "Patrols. Four hours. I start from the town hall four in the morning. Go till eight. I got to get Eddie to go with me. In pairs, see? The fellers riding before us will be there and have the route."

He got up shakily and headed for the door.

"Forgot. Got to go tell Eddie."

Tiz was there before Mike could decide to close his hand on the knob.

"Go up and get to bed! *I'll* go tell Eddie."

"Got to go right now or I'll forget," he insisted stubbornly.

"Mike, I'll *go* now."

She snatched his jacket and was out the door. Once he was satisfied she was really going, Mike stood staring questioningly around the kitchen. There was something he ought to do. Oh, yes. Satan wasn't used to lamps. If he ever knocked it over—

His first try at blowing out the lamp failed. He lost his balance and reeled against the table, setting the lamp rocking on its base.

"Jesus!" he said, horrified, and blew again.

He waded through blue moon shadows on the floor, fumbled up the stairs, thought firmly that he was undressing, and was asleep as soon as he sat on the edge of his narrow bed.

The night had turned cool. When Tiz looked seaward, she found a line of mist lying along a hollow between her and the quietly breathing water. She stopped there in the hummocky field, seeing the long finger of the breakwater cutting across the silver moon path. Inside it the paper-white hulls of boats riding quietly at their moorings looked peaceful and reassuring.

The smell of smoke was stinging in her nostrils, but Tiz knew it for the bitter, sodden smell of actual death and not the smell of dying.

The Peninsula lay hushed in the impossible light. To the south through the night the cars of the watchers would go slowly through the threatening spruces. Along the secret, hidden roads that sooner or later ended in small fields where the sea came soundless through marshy grass, or more articulate on gravel shores, or loud in the night against the ledges. Danger lay quiescent in the south and to the west; but nothing more could come upon them from the true east because there everything that could happen already had.

She took a quick, reluctant glance at the hills. To one who had never seen them before, they might have been unchanged; but she knew they were dead and looked stolidly at the cracked paint on Jasper Hanscom's door with eyes that burned dryly. Before the door opened, she could hear the voice inside.

"Come in. Come right in. Do come in."

The door flung away from her with a wide freedom and Tiz found herself facing an Eddie who obviously didn't know her from the man in the moon.

"Come in." He reached down and grabbed her wrist. Rather than struggle, Tiz went with a shrug through the back shed to the kitchen.

49

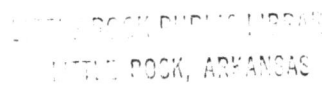

"Hanh! Now I can see who you are," Eddie said. "So dark out there I couldn't see a bloody blink."

Tiz's narrow-lidded glance at his face found the irrefutable signs of intoxication. Clearly he wasn't going to be much help to anyone at four o'clock in the morning.

"Well, well, well." Eddie smiled at her cherubically. "So it's you after all. I thought you weren't coming."

"Eddie." Ginny's voice came faintly down the stairs. "Is anything the matter?"

Eddie's face took on a still, listening look.

"Did you hear a voice?"

Tiz nodded.

"I've been hearing people talking all night," Eddie said.

"Eddie?"

"There it is again." The expression of slurred craftiness that came down over Eddie's wide, young eyes made Tiz want to laugh—or cry. "I'll tell you what. We'll just pretend we don't hear them and they'll go away."

"Eddie Hanscom!" Abovestairs there was the unmistakable sound of somebody getting out of bed.

"Don't listen," Eddie said sharply. He stood frozen and when Ginny, in pajamas and a long house coat, appeared in the hall door, Eddie didn't even turn his head.

"What—"

"There." Eddie gave Tiz a triumphant nod. "I *told* you they'd go away."

"I'm sorry, Tiz. Is there anything I can do? He's been like this ever since I got home this afternoon."

"Perhaps you don't even hear them," Eddie suggested. "I suppose that's how it is."

"I came to see Eddie about riding patrol," Tiz said helplessly. "Mike has to go on from four to eight tomorrow morning and he thought he might get Eddie to go with him."

"I would be delighted," Eddie said. "I would never turn down such an invitation from a lady—even though four o'clock in the morning is kind of an unusual hour."

"Not me," Tiz protested. "Mike."

"Oh, sure. I'd be delighted. I'm so glad you invited me."

"Eddie!" Ginny's voice sharpened.

"There, by judast!" Eddie spun to face her. "I knew I heard somebody talking. I was afraid I was hearing things. Go back to bed, Virginia. This is none of your mix. This lady has come to ask me to go riding with her. Nothing to do with you."

"All right, Eddie." Tiz gave up in desperation. "At four I'll come and get you."

"Fine. Fine." Eddie's round tones wavered. He sat down in the chair by the kitchen table and laid his head carefully on his arms. The two women stood looking down at him before their glances met.

"Do you think he'll be able—" Tiz hesitated.

"I'll do my best, Tiz. I don't know where he's getting the cussed stuff. I had him nearly sober when I went to bed and now he's worse than ever."

"Well." Tiz's doubt was clear in her voice. "I'll tell Mike to look in. If Eddie feels—er—better—"

As she went out, Eddie looked up to shout after her: "Don't forget our date. I'll be ready. Four o'—" His voice went out like a snuffed candle.

If he was ready to go at four, Tiz thought with wry amusement, it was going to be a shock to him to find Mike waiting when he expected a woman of mystery.

Her own house was dark and she lit the lamp and went

51

up to see if Mike had got to bed. He had unbuttoned his shirt. Except for that, he lay completely dressed, his head on the pillow, his feet still on the floor.

Clicking her tongue, Tiz deposited the feet, shoes and all, on the bedspread. Mike's breathing didn't waver when she covered him.

She took the alarm clock he had forgotten to set downstairs with her. In the warm, safe darkness of her own kitchen, the exclamatory ticking of the tinny, old clock kept her asthmatic company. It also kept her awake.

The sight of Mike's white, weary face tonight had reminded her of the night he had first come to her for help. He was the only one of Jack's four children who resembled him. The others all had the imperturbable, blond, smooth look of their mother.

Mike had knocked at the door at eleven o'clock one night. Tiz had stepped aside to let him come into the kitchen. Silently he had gone over to the stove and held his red, stiff hands out to the warmth. It was November and cold and he wore only a thin shirt and his trousers. His bony shoulders shook under the flimsy cotton.

"What do you mean, running around like that this hour of the night?" she'd inquired icily. When Mike turned she saw the livid bruise along his cheekbone and down the side of his face.

"Aunt Tiz—"

"Yes?"

"I—"

"How'd you do that?" She touched the shocking bruise lightly and Mike jerked his dark head away from her fingers.

"I got hit."

"Looks like somebody let you have it with a two-by-four." Absently, wondering what on earth had happened to

52

him, she reached for a cigaret. Above the match flame, her eyes met his fascinated stare and she grinned, thinking Mike had seldom seen a woman he knew smoke. The fascination reminded her that he was only a baby.

"Look," she said. "Just tell me what happened."

Her voice had grown gentler and Mike's face puckered.

"I done something awful. I don't know what they'd do to me if they ever caught me."

"Well?"

"I—had a fight with Harold. He hit me with a piece of stove wood."

"Yes?"

"It's like this. I think I killed him. I let him have it over the head with a milk bottle and blood run down all over his face. He fell down. I think he's dead."

Tiz went quickly to the telephone. When she touched the crank Mike was at her furiously.

"You can't tell them where I am! Just let me get out of the house. Just give me an hour to get out of town."

"I'm not going to tell anyone anything," she said. "But let's find out how bad Harold's hurt."

"Nita?" she said to the slow, sweet voice at the other end of the line, feeling her own clipped syllables get even tighter. "This is Tiz."

It was never necessary to say more than that to Anita. If she had anything to tell you, it would come out like water out of a jug.

"Oh, Tiz! I've just had the doctor here to put four stitches in poor Harold's head." When his mother got that far, Tiz put the receiver down to Mike's level. "That little devil of a Mike hit him over the head with a bottle. Near half-killed him. I don't know what I'm going to do with those boys if they don't stop fighting."

"Where's Mike now?" Tiz asked into the spate.

"He's run off out. Probably won't come home all night."

"He ever stayed out all night before?" Tiz raised one eyebrow and glanced thoughtfully down at her breathless nephew.

"Oh, yes." Nita's voice was unworried. "He's a regular little wildman. He'll be back by morning."

"I'm sure he will," Tiz agreed, threatening Mike. "I hope Harold's all right."

"Good night, Tiz. Oh, was there anything special you wanted?"

"No, no," Tiz said hastily, and hung up.

"All right." She turned on Mike. "Get upstairs and go to bed. Nobody's dead. You better have something for your face."

"I'm all right." Mike's shoulders stiffened. "I don't ask nothing from anyone."

But a minute later his voice floated thinly down to her, the voice of a ten-year-old, asking all that a ten-year-old would.

"Good night, Aunt Tiz."

In the morning he had firmly refused to go home and Tiz had gone reluctantly off to see his mother. When she had come back, Mike was sitting tautly on the doorstep waiting for her. Her eyes felt burned and her glance was cursory.

"All right. You don't have to go back. You can stay here with me, or else do anything you want to."

"Well." He was a little frightened at the sight of her face. "I'd like to stay here with you, Aunt Tiz. At least till I'm old enough to get a job. You have to be sixteen."

"Stay, then. Only don't call me *Aunt* Tiz."

Mike had stayed and had never called her by the forbid-

54

den name again. Nor had he ever asked what Tiz and his mother had said that morning. Funny, Tiz thought, how a family peters out. Nita and Jack were both dead. Their only daughter, dead. The three boys—Mike was here; but she hadn't heard from Harold or Ralph in years and Mike himself didn't know where they were.

At three-thirty the raucous scream of the alarm jerked her off the couch, completely awake. Hastily she groped for the clock and choked it into silence.

Without consciously deciding, she got ready and went out to the car. She wouldn't sleep another wink tonight anyhow, and she could probably do the patrolling better than Mike could because she wasn't so tired to begin with.

She saw with surprise that a figure was waiting at Jasper's driveway. The flashlight waved her down.

"Mike." The voice wasn't Eddie's. "I'm sorry, but you'll have to go alone tonight."

"It's not Mike, Ginny."

"Oh, Tiz!"

"I couldn't bear to wake him up."

"Wait till I get a jacket." Ginny's voice came floating back to her when the flashlight was bobbing halfway up the drive. "I'll go, too."

In front of the town hall, a car was already waiting. Tiz stopped behind it and the driver got out and came back to her.

"Jay," she said accusingly, seeing his worn face in the headlight, "are you trying to kill yourself?"

"Thought I better go the first night." Jay had trouble making himself realize who she was. "Mike?"

"He's where you should be, in bed. What's the route?"

"It's just the back roads. Every road not listed here is

55

closed. These are the ones where people live." His careful, tired voice stumbled.

"It's a long, lonesome ride, Tiz. Takes a full hour to cover at twenty-five or thirty miles an hour. I figured four rounds to a patrol. There'll be somebody waiting here at eight in the morning."

Tiz took the paper out of his fumbling fingers, and swung the car past him down the deserted street. The only light in town burned faintly in the the telephone exchange. Main Street changed imperceptibly to the main road. The houses drew farther apart and the the trees closed in.

"Well," Tiz said in a sort of hearty croak. "Here we go. You nervous?"

"Yes, I am. I don't know how I'd act if we really found a fire."

Tiz's mind gathered into a tight, rubbery knot and let go with a snap. She can say it out loud, she thought, and the rest of us say anything but.

When they left the tar for the first washboardy, gravel road, darkness and moonlight lay before them like a dappled carpet. A before-dawn breeze ruffled the silver-gray heads of parched grass across a field. The road pulled the car like a child's toy on a string down to the water where the cars of parkers had worn a turn-around. As they came back up there were lights in one or two houses where there had been only darkness minutes before. For Tiz the lights made it worse.

"Seeing these houses out here, tucked away under the trees." Slowly she tried to give the feeling form in words. "You'd ,think it was the safest place in the world to live. And you know it isn't. There ought to be something visible to *mean* danger. But it's so peaceful. And they're so defenseless."

56

She stopped, waiting to see if Ginny would understand what she meant. But Ginny let the silence grow until Tiz started, in self-defense, to talk about something else.

When they had finished their first round and came back past the town hall, light was growing reluctantly and the atmosphere had tightened against the coming of day. Day meant that people would be out and around; people, the only unknown quantity in the equation of danger. The air felt colder and every low-lying hollow had its deceiving, heart-stopping drift of ground mist. From a distance, nothing looks so much like smoke as ground mist in the moonlight. Even after daybreak, several times Tiz felt her heart give its betraying leap. Every nerve in her taut body would be pulling the other way; but ahead lay the hateful, lovely mist.

Ginny had turned on the radio; but there was nothing at this hour in the morning but the nerve-wracking, yodeling cowboy music. Finally she stopped fiddling with the dial and promptly fell asleep.

Tiz let her sleep. It was less exhausting than having to try to think of something to say to her. The night was quiet and Ginny was always there and easy to wake if it became necessary. Her own eyes felt heavy and she heard Ginny's even breath with envy.

It was a shame to wake her, Tiz thought, stopping at Jasper's driveway at eight o'clock. But she did and Ginny climbed obediently out of the car and went up the walk, staggering and uncertain with interrupted sleep. Tiz watched her progress with an amused smile until she had reached the shed door in safety.

Her eyes heavy, her mind concentrated on the thought of bed, Ginny was halfway across the kitchen before the amazed voice stopped her as abruptly as a heavy hand on her shoulder.

"Would it be asking too much, Virginia, for you to tell me where the hell you've been?"

If her father had been acting like this all her life, she would have been hardened and expecting it. But it was so new, only since Marm had died. Momentarily she had forgotten that he would almost certainly be waiting for her. She knew how he would look, sitting in the chair by the window, a short, stout, bullocky man, bolt upright; his smooth, sun-reddened face that had lately become the face of a stranger. His hair would be standing stiffly on his rounded skull, each spear as straight and independent of its fellows as a soldier in a platoon.

"Virginia!"

She turned slowly to face his outraged astonishment and he sat there so exactly as she had known he would that she nearly laughed.

"My reputation is pretty good, Ginny. I don't want the neighbors to see my daughter coming home at eight in the morning. Don't you understand that?"

"Look, Pa, if you don't trust me, why did you let me alone while Marm was still around?"

"It's up to a mother to tend to her daughter. I had Eddie. You were your mother's affair. Now she's gone, I've got to do my best to take her place. And I'm not going to stand for things like this, Ginny. Not unless— You weren't with By, were you?"

She shook her head against the hopeful question, wondering why that would make it any better.

"Well, where then? Who with? Answer me."

"I was wondering if you'd believe me if I told you the truth."

58

"If it's truth, I'll believe it." He was righteously sure he could distinguish between truth and falsehood.

"Oh, Pa! Honestly, you've got to stop this business. You're driving me—"

"Whatever I do, Ginny, I'm doing for your own good. Nobody knows any better than I do that women are weak. But nobody's going to get in trouble because of my daughter if I can help it."

He meant every unbelievable word he said. Since her mother had died, Jasper's constant, nagging suspicion had become unbearable; but he'd never before taken the trouble to justify it.

"I didn't go out till four, Pa." Ginny gave a gasping laugh. "Doesn't that make it worse? I went to ride fire patrol with Tiz Arey. She's standing over in her back yard this minute. I'll call her and she can tell you." And thank God, she added silently, it *was* Tiz and not Mike.

Jasper relaxed visibly when he saw Tiz; but for an awful minute Ginny thought he was actually going to call to her.

"Well, if you're willing I should ask her it must be true. I'm sorry, dear. I don't really want to feel like this but I have to. Think how *you'd* feel—if it was *your* daughter."

"I'm trying to, Pa." She turned away abruptly. "It's pretty hard to do."

The ease with which he suspected her was infectious. Thinking back, she was almost prepared to suspect herself. Last night she hadn't even tried to sober Eddie, feeling with a tinge of undeniable excitement that events would take their course anyhow. If Mike had arrived instead of Tiz, she would have gone.

What is the matter with me? she thought blankly. I don't

want to get mixed up with him again. I can't! It's not decent! In a month I'm being married.

The thought of Byron was sobering. Maybe Pa was right and a woman was nothing but a weak reed. She remembered an instant on that long ride when she had glanced dreamily across at Tiz and thought sleepily, I wonder what we'd be saying if it *had* been Mike, instead.

This morning's early rising had left no hangover in Tiz. She sat in the car at the unmarred heart of a charmed circle, looking at her house. By turning her head a degree, she could see the hole in her horizon where Jasper's barn had been. Closer to the main road and supposedly to safety was the more distant blankness where the broken-backed dragon silhouette of Powder Tilton's red buildings was no longer. Not a mile away rose the stripped and blackened hills. And only three hundred yards across the field were the burned trees.

She put her hand on the trunk of the old Northern Spy tree and looked up into its sprawling fountain of branches. The leaves had thinned through the drought. In the top of the tree a flock of starlings discussed the coming winter as articulately as they had every fall before.

A car turned the corner and came coasting silently down the road to stop beside the picket fence. Tiz didn't know how long it has been there when she turned and met Clyde Amory's amused, interested stare. He was leaning forward over the wheel of the police car, his flat, newly shaven cheeks looking scrubbed in the brash, morning light, his eyes shadowed by the visor of his cap.

"What you doing, Tiz?" he inquired pacifically.

She blushed and took her hand off the borer-riddled trunk of the tree.

"I guess I was just being grateful for small favors."

"You *were* one of the lucky ones," he agreed. He gave the visor a shove and the threatening shadow no longer hid the steadiness of his gray eyes and they still said something he himself had said only once in so many words.

"Well," Tiz said hastily. "I guess I'll have some breakfast."

"I had some." He paused reflectively. "About two hours ago."

"You'd better have some coffee." She couldn't see how to avoid the invited invitation.

"Maybe so. My stomach's beginning to think my throat's cut." He got out of the car, groaning. "Lord, Tiz, I don't even begin to feel my age until something like this happens. I've been on the hump for the last week and, believe me, I know it."

He looked more than his fifty years. The whites of his eyes, usually as clear as bluish glass, were veined with tiny red lines and he walked with a careful settling of his weight on each foot that wasn't like him.

"None of us are getting any younger." He answered her unobvious glance apparently without seeing it. "Nobody lives forever, Tiz. Or leastwise, nobody stays young forever."

"I don't think I'd want to," she said sharply.

"Maybe not. I don't know's I would myself—specially if everyone else didn't. I'd want to keep up with you, Tiz."

"Amory—" she began with anxious desperation.

"It's all right," he said quickly. "I'm not saying anything. I just wanted you to know that there's a lot doesn't change even if we *do* get older. Some things seem to get stronger the longer we live."

"I'm sorry."

"You know you don't have to say anything to me, Tiz. We had it all out. But sometimes a man kind of has to re-affirm the things he believes in."

"I wish you'd—" It was harder for her to find anything to say to him now than it had ever been. It didn't seem important that he should stop talking to her like this.

"I wish you'd settle down," she said lamely.

"Well, I won't and you know as well as I do why." His big, weathered face twisted into a surprisingly sweet smile.

Tiz knew as well as if he had told her that he would never let unrequited love keep him awake nights. Nor would he let it make him sleep alone. In a way she was glad he was so honestly himself. There would be no false protestations of complete, physical fidelity from a man like Amory. He hadn't made them even on that first night when he had told her in brusque, clear, surprising words how he felt about her and how he thought he would always feel.

Knowing his reputation, she had taken his declaration of permanence with reservations that time had erased.

"I'm sorry," she said again, weakly, because the inade-quacy of the answer she had always had for him had become too apparent. "I wish—"

"You needn't wish for anything. I'm willing to take what I can get. And right now I'll settle for a cup of coffee."

"Don't bring him here," Mike yelled. He was standing beside the stove and his black hair might have felt a comb. His face looked swollen and numb with sleep and only his eyes were fully awake.

Amory grinned and shied his cap at a peg behind the door. It clung hopefully for a moment and slid to the floor. "Signs and portents," he commented thoughtfully.

"You look kind of pooped," Mike said.

62

"Well, probably because I am." Amory sat down, letting out a sighing breath.

"*Has* been kind of a hectic week," Mike agreed. He filled their cups, looking accusingly at Tiz.

"I might have known you wouldn't wake me. Did you ride my patrol?"

She nodded.

"Alone?"

"Oh, no, I had company."

"Eddie, I suppose?" Mike insisted.

Tiz shook her head.

"Well, *who?*" Mike roared.

"Ginny." She regarded his deep interest with amusement. "Nothing much happened. About eight o'clock, I saw a fine smudge of smoke and rushed up just in time to point the fire the janitor had just built at the Bartlett's Cove schoolhouse."

Amory let out a bark of laughter.

"I'll get along, I guess. Thanks for the coffee, Mike," he added from the door. "If you could only cook, you'd make some girl a fine wife."

"What're you going to do today?" Tiz said after he had gone. "Going to haul?"

"Well, I don't rightly feel like going away from home. Pretty late to start hauling, too."

"I'd be glad to have your ugly face around, if you want to stay." She tried to sound chaffing.

"I don't feel much like doing anything till I know whether it's going to be any use." Mike grinned shortly.

"I know what you mean. But we could get the vegetables in, pick the apples. Stuff like that. If I could make myself think it wasn't going to happen, I'd feel better."

"Yeah," he said indecisively. But when she looked out the window a few minutes later he had started on the first fern-topped row of carrots. Behind him they lay on the dry ground, nubbiny, but yellower than gold.

She was just on the verge of going out when she heard a stirring overhead and the sound of cautious feet on the stairs. Lord, she thought contritely, I forgot all about Polly!

"Tiz. Tiz. Are you alone?"

"It's safe." Tiz stifled a smile. "Everyone's gone but me."

Polly was fully dressed and already looking harried.

"I been up since six. Where on earth you been, leaving me alone with that young fellow? I got to go right home. Pa'll be crazy, wondering where I am." Her natural curiosity overcame her. "*What* did Clyde Amory want? What did he say?"

For an amused minute Tiz wondered what Polly would do if she told her what Clyde Amory had been saying as they came up the walk.

"He just wanted some coffee."

"The *cop!*"

"I'll get Mike to run you home, Polly." Tiz cut her short.

"Oh, no. I'd much rather walk. Thank you for everything, Tiz. And please come and see me as soon as you can."

Polly's invitation was more than the conventional request.

She went down the walk, her eyes carefully averted from Mike. Tiz was watching him disapprovingly from the door.

"That woman makes me feel like I wasn't even here," he complained.

"She's pretending you aren't," Tiz said. "She didn't want to compromise you."

She went out to join him. He needn't think he was going to have all the fun. She usually saved getting in the
64

vegetables for a day when she didn't feel quite up to snuff, and this was it.

The southwest wind that had begun before daylight was freshening and the sea, which for the past two days, had been as calm and shadowless as a goldfish bowl, was raising a few whitecaps. Tiz sifted the scent of smoke from the rising wind, wishing it would never blow again.

After she started working along the garden rows, she managed to forget that threatening smell of smoke which must be coming from somewhere to the westward.

At noon Mike went down to the store and came back with two bottles of beer. Tiz found a can of corned beef in the cupboard and they sat in the lee of the woodpile eating in peaceful silence.

Mike had finished the last sandwich and was lighting his cigaret when he heard the screech of brakes at the gate. Jay Stone's car, loaded to the gunwhales, was making a U-turn before the house.

"Come on, Mike," Jay yelled.

Mike didn't stop for questions; but Jay explained briefly for Tiz.

"There's a fire in the cutting on Hardwood Point. Small yet. If we get to it in time—"

She lost the last few words as the car pulled away. It swayed crazily around the corner and vanished with a scream of rubber on macadam.

She stood staring to the south, trying to find smoke over the trees; but she could see only the southwest haze.

PART TWO

*Tomorrow fair. Gentle northeast winds,
changing to southwest late in the day.*

J AY STONE stood at the northeast corner of the old,
pulp clearing on Hardwood Point looking back down across
its blackened smoking vacuity toward the water, and the
hair on the back of his neck rose like the hackles on a dog's
back. The sickening smell of salt-water steam was gagging
in his throat.

It beats the devil, he thought wearily, how anything like
this happens in just the right place at the right time. If the
boys on patrol hadn't been more than on their toes, the
south end of Frenchville would have gone up in smoke this
afternoon.

Damn the pulp cutters to hell, anyway. Leaving a mess
like this behind them. But God bless them for at least ob-
serving the letter of the law. For fifty feet back from the
road they had cleared away their slash. That fifty feet of
young birch and alders, growing free of the snatching, tearing underbrush, had been one of the major reasons that
the fire was stopped now. If, with that wind behind it, it
had crossed the road into the second-growth spruce, the fire
wouldn't have stopped until it hit solid, salt water on the
other side of the Peninsula.

66

Jay wiped the back of his neck with a black handkerchief and found the skin tender. Gently he sopped at the mixture of sweat and accumulated dust. He discovered that his knees were shaking.

He couldn't see yet how they had managed to keep the blowtorch of fire within the clearing. On each side of the blackened strip the spruces hung, brooding and dark, their limbs halfway up the trunks as dead and brittle as the branches of trees long gone.

Four hours earlier this whole clearing had been hip-deep in five-year-old slash, laced into near solidity with raspberry and blackberry thicket, so dry it sent up clouds of dust behind each step. Now it was as clean as the palm of his hand.

He could hear the pumper going steadily down on the shore; and, remembering the steep bank, he wasn't sure how they'd managed to get it down there. Halfway across the clearing, between him and the water, a group of creatures resembling devils out of hell managed one hose line which was still pouring gallons of salt water into the hot spots.

He stumbled tiredly back over the singed ground to the hose crew. The cold water brought up an answering spurt of steam from crevices among the boulders where fire had driven stubbornly deep.

Allen Carter came just as tiredly up from the shore.

"You didn't leave that pumper alone, did you?" Jay asked.

"Think I'm crazy? Mike and Powder are down there. I told 'em one could leave at a time; but I'd kill both of them if they went together. They'll watch it."

"Better leave the pumper here with a crew all night."

"I feel like leaving it till the damn place freezes over," Allen's face was a mask of dead black and dead white. "It'll be here till the fire's out. Rely on it."

"I don't know but it's pretty well out right now," Jay said judiciously.

Allen grinned.

"Take a look behind you," he suggested gently.

Jay spun and stared. A patch of ground a yard behind him and about a yard square was turning black. There was no smoke at first. The center of the small space fell inward with a soft, puffing noise, leaving a glowing cancer of fire burning a foot deep into the punky ground. The duff around it singed and began to smoke. Jay let out a yell and sprang away from it.

The two men on the hose nozzle filled the circle with cold salt water.

"We were lucky it was so near the shore," Allen said as casually as if the earth had not just opened up in fire under his feet. "If it'd been inland, we'd have been hard put. With everything so dry, the only thing you can use is water and plenty of it."

"Wells," Jay said flatly.

"What wells ain't dry already, that pumper would suck dry in a matter of seconds."

"Oh."

"If anything else breaks loose tonight, you'll have to get a bunch of the boys to go out and spit on it. We're staying right here till I'm satisfied there isn't anything else to wet down."

Jay went at a swift, stumbling walk down the hill toward the shore, his sweat turning cold in the warm, late afternoon. This fire niggled at him. Back in a corner of his tired mind there was something he couldn't put a word to.

The southwest wind was dying with the sunset. The rays of the setting sun, level with his eyes, fell like a blow against the anguished lids.

68

That idea was starting to come out into the open. A fire starting down in the southwest corner of a slash clearing where there was no earthly reason for anyone to be, not even berry pickers at this time of year!

He could see about where it had started, to the east of a ledgy outcrop. With the wind behind it, blowing strongly, the fire had fanned out rapidly to take in the entire clearing.

He knew about spontaneous combustion and that there was no finer fire glass in the world than the neck or the heavy bottom of a beer bottle.

If every broken bottle was a potential danger, they were living in a powder keg. Along the main roads the kids scavenged like gulls and missed nothing in the way of a redeemable bottle. But through the woods anything could lie undiscovered until its potential was generated into animation by the four, hot hours of overhead sunshine at noon.

He reached the brink of the drop to the shore and made his way along it, knee deep in fine grass as soft and silvery as the hair of a clean old man. His feet made a sound not so soft as a hushing, but drier, sharper, more dangerous. He saw the two men standing on the shore beside the throbbing pumper and wondered again how they had got it down there and how in the name of God they were going to get it up.

Mike and Powder were all right now. Funny. No matter how allergic two men were to each other, let a crisis arise and they forgot all about it. Jay accepted the fact thankfully. So long as they put off their battles until things quieted down, they could tear each other apart later for all of him.

He moved slowly up toward the beginning of the burn,

69

through a small island of unsinged spruces. He wasn't watching the path; and the round thing that rolled, then gave under his weight, threw him heavily off balance.

He stooped to pick up the big tin can that had flattened under his foot, giving it a brief glance. Still holding it, he stood watching the stream from the hose far up the hill as it caught the last rays of sunlight, and he waited for the ache in his ankle to subside.

Well, he thought wearily, as long as we have a day or so between fires, maybe we can hang on. He wasn't sure. The way he felt, there wasn't much left in him with which to hang on.

Then suddenly he sniffed. There was something terribly wrong. The smell of smoke had an accompanying odor, which was the smell of treachery.

With the strong, unmistakable scent of kerosene in his nostrils, Jay knew there had been nothing accidental about the time and place of this fire.

He stood staring wildly about him. When his eye fell on the big can he still held, he lifted it and sniffed once. He jerked his head back as if he had found a nest of rattle-snakes curled comfortably inside the tin. Slowly he lifted it again and looked into it. There were a few drops of nearly colorless liquid in the seam at the bottom of the can and he tipped them out into the cupped palm of his free hand. Feeling as if his hand were burning, he hastily wiped the wet palm on the seat of his pants.

Dear loving God, he thought, what'll I do now?

His immediate reaction was to tell somebody. He turned to run; but years of training held his feet right where they were. There were a good many other things to consider besides knowledge and he knew them all.

First there was the town itself. Frenchville depended

largely on its summer trade. Once you let a story like this get out and it wouldn't do the town any good. How many times in the last few years he had heard that particular phrase. Conceal. Hide. Keep to yourself. He could remember the time a few years back when four cases of scarlet fever had broken out in July. A deputation from the board of health had come to the selectmen's office. They had suggested loudly that the information be kept quiet. If it got out, it wouldn't do the town any good.

Panic was another thing. The way people were feeling, panic would go through the town the way fire already had. If they ever found out this fire had been set! If he kept it to himself, it would be better for everyone. He could watch. He—

But he couldn't. Even as he thought it, Jay knew that this thing was too big for any one man to handle. Before he could think what was best to do, it was already too late to do anything.

Mike, who had come up the bank when he saw Jay, stood watching him curiously, eyes narrowed to take in whatever meaning there might be in Jay's look of distraught horror.

"Jay," he said sharply. "What is it?"

Jay glanced at him and shook his head; but that look drove Mike back an involuntary step.

"What's wrong, Jay?"

He came slowly along the few feet of path between them. Jay, realizing suddenly how it would look to Mike, finding him here with the evidence hot in his hand, felt like a man caught burying the body.

He thought he might divert Mike's attention from that betraying can and as he thought it, the can seemed to grow to proportions so great nobody could miss its significance.

Better face it out and rely on Mike to understand that it must be kept quiet.

He held out the can.

"What's so special about this?" Mike took it helplessly.

"Smell it," Jay said, his eyes blank and watchful.

Mike did, and Jay read correctly the swift passing of expression over his face: first comprehension, then horror; then, inevitably, suspicion.

"Where'd you get it?" Mike asked carefully.

"Right there." Jay pointed out the spot.

"Did—how did you know it was there?"

"I nearly broke an ankle on the cussed thing."

"Seems funny you'd know right where it was," Mike said clearly. It seemed to Jay that Mike had hunched inward, almost as if he expected Jay to fly at his throat.

"No, you blasted fool!" Jay yelled. "I didn't set the fire. I didn't come out here with a can of kerosene and try to burn the town up."

Mike accepted the denial with such alacrity that Jay realized he hadn't really believed for a minute what he'd seemed to be saying.

"Well." Mike held the can as if he expected it to come to life in his fingers. "I don't see why you— Why didn't you say right out what it was?" His shoulders relaxed; but his eyes were still furious and accusing. "Oh," he said into Jay's intent silence. "*I* see. You weren't going to say anything, were you? But if there's something like this going on, then we have to know it."

"It's like this." Jay tried to explain the inexplicable. "I —well, it wouldn't do the town any good to have a story like this around."

"Do the town any *good!*" Mike roared. "I suppose it'd be better to hide a thing like this and let people get burned alive in their beds, hanh? Do you suppose if there's anyone around would set a fire here, he's doing it for fun? Do you think he won't do it again? My God, Jay, we *have* to know. We'll have to watch every second."

"I didn't want to start a panic," Jay said, the words sounding stumbling and ridiculous to him. "I thought I could take care of it myself."

"Would you set out to fight a fire like this by yourself?" Mike's voice lowered a little. "No. And you may be a big man; but you aren't big enough to handle everything alone. You got to tell people. You *got* to."

"I won't do it," Jay said flatly. "I'm first selectman of this town and I'll take care of this. This is my business. You stay out."

"I don't care if you're King Tut himself. You couldn't take care of this alone. And I'll tell people if you won't."

Mike started up the hill toward the hose line with the can in his hand. Jay shrugged and followed slowly. It was out of his hands. Once you told anyone else anything at all your authority was divided and never so complete as it had been at first.

Mike glanced back, and when he found that Jay had started after him, he stopped to wait.

"I guess you're right." Jay came up with him. "Anyway, I can't stop you without a fight."

"No, you can't," Mike agreed.

Allen Carter was standing on the rise beside the hose crew watching them come and there must have been something revealing in the way they walked. His singed, black face was tight and his eyes watchful and showing a lot of white under the brows.

"Who's down there with the pumper?" He stared at Mike.

"Powder," Mike said soothingly. "Powder's there, Allen."

He passed the treacherous can to Jay who took it casually and put it into Allen's outstretched hand.

"We got something to show you, Al," Jay said quietly. "I found this down where the fire started. It had coal oil in it this morning. Not now."

"I didn't feel right about this fire," Allen said slowly. "It was too perfect. Everything against us."

"I guess we got us a firebug on top of everything else." Mike looked from one worn face to the other.

Jay could feel the change in the hose crew. A moment before they had been slack from weariness; now they were taut and their black faces fierce. Lord, he thought, I'm glad it's not me. There isn't a one of them wouldn't shoot me where I stand if he thought I'd done it.

It was exactly seven-thirty by the big clock in the post office building gable when Jay parked his old Studebaker in front of the town hall. He was still black and grimy and he hadn't even had time to comb his hair which stood in wiry wisps and at odd angles over his hard skull. He had dropped the last of his disreputable passengers and was going up to the office to wash off the worst of the grime before he went home to supper.

As he got out of the car he glanced up and down the length of the quiet street, dreaming and deserted in the afterglow of sunset. He shook his head vigorously, trying to clear out the cobwebs that seemed to be behind his eyes, and stared at another face on the other side of the big glass door. He turned the knob.

"I'm not a ghost, Jay."

The familiar voice was all Jay needed to bring him back to normal. He managed a grin that was a little uncertain around the edges.

74

"Great Scott, Byron, I don't know whether I'm on my tail or my elbow. Seemed to me I hadn't ever seen you before. You waiting for me? Come on up to the office while I wash my face."

Jay disappeared into the tiny washroom off the inner office. When he came out again he was scrubbing his face with a dirty towel and the tender, abused skin glowed as if the blood under it were three or four layers nearer the surface than it should have been. His hair was tousled and limp with water.

"Well, I may not look any nearer being human," he said. "But I sure feel better."

He glanced curiously at Byron's clean face and hands and Byron flushed darkly. There was no accusation in Jay's straight glance, merely wonder that Byron had managed to be so clean. The accusation that wasn't there; Byron's mind put it there.

"I went over to the weir today," he said quickly. "I never dreamed anything would happen in the daytime. I don't know. Seems as if you expect anything like a fire to happen at night. I never got in till it was all over."

"Heck, Byron, you don't have to explain to me where you were. Nobody's accusing you of anything."

"No. I know it. But it looks kind of funny, anyone who doesn't pitch in and help. I just wanted you to know why I didn't."

"Look, don't any of you boys get the idea that I'm God Amighty and you have to explain to me everything you do. Because I ain't. And if my job comes anywhere near ending where His begins, I can tell you right now, I sure don't want to be."

Jay could hear his own voice burbling on and he wasn't quite sure what he was saying; but it was all right because it seemed to him Byron wasn't listening. He was like everyone else, so engrossed in his own thoughts he didn't even bother to hear what anyone else was saying to him, just went right on thinking until the other voice stopped and he could fill the silence with words of his own. "Jay, I'm supposed to ride patrol in a few minutes; but my car's in the garage with a burned-out main bearing. I didn't know but what you'd let me take yours just tonight. I'll have mine back tomorrow, the next day."

"Sure," Jay said quickly. "Take her. I wouldn't let her stall on me, though, because the battery's kind of low and she might not start again."

Suddenly he remembered the thing he had thought he would never forget and had forgotten for nearly ten minutes. Looking at Byron's clean face and hands, unsullied by fire fighting, he felt the first stirring suspicion directed at a particular person. Maybe Byron *had* been over on Hardacre Island this morning. But maybe he hadn't. And if he hadn't, of course he would make a great point of explaining his cleanness. Why, if Byron didn't know that fire had been set—and Jay didn't see how he could know yet—had he reacted so sharply to a casual glance? Standing there, hating himself for the position he was in and the necessity for watching Byron's face so closely, Jay said:

"Byron, we've really got trouble now."

Might as well tell him, he thought. It'll be all over town in half an hour. And if he *don't* know it already, he better get it straight from me instead of exaggerated from half a dozen others. Byron's expression of harried bewilderment was exactly the one Jay himself would have worn if anybody had said the same thing to him.

"Why? What's happened?"

"Plenty." Jay felt himself relax slightly. Byron certainly

wasn't behaving like a guilty man and Jay was pretty sure he wasn't that good an actor. "That fire down on the Point today was set. It didn't just happen."

"Oh, Jesus!" Byron said, his voice fading thickly. His face looked unrelated, like a loose collection of features that happened to be arranged in juxtaposition with no reason like an actual face for their being there. It was only for a second, before Byron had a chance to get his expression under control again and then he looked very young, but there was a new, quick, wolfish look about him that gave Jay a cold shiver.

"You got—how d'you know?" Byron asked.

"I found where it had been set. There was an empty can that had kerosene in it. I don't know what more you'd want."

"No, I guess you're right." Byron was staring out the window but he wasn't seeing the quiet street.

"Okay," Byron said. "I always like to know what I'm up against."

"Yeah."

"Guy must be crazy!"

"My idea, too. Trouble is, there's no way of knowing who it is, see? I don't like what may come of it. This is no time for any man not to be able to trust his next-door neighbor."

"Well." Byron looked at him bleakly. "All there is to do is watch everyone like a hawk. Just remember who you happened to be looking at when the next one starts. That's all. If you're looking right at someone when trouble starts, then you're pretty sure he's not starting it."

Byron's tough, unquestioning acceptance of this information and his taking for granted that where there had been some trouble there would likely be more made Jay see clearly the lack of wisdom he had shown this afternoon. Hiding the unwelcome knowledge would have been one of the dumbest things he had ever done and he accepted humbly the fact that his making it public had been forced on him.

They went together back down the stairs to the street. As they stopped beside the Studebaker, which was still muttering away like a faithful but crochety sewing machine, Byron glanced hopefully at the mackerel-clouded sky.

"Wind's shifting to the east again," he said. "Maybe we'll get a little rain from it."

"Don't count on it before it drowns you," Jay told him. "That wind's been boxing the compass all summer long. Twizzle, twizzle, twizzle! I should think every weather vane in town would be worn right off its bearings."

"It ain't decent." Byron scowled. "All this east wind without a drop of rain in it. Why, my garden this year didn't hardly get above ground. Not a green thing in it. Course, I didn't get it in until late and then there wasn't even enough dampness to make it grow once it come up."

"Yeah."

The patrol car on duty drew up to them. Anse Barker's flushed, weary face appeared in the driver's window.

"It's all yours, boy," he told Byron loudly. "The whole cussed mess." Byron grunted, climbed into Jay's car, sat waiting while Anse and Charley Kelly loaded the Indian pumps into the back seat. Without a word, he pulled off down the street to get his second. Charley stood looking after him, his red face beginning to be a little angry, too.

"What ails *him?* Can't he speak English?"

"He just had some news that didn't set too good with him," Jay said heavily. "I guess I better tell you boys, too, so you'll know what we're up against."

He told them, seeing their faces undergo much the same metamorphosis as Byron's had.

"All right," Anse said slowly. "I'm just as glad to know exactly what we've got to contend with. Only I hope to the living Lord I ain't the one who finds him because they'd have me up for first-degree murder, premeditated."

Charley didn't say anything; but he didn't have to. The quick glance Jay took at his congested face was all he needed to know how Charley felt.

Standing there alone watching them drive away, Jay felt as if a huge, cold-fingered hand had closed around his heart and was squeezing it like a sponge until every drop of blood had been wrung out of it. Oh, my Lord, he thought, what am I letting loose in this town? The responsibility for turning neighbor against neighbor was his and it was almost too much for one man to bear. He felt as poorly equipped as a child to handle whatever hysteria of violence might come of knowledge. The result of this business could be nothing but violent, and his whole soul shriveled away from the idea.

Here in this quiet street where peaceful men had lived their sane, steady lives, the mere idea of violence was an intrusion. The light that lay across the time-mellowed houses denied its validity. The great elms that had shaded those houses for a century or more claimed immunity from violence.

He thought suddenly of the men and women who had lived in and loved this place and died long before he himself had ever walked under these elms, past these houses they had built. He thought of the big, old, square, white house on the hill where he lived himself, where his father's father had been born one hundred and ten years ago. He remembered himself as a child in this place that had always

79

meant security and the ultimate of safety to the child, where now the man walked in fear and trembling because of what he was doing to something as calm and established as two centuries of safety.

Then he caught himself wondering if maybe something like this wasn't necessary every generation or so. Maybe the life they lived in places like this was too safe. Maybe they needed crisis as a laxative to do away with the underground fights, the old grudges that live on in the succeeding generations of a family when the original instigators and the original reasons have been long dead. In a place where time had come to matter as little as it did here, maybe that unimportance was a sign of underlying evil.

Above the kitchen ell roof of Ray Spalding's house, he could see the high, unpruned, age-massive branches of the Yellow Transparent tree from which he himself had stolen apples long ago. And the tree then had been as big as it was now and looked as old.

Between the white house where Miss Lizzie Goodwin lived all alone and the mansard-roofed, once-elegant minarets of the house Captain Baker had built years ago when he retired from the sea lay the hummocked, alder-grown pasture where Jay had broken his leg once, trying to ride Miss Lizzie's gentle Jersey cow.

Beyond the Baker house, overgrown and nearly invisible, was the empty cellar where the Seaforth place had burned twenty years ago and had never been rebuilt because the two Seaforth boys hadn't had the money to put it back the way it once was. Being family-proud, they wouldn't rebuild on any other scale. The cellar slowly filled in with the years, the mortar runneled down, and the burdocks grew rank.

If you knew the Main Street of a town and what lay behind it, you had its whole history there—each house, each tree, each cellar, each vacant lot was a chapter, and the people whose names had been written on the deeds were the characters. In nine out of ten of these houses, tucked away in a desk drawer somewhere, the old, original deeds were lying and at their heads the words: Commonwealth of Massachusetts. That was before Maine was a state. Good for nothing now but curiosities, yet somehow they never got destroyed. They were important. Just knowing they were there.

There was a deed like that in the right-hand side of the old Governor Winthrop desk in his own front parlor. The record of ten pounds cash paid to the Commonwealth of Massachusetts by Jathro Stone in 1789 for fifty acres of land.

This land, Jay thought, setting his foot firmly on his own place. This land I'm standing on right now.

Maybe we're too old and ingrown. Maybe the evil is coming out.

He looked up and saw Addie in her crisp, clean, blue, cotton dress sitting on the front porch waiting for him and knew that he *must* be crazy to think that what he had here wasn't good. Maybe, when the human organism reached a certain point in exhaustion, craziness was a safety valve.

Any place about which people felt as they did about this one—Jay had no doubt that everyone else loved it as much as he did—must be good. But it was changing and perhaps the people were changing, too. A man was his own boss; but having been many different things was nothing against him any longer. It meant merely that he would try his hand at anything before he'd leave his native place where once a man could spend his lifetime at one job and make a good living and a little more. But the jobs were shifting sand and going out from under a man who found his toe-hold anything but steady. Jack-of-all-trades he had to be—and master, too. Because most men did all their own work instead of paying out money to the men trained to do it. They either did it themselves or it didn't get done —and the man who was willing to do it wanted to be able to take pride in what he did for himself at least, since there was little else left to be proud of.

"Jay," Addie said gently as he came stumbling up the hill. "You must be nearly dead. There's supper in the warming oven for you."

"I'll eat in a minute," Jay said. He sat down on the top step like a doll collapsing at the joints. "Just a minute, soon as I get my breath."

He was worrying over a new and nasty idea that had just occurred to him. Why would a man set a fire if he wasn't crazy? Money, of course! Insurance. But who ever insured a pulp clearing? No, that wasn't it. Whose buildings would have burned if they hadn't stopped that fire? Pop Danforth's, for sure. He wouldn't have much insurance, though. His place wasn't worth more than three or four hundred. By's might easily have gone. But Byron was well off for a young fellow. Pretty well extended, though. Finger in every pie he got close enough to smell. That was quite a place he had, too. How in thunder could you find out how much insurance a man carried, short of asking him?

Addie didn't speak to him again. After a glance at his face, she let him sit there in silence, watching the light fade in lovely color across the ruined hills.

"Did Jay think of looking for fingerprints on the can?" Tiz asked.

Mike opened his mouth and sat staring across the table like an idiot.

"Fingerprints!" he repeated, making the word sound profane. He had a momentary vision of that can passing rapidly from hand to hand after Allen had looked it over. He gave a short, distorted yell of laughter.

"Judas priest, it never entered our heads! And if it was tested for fingerprints now, there isn't a man there who wouldn't be hauled in. Jay's are on it. So're mine. Every guy on that hose line had that can in his hands some time or other."

"That was bright!"

"Wasn't it?" Mike agreed.

He sat cursing them all for fools before he thought of the obvious thing.

"But, Tiz, it wouldn't have done any good. If there *had* been fingerprints on it, they wouldn't have told anything without something to compare them to. It's not like a face or anything you could recognize. There couldn't be anything more anonymous than a set of fingerprints without any idea who they belonged to."

"Lord, that's right, too."

Mike leaned comfortably back in his chair, bringing the front legs off the floor. It was surprising what a bath and a good meal could do for anyone. Now that an agency recognizably human had entered into this business, Mike, to his own surprise, felt better. It wasn't that the danger had decreased—it had done the opposite. But he felt less as if the Lord Himself had declared war. A man, no matter how crazy, was still something you could recognize and touch and sooner or later grapple with. Brought to a focus, impersonal fear changed, took on a dogged, stubborn wrath that made it easier to bear. The fear was still there because the cause and result had not changed; but as long as the anger lived, fear would never turn to panic.

There was another inevitable presence that had been bred by knowledge; and Mike, recognizing its shadow over his thoughts, didn't care for it. Suspicion would be harder to live with than fear.

When a man needed the support of his neighbors most of all, first in his mind would be suspicion of those neighbors. But he couldn't point to any one of his neighbors and think directly: *He* could be the one. There was only one person in the entire town of whom he could believe such a thing. Hokey Mitchell, the half-wit, who lived in that old pulp-cutter's shack down by Anse Barker's house. He might do it just for the excitement. But when he really stopped to think, it was hard for Mike to believe it of Hokey, either. Hokey had to tend to his own business with a single-minded purpose to get himself a living.

There was nobody.

But there *had* to be someone.

The October night pressed close against the shining kitchen windows. Outside, in the branches of the Spy tree, the wind shifted idly through the dry leaves, making a faint whisper of sound. Hushed and waiting, impersonal and all-concealing, night lay over the Peninsula a solid blanket of blackness, blacker than ever just before moonrise.

"The trouble is—" Mike began aloud when they both heard the hurried footsteps on the clamshell walk. He stiffened in his chair and sat staring at the door. Whoever it was, was coming fast; but there was none of the expected urgency in that walk—no hint of emergency, just purpose.

Mike had already relaxed when knuckles touched the door panel lightly.

"Come in," Tiz yelled.

"Hello." Ginny Hanscom's voice preceded her.

84

"Pull up and have some coffee," Tiz said hospitably. "Sorry there's nothing more to offer; but Mike and I, between us, have licked the platter clean."

"I just finished supper. I'd like coffee, though."

Composedly she sat down between them. As she came within direct range of the lamplight, Mike could see the tiny twitching of a muscle beside her right eye.

He sat watching her face with an old, remembered hunger. In this light, her eyes looked larger and darker than they were. He knew so well how they really were—clear and a sort of topaz color like brook water running over dead maple leaves. He could see the small, quirky line at the corner of her wide mouth, a line that looked tight now but might dissolve into laughter. That was new. There was a lightly traced fan of finer lines at the corner of her eye, too.

She faced him and her lifted brows told him she had been aware of his scrutiny from the beginning.

"Mike," she said directly. "I had to come over and find out what happened today. Eddie came home with the darndest story. He says it's all over town. But he heard it from Allen Carter."

"What story's that?" Mike thought it might be interesting to see how it had been distorted since the actual incident. Surprisingly it was not distorted at all, and he realized that when a thing is really bad, it needs little exaggeration.

"They're saying Jay Stone found a can that had kerosene in it. They're saying the fire today was set."

"Well, it was."

"I do *not* believe it."

The nerve beside her eye set up a quick, betraying movement and she put up one hand to hide it.

"I wish *I* didn't," Mike said soberly. "I was right there and it's true."

"It—" She took a deep breath as if the air were laden with a substance that made it hard to breath.

"Yes," Tiz agreed wholeheartedly with her unspoken reaction.

"It's hard to believe anyone would—"

"Anyone who would," Mike said brutally, "is crazy and you can count on that."

"Or broke," Tiz suggested stolidly. Their blank reaction denied the validity of that.

"Could it be— It might be somebody from away. Some of those crazy kids looking for excitement." Desperately Ginny tried to convince herself.

Mike shook his head.

"That's possible. But it seems to me whoever set that fire knew just where to do it. He knew what he was doing and he knew the lay of the land as well as I do. You take a stranger, he'd have to do a lot of prowling around to light on a place as good as that one—and anyone doing that kind of prowling right now would be laying himself open to a lot of misunderstanding. No." His head shake was weary. "I'd like to think you were right; but the man who set that fire wasn't anyone from away."

"What are they going to do?"

Mike shrugged.

"There's nothing *to* do. Except wait and watch and pray to God it'll rain. I guess Jay plans to make the patrols tighter. He's got some idea in his head. But he better do it and do it fast or we'll be having a few self-appointed vigilantes horsing around and Lord knows what'll happen then."

"Well," Ginny said slowly. Indecisively she got up and started for the door. "I guess I'll go along. I wish it would rain. I just wanted to get the rights of it. I don't really

86

know for sure whether Eddie knows what he's talking about half the time."

"How's your father?" Tiz asked suddenly.

Ginny gave her a quick, searching, furtive look.

"What—how d'you mean?"

"Why, I mean how *is* he? How is he bearing up?" Tiz's astonished reaction gave Ginny back her confidence, mixed with embarrassment at having been so defenseless as to think for a moment that Tiz might know more about her than anyone else had a right to know.

"He's awfully upset about Eddie." She was saying more than she would ordinarily have said to cover her slip. "Outside of that, he seems sort of resigned to anything. I guess he feels nothing more can happen to him. Even when he saw the barn was gone, all he did was stand there and shake his head. Eddie bothers him terribly."

That was true enough, Ginny thought, as far as it went. She didn't have to go on and tell them the other thing Jasper cared about with a single-mindedness that had come to its full strength since her mother died. She couldn't say: His suspicion is driving me crazy. He doesn't trust me out of his sight.

Tiz, sensing the withheld, looked at her sharply. Eddie had always been his father's favorite, with reason, she admitted. That wasn't something that Jasper could hold against his daughter, but apparently he did. At least, he was making her miserable in some way.

"Is Eddie straightening out any?" she said brusquely, knowing it was none of her business and Ginny had every right to tell her so.

"No, he's not," Ginny said hotly, glad to be away from a more dangerous topic. "I don't know what's got into him. He just gives himself time to sober up into a good hangover and then he's off again. I don't know where he's getting the cussed stuff, and if I could find out, I'd kill the man who's selling it to him."

She put her hand on the latch and Mike got up slowly.

"I'll walk over with you," he announced and, against her quick protest, robbed the offer of any personality by adding: "I don't feel as if anyone ought to be wandering around alone."

"Oh, fine!" Ginny's voice was tart. "I suppose you'll tell me next you want to be sure I don't stop to set any incidental fires on the way."

"That, too," Mike agreed. He let the words hang in the air, unaccompanied.

"Mike, for heaven sake!" Tiz protested. "If that's your idea of a joke—!"

"I know." Suddenly penitent, he grinned. "I've got a primitive sense of humor."

"The remains of one!" Tiz corrected icily. "Ginny, just disregard him."

"You forget," Ginny said. "I knew him when. Him *and* his sense of humor, such as it is."

For a second the two women looked at each other thoughtfully, measuringly, and without either liking or dislike. It was a completely impersonal exchange of glances that told each of them more about the other than Mike could have learned about either of them in weeks. When the young answer you with that particular, impersonal suspicion, Tiz thought, that means you've crossed the line. You're authority. Dispassionately she examined her conclusion, seeing that the momentary friendliness they had established on that long, lonely ride the night before was unimportant. It had been merely the friendliness of being

88

together and being alone and more a form of politeness than anything that mattered.

Ginny went out the door as unobtrusive as a shadow and left Mike staring. Grabbing his jacket from the hook, he caught her just as she reached the front gate.

"Ginny, I'm sorry."

"Oh, Lord, Mike, don't make so much out of so little. I *did* know you when, if you remember."

"I remember a good deal," he said with meaning and when she made no answer to that, he thrust his hands into his pockets and strode moodily along beside her in silence.

"It really isn't necessary for you to walk just over there with me."

"I know it; but you know the old saying about all work and no play—"

"Well." Her voice was lower and had a different timbre than it had had in Tiz's kitchen. "Of course, I won't say I'm not glad of your company."

"Thanks for the 'your,' anyway," Mike said.

He thought she was laughing, but it was too dark there in the shadow to be sure. Once they moved out of shadow and into the light of the just-risen moon, he stole a quick glance at her. Her face was sober and he remembered that she had always had the disconcerting ability to change her expression on the instant.

"How did you get home from the Harbor yesterday?" he asked suddenly, remembering that she had had no way to do it.

"I came down with Byron."

"Oh?" Mike wasn't really interested; but the inflection of his word made her flare up at him.

"Well, things were quiet then. He felt it would be all

right for him to come back. I can tell you, Mike, it wasn't any easier for him to be up there where he couldn't fight, or anything, than it was for you. After all, Jay *did* tell him to stay there and keep track of things and he was nearly crazy all the time the fire was going on."

Mike couldn't have answered her or he would have laughed aloud. So that's why he'd been able to touch old By up so easily last night. By the Lord Harry, he *had* spent three days in Barrett's Harbor tending out on the women and children. Seemed funny, though, that Jay would spare a good man like that when the Red Cross had taken over so well.

She didn't speak again until they reached her driveway and then she said it over her shoulder: "It's easy for me to remember, too," and kept right on going.

"Virginia!" Mike said loudly.

He grabbed her wrist just as she turned to face him and in that moment learned more of the change that had taken place in her than he had in the fragmentary conversation he had tried unsuccessfully to use for the same end. Once she would have come willingly to that touch, letting him see her willingness; or she would have resisted, half-heartedly, admitting resistance as willingness. Now she merely stood and accepted it, showing him that she thought it not important enough for comment.

"Don't try anything with me, Mike." She let her smooth voice build a fence around her.

"You're so different," he said in puzzled surprise, staring down at the mystery of light and shadow that was her face.

"Why on earth wouldn't I be?"

"Just tell me one thing," Mike said, thinking to get by direct question what he hadn't been able to find out any

90

other way. "Why did you come down to the house to-night?"

"To find out for sure about the fire—partly."

"Well, what was the rest of it?" Insistent and triumphant, he loomed over her.

"I think you know as well as I do." Her head moved restlessly as if she wanted to turn away. Mike, thinking he recognized in her the same unrest he felt in himself, tried to drive his victory home.

"Go on."

"I don't want to," Ginny said miserably, watching him, reading his triumph and even now unwilling to deflate him. "But if you won't let me go until I say it, all right. I came to find out whether I was right—about you and me."

"And were you?"

Her answer took the elation out of him like a siphon. It was so unlike what he had expected her to say—it was so far from the answering mood he had thought he sensed in her. Listening to her careful, slow words, he felt his own pride curl back upon him like a taut wire suddenly cut and stinging like a whip lash.

"I'm afraid so, Mike. In a way I'm sorry. It would have been fun to play around with you, now." Her silence added: Now that I know better than to let you matter. "But something's happened to me. Two weeks ago I could have done it and enjoyed it; but right now I don't want to play."

Slowly, to let her think he accepted, but still intent on his own purpose, Mike leaned forward trying to surprise her into physical contact, trying to betray her into admission he still thought she could make.

Her own sudden, flurried retreat surprised Ginny, too.

"Won't you even kiss me good night?" Mike didn't move. "Just to show we're still friends."

"I'm not so sure we are. You don't expect a friend to try—to—" The only words she could think of were too strong. There was "betray" but that made it too important. "I don't see any need of it."

"I've kissed you before."

"I know, Mike." As if she wanted to say the thing that would cut his pride deepest, she went on: "Others have, too, and I don't deny for a minute I enjoyed it."

"Didn't it mean anything?" Mike pulled out another hopeful stop and was astonished at her flashing anger.

"You know it did," she said furiously. "I guess I'm pretty unsophisticated, Mike. It always means something when it's happening and I'd be lying to you if I said it didn't. But when it's over, it's over. I can't go backwards. There isn't time now."

"Whatever it was happened between us, it was never over." Mike said hotly. "But it must have meant a lot more than I thought it did. If you can't even let me forget it now. Seven years. We've both changed, Ginny. I'm no more what I was that long ago than you are."

"It's a little late for apologies," she said in a stiff, polite voice that held him away like a hand set hard against his chest.

"I'm *not* apologizing," he said loudly. "How in Heaven's name can I apologize for something someone else did? That's how far away it is."

"I guess a woman's memory works differently," Ginny said evenly, showing him that it did. Whatever she was remembering was clearer to her than it had ever been to him, and as painful right now as it had been in the beginning. He saw her distrust and actual resentment as physical as a thorn in the flesh.

92

"Ginny." He put his hands lightly on her shoulders, letting her see that there was no force in him. "Maybe I could understand better now. Let me try?"

"I'm sorry, Mike." She went out from under his touch as easily as a shadow or a flame. "Besides, there's Byron." She summoned up his name like a wall to lean against or hide behind.

"Yes, so you said." Mike let a little of his own resentment out in the sarcastic agreement.

"Well, what did you expect? Did you think I'd sit around and wait until you got good and ready to come back and claim your own property?"

"Don't you ever read the ads, Ginny? They tell you never to accept substitutes."

Her instant stiffening told him he'd said the wrong thing. He had let himself be flip and she had never understood and had always hated that flipness.

"It makes a difference to me, if it doesn't to you."

"I warn you right now, Ginny, it won't make any difference to me till I see you married to him legal."

She moved away.

"It's an open field," Mike said after her, knowing that she heard him though she didn't give the slightest sign of it.

She heard his steps grow fainter down the street, but couldn't bring herself to turn and look. Her mind was a turmoil of shamed distrust of her own body. The nerves, she thought bitterly, will remember and betray you long after your brain knows better. Hers had betrayed her only to herself in the second when Mike's hands lay laxly on her shoulders and she hated her own weakness for that involuntary response. Knowing it so well for what it was

93

made her want to throw something, to reach out and hit him hard, to react in any basic, physical way but the one she had.

Mike himself was still thinking about her when he went slowly up the long flight of stairs to Jay's office. But as he opened the door and stepped inside, he met an atmosphere that nearly drove the breath out of his body and certainly drove all thought of Ginny out of his mind.

Sensitive to mood as a cat, Mike could feel his nostrils twitch as if there were a smell to this one. Maybe fear and suspicion did have a smell.

There were only four men in the room: Jay, Allen Carter, and Ralph Swain sat together, ranged around the desk. In a solitary chair, canted back against the wall, as detached as he always was, Anse Barker watched them as enemies, and listened, but said nothing. The second Mike's hand touched the door knob they stopped talking and looked and their eyes built a solid wall.

He read the same thing in each glance: Are you it? And he was pretty sure that question was in his own face.

"Hi, Mike," Jay was the only one who spoke. The others just sat waiting.

Mike nodded and jerked a chair out a little from the wall to sit down.

All their physical and mental resources were gathered in this room, concentrated and hot as the rays from a burning glass. The life-giving current of their safety, their defense, rayed out from this vital and living center.

Mike's eyes rested on Ralph Swain's gleaming, blond head and since Ralph wasn't looking at him, Mike let them stay there. He knew pretty well why Ralph was here. He lived in Barrett's Harbor; but there weren't many towns

94

anywhere along the coast where he didn't have an interest of one kind or another. Here in Frenchville it was pulp land. Nobody but Ralph and the tax assessors knew exactly how many acres of land he owned on the southern end of the Peninsula. He had the unmistakable look of a successful man. Every hair on his curly head was stiff with assurance. With Ralph, sitting still had nothing to do with physical repose. He sat without moving, not even turning his head; but his eyes went from face to face, watching the others the way a cat watches a mousehole. After the ranks had opened and taken Mike in, Ralph, who had been talking, leaned forward again. His eyes were on Jay, but what he said was addressed to them all.

"Now, Jay, you got to be reasonable. This business today proves to me that you fellows down here aren't on your toes."

"It proved just the opposite to me," Jay said hotly. "The patrol spotted that fire not ten minutes after it started. Been any later we'd never of stopped it and you can count on that!"

"All right, if you say so." Ralph's uplifted hand, palm out, was a sign of peace. "Maybe I was a little hasty. Perhaps what I meant was that you really haven't got the equipment to take care of anything big. Not alone."

"That I'll go along with. But what do you suggest? We can't go haring off on the spur of the moment and buy us a fleet of tank trucks, can we? I don't know what you expect."

"For the taxes *I* pay this town—" Ralph's voice took on a new note. Money was important. Money bought things. And his money should get him more than it did. "—I expect better protection than I'm getting right now."

"All right," Allen Carter interrupted bitterly. "Why

95

don't you come right out and say what you've got to?"

"I don't like to hurt anyone's feelings," Ralph said gently. "I don't want any of you boys to feel I'm stepping on your toes."

"At a time like this I think you can disregard feelings, Ralph." The only thing that betrayed Jay's anger was a narrow line of red just above his eyebrows, as if he had just taken off too tight a hat.

"All right. This is what I want to do. I have a crew of men lying idle up to the Harbor. They're not letting logging crews into the woods up there. I want to send them down in here. I know I can do it without permission from any of you—" the claw showed a little—"but that's not the way I do things."

"What would be your idea in that?" Jay asked quietly.

"The boys are all trained woodsmen. They could work by themselves without bothering any of you. They'd have a couple of handy-billys and some hose. It'd be a help."

"Yes, it would." Jay was willing to admit the obvious; but he didn't trust the offer and was looking cagily for the catch. "It would be a help, provided we could use them when we needed them."

"I'm sorry." Ralph shook his shining head decisively. "If I sent them down here and was paying them, I'd have to have the say of what they did. I'm being pretty hardheaded about this, Jay, and those men would be here for my protection. I'd have to decide if I could take them off my land and let them go off somewhere else, leaving me uncovered. That's flat."

"In other words—" Jay's face reddened slightly—"what you're saying is that you want to send a crew of hooligans down into the Peninsula here to act as your private vigilantes."

96

"I suppose, if you want to put it that way." Ralph's open face hardened a trifle.

Jay shook his head.

"If you're asking my opinion, Ralph, I would say: Don't do it. I can't order you not to. It's your private business. But if you send them down here understanding they're to take nobody's orders but yours, I won't guarantee what'll happen. Right now we can't afford to have any split authority. And we certainly don't want any vigilantes. No matter what the circumstances are, there isn't going to be any private law taking over."

Anse Barker lit a match with his thumb nail. In the quiet room, the sound had the effect of a pistol shot. Anse held the light to the end of his cigaret and looked thoughtfully at Ralph through the cloud of smoke.

"When *I* ride patrol from now on," he said, his steady voice gaining importance from its quiet, "I'm going to have me a shotgun in the seat beside me. And law or no law, it's going to be loaded. I think if I saw a stranger wandering around in the woods, I wouldn't stop to ask him what his reason was for wandering. Not till he had a broken leg, anyway."

Jay gave him a straight look that said, We'll discuss that later.

Ralph got up. He stood towering over the seated men, his square shoulders bulky under the gray Harris Tweed jacket. Casually he leaned to brush a fluff of dust off one knee.

"Well," he said easily. "I'll tell you. I probably know more about the financial condition of this town than any of you fellows—but maybe Jay. I know what your taxable property amounts to. I know how much you've lost. And I know what percentage of your taxes *I* pay. *Your* nose isn't

97

so long that you can afford to cut it off to spite your face."

He started for the door, walking through the icy water of their combined distrust and dislike. Once there he turned to look back at Jay.

"I know when I can afford to forget anything," he said softly. "When you come to your senses, just let me know. The offer stands—unchanged. I think you'll see my point as soon as the inspectors get on your tail. Word gets around, Jay, especially about a thing like arson."

The latch clicked gently behind him and Anse said into the vacuum he had left: "I wouldn't trust that son of a sea cook not to set a couple fires himself, just so's he could send his crew down here to take over."

"Look, Anse, about that shotgun—" Jay began.

"If you don't look in my car, Jay, you won't know anything about it."

"It would be better if it wasn't there to know about."

"After that fire today, knowing it was set, if I see my own brother lighting a cigaret in these woods around here, I'd let him have it without a second thought."

Their steady glances tangled for a moment and Jay, with a slight grin, gave up.

"I've been trying to think of the worst danger spots," he said. "It's the woods that hasn't burned that's our worst headache. There's the dump. We'll have to watch that pretty sharp. Not only because of the intentional fires, either."

"Judas, yes! After the way the big one started."

Already, Mike's mind said thoughtfully, it's 'the big one.' That's to tell it from the others, the ones we're getting ready for.

"Be just like some fool to go up there with a pile of trash and set it off." Allen Carter was suddenly furious. "Here

98

we've had a fire ban on in the whole state for more than a month and some dimwit up on the Sanger road had to go and burn a pile of brush."

"That really how it started?" Mike asked. "I heard that, but I didn't know whether to believe it or not."

"That's how it started all right," Allen said. "And the fellow that started it is sitting in the jail up to the Harbor right now, thinking it over."

They seemed to have a compulsion to talk about it.

"Lessee, it blew up five days ago, didn't it," Jay said, counting back on his fingers. "Five days! My judast priest!"

"The night before that was calm if you remember," he said. He whistled a soft incredulous note. "There wasn't a breath of wind anywhere. Quiet as a clock.

"I was up on the fire line just south of the Peninsula turn where the road block was. We was just sitting there because you couldn't do anything else. From where we were you could look down the Southeast Valley and, so help me God, that whole valley was like a big, flaming ocean. I never in my life saw so much fire and I don't want to again."

The others were listening to him, breathless, apparently forgetting that they had been there, they had seen it, too.

"Jay," Allen said quickly. "Were you scared?"

At the word brought baldly into the open, they all looked hurriedly at Allen. All except Jay. He turned his head slowly and his eyes were sober.

"It scared hell out of me," he said. "If there was anyone looked at that fire and *wasn't* scared, tell me who it was and I'll show you a pure, cussed fool."

"That's a load off my mind," Mike grinned feebly at the memory. "I know now I'm not a cussed fool. I was so scared I puked and Jay's a witness to that."

"I'm not over it yet," Jay said. "I'm still scared. But I

want to do something about it. I want action. I want a man on every pulp clearing in this town twenty-four hours a day. I want somebody on every hot spot we can find."

They nodded owlishly sober agreement.

"The main thing is, keep your heads." Jay's voice, flat and steady, impersonal as ice water, told them that no man could take the law into his own hands no matter what the provocation. "I don't want any careless shooting around. If you're going to be crazy enough to have guns with you, the first man who takes a wild shot is on his way to Barrett's Harbor. Ralph Swain can't do it—no more can we. Unless martial law is declared, then the law we already have is what we go by. Keep that in mind. Any one of you who feels he can't abide by the law, say so now and he won't be asked to patrol."

They heard him out and nobody disagreed with what he said; but each one was thinking: That's all right for the others, but I'll take care of myself.

"The man we're looking for is probably one of your neighbors. Keep that in mind, too. I'm kind of set in the opinion that he's been driven off his rocker by the big fire. Or we'd have had trouble before. I think this is something he can't help."

"Well, Jay, if you're so strong for the law, what *do* we do with him?" Anse asked.

"You catch him first," Jay told them straightly. "The law covering arson is pretty strict. But it also says that you practically have to catch your man right in the act to convict him. You can't use the accumulated evidence of two or three fires. You can't do a lot of things. The safest thing is to catch him in the act."

"And in the meantime—?"

"In the meantime, keep your eyes open and—well—"

100

Jay stood up.

"I don't want any careless talking either. If you've got any ideas, then keep them to yourselves unless you've got your proof to back it up. Once a story like this gets around about any particular man, whether he's guilty or not, he might's well be."

In silence the five men filed down the dark stairs to the street. They stood in an undecided knot, hearing a car come up the road fast from the south. As it drew abreast of them, the driver flipped a live cigaret out his window. Frozen, they stood watching. The car squealed to a stop. The driver got out and hunted along the gutter until he found the butt and mashed it out with his toe. Not looking toward them, he climbed back into his car and drove away. Through the night they could hear his motor gaining speed until the sound of his passage faded altogether.

"There'll always be fools," Allen said bitterly.

"As long as the fools stop to think better of it," Jay's voice was pacific, "that's all you could ask of anyone."

Allen and Mike turned to the right, leaving the others, and walked slowly down the road home. The moonlight cast their crippled-looking shadows ahead of them.

There was a slight haze over the sky. In the west a long, black cloud bank hung lowering above the horizon and the faint stirrings of wind were from the southeast.

"It sure looks like rain to me." Allen squinted thoughtfully.

"All signs fail in a dry year."

"You're such a help!" Allen gave him a light but bruise-raising knuckle rap on the soft part of his arm above the elbow.

"Don't tangle with me. I'm poison."

"According to Powder Tilton, you are," Allen agreed.

101

"Why?" Mike stopped and stared. "What's *he* been saying?"

"Told me in all confidence you tried to drown him the other morning."

"Well, I did." Mike was wondering just how much more Powder had told. "In front of witnesses, too. Jay was standing there watching the whole thing. Tried to drown himself first, though, Powder did; but he knew full well we'd haul him out."

"Surprised he found water enough." Allen stopped in front of his own house and looked thoughtfully at the light shining from the window. He could see his wife's gray head glowing softly in the lamplight. "Don't know's I really blame him, though. Nine kids and no place to put 'em."

"Where's he keeping his kids, anyhow?" Mike asked.

"Well, somebody told me—forget who—he'd farmed them out with his wife's folks in Barrett's Harbor. Till he got some kind of a shack put together, anyway."

"I guess I better make peace with him," Mike said thoughtfully. "I'll go see what he plans to do, then maybe a bunch of us could get together and give him a hand."

"Sure." Allen agreed heartily. "At least we could get a tar-paper shack up before snow." He stepped inside his gate. "Well, I've had my stint for today. Guess I'll get to bed."

Mike walked on alone, aware that Allen stood looking after him for a minute before he went up the walk. What's he staring at me for? he thought angrily. Then he realized that he, in the same place, would have stared after Allen, allowing himself one minute to wonder: Is he the one?

After the others had gone and the sound of their steps had faded along the hushed street, Jay and Anse stood indecisively where they were. Anse's impersonal rage was heard to bear.

"Thing makes me maddest," he said for at least the tenth time, "I never sold that stand of spar spruce on Sebois. Ralph's been after me for years to sell that. Now it's all gone. Makes me feel kind of crazy, thinking about it. By judast, I could kill the guy that done it with my bare hands!"

He probably could, too, Jay thought, looking at Anse's huge fists.

The living shadow that detached itself from inanimate shadow behind them took them both by surprise. At the sound of an unexpected voice, Jay felt his throat tighten. Anse jumped visibly and spun to face the sound.

"Jay," Powder said. "Could I talk to you a minute?"

"Why sure, Powder. Only don't sneak up on me like that!"

Powder started to speak, looked at Anse, and stopped.

"Go ahead and talk your head off." Jay tried to keep impatience out of his voice and knew he'd failed.

"Well, it's kind of private."

"Is it—what's it about?" Jay looked thoughtfully at Powder's pale face.

"That fire today. I wanted to ask you something about it."

"I guess that's as much Anse's business as it is mine. Matter of fact, if you know anything about it, Powder, why you better make it public just as quick as you can spill it."

Powder shrugged.

"Okay, if you feel that way. Feller's kind of a friend of yours, Jay."

"All right," Jay said firmly. "This is just the sort of thing we want out in the open. I don't intend to have anyone talking behind anyone else's back if *I* got anything to say

103

about it. So you just say whatever you've got to say, Powder, now and right out loud."

"When you walked down along the edge of that clearing," Powder blurted. "You know, down there where the fire started, I was right down on the shore below you with Mike Arey."

Once the name was out, he stopped and took a deep breath. "I saw you," he said, when Jay was expectantly silent. "Then I looked at him and he was whiter than a ghost. He went up over that bank after you like a scairt rabbit. It seems to me that for a man who didn't know what you were going to find up there, he acted mighty suspicious."

His voice stopped and when Jay still said nothing, Powder added: "Did you ever stop to wonder why it was he followed you?"

Jay drew a deep, sobering breath.

"Powder," he said carefully, "the easiest thing in the world to ruin is a man's reputation. All it takes is a little easy talk. I want you to stop and think what you've just said. Actually, all you have said is that Mike Arey happened to come up there just after I went down to where the fire started. For that you want me to believe he started the fire, don't you? Isn't that what you mean?"

"Why, no, I don't know as it is. All I'm saying is that he was in a God-awful hurry to see what you were up to. I didn't see any reason for it."

"I think you've got your answer right there," Jay said stoutly. "I don't think there *was* any reason for it and I think there was less reason for you to make any kind of a story out of it."

"It's just as well to know things like this, though," Anse said.

Jay felt as if somebody had thrown a net over his head—

too fine for him to see; but not so fine that it didn't strangle him.

"Things like what?" he shouted and, startled at the sound of his own furious voice in the silence, quieted. "I never in my life saw people so willing to make something out of nothing. I warn you here and now, Powder—and you, too—" turning on Anse—"this is not the time for gossip. We can't afford the luxury. We need every reliable man we've got. And if I hear any gossip that could have come out of a thing as ridiculous as this, I'll have the skin off the pair of you to make me a bull whip to use on the next man I hear making such tomfool talk."

"We can't afford to ignore anything," Powder insisted. "We can't afford that, either."

"True enough. And when you bring me something, I won't ignore it. But when you come to me with nothing at all, then, by the holy old mackinaw, I will not stand for it."

"All right, Jay," Powder said softly. Turning, he faded easily down the street.

Judas, Jay thought, it's so easy! This time he had seen the trap opening softly beneath his feet; but if things kept getting tauter and more uncomfortable, he wasn't sure if he *would* see it the next time.

"Good night, Anse," he said sharply and left Anse to stare after him in surprise as he strode away toward home and sanity.

Midnight lay quietly along the street when Mike pulled up in front of the town hall. He hadn't bothered to go to bed when he got home, knowing that three hours of sleep would leave him groggier than none at all. He had reached a light and dreamy and highly pleasant stage in fatigue, al-

105

most like being a little lit. He had barely stopped when he glanced up and saw the telephone wires overhead begin to gleam. That meant another car was coming, its headlights picking out the wires before it topped the rise and came coasting down Main Street.

Whoever had the shift before him tonight was conscientious enough to make the full round. He was just on time. When the Studebaker rolled abreast of him, the conscientiousness was explained to Mike before his mind told him that Jay Stone couldn't have been riding patrol tonight. This shift had gone on at eight o'clock and at nine Jay was just leaving his office.

Cautiously Mike got out and went around to peer in through the Studebaker's window. It took him a moment to adjust himself to Byron Sawyer.

"Oh," he said blankly.

"Surprised?" Byron's white teeth flashed. "Did you think I might be home in bed instead of riding patrol like the rest of you poor dogs?"

"How'd they get you out—with a derrick?"

"Oh, nuts!" By's jaw cracked slightly under the wide yawn. "Take the chip off your shoulder and give the rest of us a break, will you? It's bad enough having to run a rig like this without having you to contend with, too."

"I'm blessed if I see how you accomplish everything you do," Mike said nastily.

"Look." Byron's weary patience was infuriating. "I don't know what's chewing you, Mike, but as soon as things settle down, I'll be glad to play drop the handkerchief with you any time you say. Right now I'd like to get a little sleep, if you can bear it. The pumps are in the back seat."

Smarting under the dismissal, Mike hauled them out.

"You find anything tonight?" he asked, his voice surly.

106

"Nope. And I thought I'd give you a break so I didn't start anything, either."

He pulled away fast.

He's scared, Mike told himself, still furious, and knowing that Byron wasn't scared. He had simply brushed him off as a buzzing annoyance. Mike knew that, if he could only keep his temper when they met, Byron might begin to take him seriously. But some involuntary and wild instinct drowned his good sense, and Byron obviously didn't intend to fight back until he saw a reason for it.

If I could only find something wrong with him, Mike thought, trying to justify his own unreasoning and childish reaction to the sight of that handsome, blond head. Oh, thunder, I meant to ask Jay what was the truth of that story about By having to be in Barrett's Harbor during the fire. That had been a funny performance. Maybe there was something there. But Ralph Swain had driven it right out of his head.

Well, anyway, Mike told himself, trying through his own firm acceptance to make himself believe it, there's something phony about that guy's top layer. Byron's surface was too good to be true. There *had* to be something more nearly human underneath it.

Anxiously he totted Byron up in his mind, trying to see what it was By had and what he was going to have to overcome. As far as looks went, By had the advantage, hands down. He also had a long, steady history of reliability.

Childishly, Mike felt deep triumph at his own advantage in their meeting. He knew why he wanted to fight Byron on sight. His trouble was jealousy; but Byron didn't know it yet and that, it seemed to Mike, gave him the upper hand.

His round that night was so quiet it was almost impossible to remember what he was looking for, or to think that

107

it might happen. When he reached the town hall at the end of the third circuit, he considered calling it quits for the night, just leaving the pumps there for the next comer and going home to bed. There would be no way for anyone to know he hadn't left them minutes rather than an hour ago.

He started on the fourth round, undeservedly aware of his own nobility.

It was nearly quarter of four in the morning and Mike was three miles out of town on his last return trip, when his headlights picked up the motion ahead of him on the road shoulder. At first he thought it was a deer, but as he neared it, the misshapen back turned into Hokey Mitchell with his eternal crocus sack slung over his shoulder.

When the full strength of the lights hit him, Hokey stopped dead. Mike could see his big head swinging foolishly from side to side and knew that blank, unformed brain was trying hard to make a decision. Hokey couldn't make up his mind whether or not to dive for the underbrush and before he could, Mike had overtaken him.

"Hokey, you going home?"

Hearing his own name gave Hokey confidence. Shamblingly, he came over to the door, the rank, unwashed, animal smell of him coming first. Mike's nostrils reacted impersonally to that smell.

"Ah-ah jus goan home." Hokey's high, nasal voice mumbled over the half-formed words.

"Well, get in the rumble," Mike told him. "I'll take you uptown."

Uncomplainingly Hokey deposited his precious sack in the front seat and scrambled up into the rumble seat which was open. Even back there, his smell was strong; but as soon as they started to move, the wind would be from Mike to Hokey. Hokey had quite a time getting into the small seat.

His motions, like his words, were undisciplined as if the vestigial brain behind them could accomplish only half the necessary impulse.

Mike glanced down at the sack and found to his surprise that it contained a good deal more than the usual collection of redeemable bottles. Cautiously he put out his hand and touched that square, large thing in the bottom of the bag, feeling through the rough material a polished surface with knobs distributed over it.

Hokey let out a yell, seeing Mike's hand. Instantly he was converted by discovery into a quivering jelly of fear.

"Ah-ah-ah-"

"Calm down, Hokey," Mike said casually. "What's in there, anyway?"

"Rur-rur- One of them— Ah neve steal—"

"No, I know; but what is it?"

"Rur-rur-" Hokey started again, hopelessly. "Talkin' box."

"Radio!" Mike said with a distinct sense of accomplishment.

Hokey nodded violently: "Ah couln' say tha word."

Listening to the foolish, panicky voice, Mike tried to make his own tone usual. If you didn't let Hokey know you were suspicious or excited yourself, he managed his tongue pretty well. Once he sensed emotion in you, he went up like a firecracker taking light, and his tongue made no sense at all.

"Where'd you get it?"

"Mist Perry ga me." Hokey managed that almost normally.

"*Gave* it?"

Hokey nodded.

"You mean you stole it, don't you?"

Hokey saw instantly that Mike would never believe the truth, never believe the miracle that lived for him yet, though he couldn't have twisted his rebellious tongue to tell about it in a hundred years. He didn't know himself what the minister had said. Lost in his own delight, Hokey had let the words pour past him like a wind blowing and they meant as little to him.

Yesterday afternoon, he'd been spudging along, minding his own business, whacking the bushes alongside the road for the rewarding sound of glass, when he'd heard the voice.

"Here, you! Stop!"

Looking up, Hokey found that he was in front of the Congregational parsonage. Unless his attention was forcibly called to his whereabouts, he seldom knew exactly where he was. He glanced once at the black-clad figure in the open door, accepted the fact that the minister simply couldn't be addressing him, and started along again.

"Stop, you! Hokey!" the minister called again.

This time terror replaced disbelief and Hokey began to run. His coordination turned running into a lurching stumble. He didn't look again. Knowing only that he must have done something he shouldn't have, Hokey just ran until he felt the hand on his shoulder. Even then he didn't look up, standing there trembling, waiting for the bolt to fall.

"Ah-ah-ah neve done it," he babbled hopelessly.

"No, no, you haven't done anything," Perry said quickly. Hokey wouldn't look at him so he had to push the thing he carried into Hokey's line of vision. Perry saw the blank, whiskered face break into creases of wondering delight. Hokey knew what the box was; but he couldn't believe it was being held out to him.

He stretched out one shaking finger and touched the

110

beautiful polished surface, instantly delighted by the feel of it.

"This is for you, Hokey," the minister said, pronouncing his words with a sharp distinction, trying to pierce Hokey's fog. "This is a lying thing—good only for you because you're one of the Lord's naturals and it can't make you covetous and evil."

Not understanding, but pleased and used to obedience, Hokey took the radio and put it carefully into his sack. When he looked up at last to see the face of his angel, the minister was gone and Hokey was alone on the long road.

As Hokey tried to tell Mike about it, his brain was able to make him see that Mike wouldn't believe what Hokey himself accepted unquestioningly.

"Ah-ah-ah work for 'im," Hokey gasped finally. "He guv me."

Mike let it go lazily.

"How you going to run it, Hokey? You haven't got electricity in that shack of yours."

"Ah-ah-ah don care. Ah-ah look at it."

Mike didn't try to say any more to Hokey while they were going. When the car drew up in front of the tar-paper shack where Hokey holed up, he got out quickly, half-falling, and hauled his sack after him. Mike heard the radio hit the ground with a tinkling crash.

Hokey leaned forward and grasped the top of the door with both hands. His eyes were wide with effort and his big mouth hung open, the lips not even moving to form the sounds that came out of his throat. Willing for some unknown reason to take the trouble, Mike groped through the thicket of babbling sound for whatever sense it might contain.

He gathered that Hokey was expressing his gratitude.

Mike, he said, was the only one who ever bothered to give
him a ride and now Hokey could do something in return.
He knew why Mike was out riding this time of night. It
was about the fire, wasn't it?

Mike's attention sharpened.

Hokey said as well as he could that he had seen the fire
on Hardwood Point being set. His voice died away before
the lack of breath; and Mike, not daring to speak, not daring
to move, afraid to frighten him back into his mist, sat waiting, clutching the wheel with hands that itched to grab
Hokey's skinny shoulders and shake the reluctant words
out of him.

Hokey said at last that he had seen the man setting the
fire. But only back to. He had been too scared to stay. He
had hidden. But if he ever saw the back again, he would
know it. He would tell Mike who it was.

Mike's disappointment made him snort with thwarted
laughter. But, at least, it was a link. He made his voice carefully casual.

"You go to Jay Stone, Hokey. You know him."

Hokey chattered that he did.

"Don't forget, Hokey. You go tell him tomorrow just
exactly what you saw."

"Ah-ah-ah better tell Mist Stone," Hokey suggested, as if
it were a totally new idea and his own.

"Yeah, you do that, Hokey. You tell him right away."

Assured that Hokey had the idea firmly in hand, Mike
could only think now of getting home to bed. Jay might
be able to get something more out of Hokey; but he doubted
it.

It was growing light as he drove into the yard.

Mike slept until noon and would have slept longer if

the babble of voices downstairs hadn't wakened him. It sounded like a ladies' sewing circle.

While he'd been away from Frenchville, he'd wondered occasionally if Tiz, back here alone in her house, was ever lonely. Now that he was back, he found there was always somebody to come in and sit, using her time as freely as if it were a public utility. She would go on with what she was doing in a sort of receptive silence, making whoever had stopped in know she was listening with deep attention to whatever he might be saying.

Mike found the noises this morning a little surprising. One of the several voices belonged to Tiz and she was holding up her end of the conversation volubly.

The minute his feet hit the floor, he sensed the sudden change in the talk. It flurried, hesitated, stopped. In the kitchen below him was listening silence.

Mike pounded down the stairs, opened the door and cautiously peered around it. Unbelievingly his eyes met the startled but expectant stare of the only other occupant of that room. Jonesy Dawes was perched on the edge of a kitchen chair, as close to the door as he could get without actually sitting out in the yard.

"Hoy," Mike said, his glance curious on Jonesy's taut, small, poised-for-flight body.

Mike had a sensation of having stepped into the middle of something that had been happening but that had ceased to happen upon his appearance and now that he was actually here, wouldn't go on.

"For pete sake, Jonesy, you weren't making all that noise by yourself?"

Jonesy made a half-completed gesture toward the dining room. Mike stepped to the door and looked in.

Tiz was on her knees at the far end of the room, painting

113

with furious intensity. Under her wide brush, the calm, gray floor was turning a bright, Chinese red. Mike moaned softly and Tiz whirled to face him.

"For the *Lord* sake, Tiz—"

"Oh, hello. I thought you were good for hours yet."

"Well, with all this rumpus going on down here! How d'you expect anyone to sleep?"

Tiz got stiffly to her feet and came over to glance out into the kitchen.

"Where did—" she began. Mike, who was still fascinated by that floor, didn't hear her; but Jonesy made a quick, denying gesture and Tiz stopped short. Her mouth curled into a delighted, half-scornful smile.

"Tiz, *what* are you up to?" Mike protested.

"Well," she admitted thoughtfully, "I *do* have the feeling Mattie's leaning over my shoulder counting each brush stroke."

"Should think you would!"

Mike headed for the sink. He glanced around to find them both watching him intently.

"I'm just going to wash my face," he said blankly.

"All right." Tiz went briskly to the stove. "Then you sit right down and I'll get your breakfast for you."

Mike couldn't rid himself of that feeling of having interrupted. He felt as if somebody had quitted the room so rapidly at his approach they'd left behind some undeniable clue to identity. When he sat down at the table, he looked blankly at Jonesy and the meaningless glance flicked Jonesy into nervous talk.

"I see you never come down for the mail this morning, so I brought it up. I thought you was probably on patrol last night. You'd be too late to get it. I brought it up."

"Anything for me?" Mike asked politely.

114

"Only a postcard and that wasn't nothing but an ad."

"Well, thanks for saving me the trouble of reading it."

Jonesy flushed and took his wounded glance quickly away from Mike's amused face.

"Tiz's floor is real pretty, don't you think?" he asked with bright, defeated hopefulness.

"It's different," Mike agreed.

"You going to have birds on the wall in there, too, Tiz?" Jonesy called.

"*Birds* on the *wall!*" Mike echoed heavily, wondering if he were the one who had gone crazy.

"Why, sure. Like out here." Jonesy gestured at the brilliant kitchen and Mike's eyes, following that gesture, searched hopefully, knowing that he had to find those heretofore invisible birds to restore his own equilibrium.

Two months ago, after a week end at home, he had left the friendly, shabby, familiar old kitchen, its walls off-white, its woodwork dark brown, just as it was when Mattie Arey had lived and died in it. A month later, when he had come home to stay, the colors, when he opened the door, had slapped against his unsuspecting eyes like a flash of unbearable light. He had never seen anything like it, and had never expected to see it in Tiz's house. It was like stepping into a room papered with circus posters. Every flat surface had been adorned with brilliant enamel. Even the brightwork on the black iron stove had been painted blue.

On the wall, just below the joint of the ceiling, like a border for wallpaper, was a row of calendar pictures, apparently also picked for their color. Neatly cut out, their lower edges square and true as the edge of a spirit level, they made Mike feel at first as if the ceiling would be down on his head at any minute.

115

"All them pictures of birds," Jonesy said with a tinge of impatience. "All them pictures around the top."

Now, looking at that fringe of lightly dismissed calendar pictures, Mike saw with surpirse that there was a relationship among them. In each one there were birds: in flight, sitting, standing; but birds and he had never noticed them before. There were herons, stalky and stiff in a marsh; gulls, white as snow falling from a blue sky against the dark spruces; ducks floating to their reflections on secret waterways; great, misty *V*'s of wild geese going north; even a pelican in flight, looking like a pterodactyl, a remainder of some dark, distant age beyond the memory of man.

He sat with his mouth foolishly open.

"I be blessed!" he said. "I never noticed that before." Before he had a chance to look at Tiz, she had turned hastily away.

"Ye-ye-yes," Jonesy said. "Well, I got to be going." Before he closed the door he looked back at Tiz.

"You talk to Mike about Powder. See what *he* thinks."

"I'll do that, Jonesy," Tiz reassured emptiness. He hadn't even waited to hear her.

"Pete sake!" Mike stared from Tiz to the door.

Tiz laughed.

"Poor Jonesy! There he is, living with that half crazy old woman. I don't know but what he's half crazy himself. But no matter how low anyone goes, they can always find somebody worse off. He's worried about Powder Tilton's kids not having any place to live this winter. He was wondering if there wasn't something we could all do about it. He says Powder's too shiftless to do it by himself."

"*Powder* shiftless!" Mike said with unconscious cruelty.

"Well." Tiz allowed the likeness. "But at least, Jonesy

116

tries hard enough. If he doesn't get anywhere to speak of, it's not for want of trying."

She went quickly back to her painting. Mike still could not get rid of the feeling that he really wasn't alone. That room, usually so relaxed that the least feeling of tension was amost unbearable, made him feel as if the walls were imperceptibly closing in on him.

He got up and went over to the door so that he could see Tiz and know to whom his words were addressed. He stood there, hands thrust into his pockets, teetering back and forth on the threshold.

"I only wish I had some of the dough I flung around while I was in the service. Why—" a reminiscent grin fluttered across his face—"I remember once we got into San Francisco the morning after an all-night poker game. I was four hundred to the good. We lit with a seventy-two and a bunch of us went down to San Dago and that four hundred dollars lasted about five hours."

Tiz heard him out in silence, listening with a stiff, uncomfortable smile to his pleased voice, thinking: Four hundred dollars. She remembered winters when she had started out to winter through on less than that. She remembered the war years and high prices and not enough money. She remembered a frantic telegram he had sent her once from the west coast: "Please wire fifty dollars at once. Urgent. Letter follows." She had sent him twenty-five only because she didn't have fifty. And there he stood, talking about that same period in time, telling her how four hundred dollars had gone through his pockets like water through hands cupped loosely to hold it. Sitting back on her heels, she stared unseeingly with that same tight, angry smile at the brilliant floor.

Why haven't I got the courage to say to him just what I'm thinking? she asked herself bitterly. Why can't I say to him: You bragging, young idiot! Why can't I tell him what four hundred dollars would have meant to a good many people in this town?

She couldn't tell him in words; but her shoulders, stiff under the white, cotton shirt, told him he'd made a mistake somewhere. Hastily he said: "I don't know why everyone feels so responsible about Powder. I do myself and I'm condemned if I see any reason why I should."

He looked at her with eyes astonished at his own humanity.

"*I'm* condemned if *I* know why you feel responsible about anything," she told him with commendable restraint. "It's certainly something new for you."

"Just because I haven't gone around all my life wailing about the hardships of the unfortunate—" Mike grinned.

The glance she gave him this time was quizzically amused.

"Well, go up and see him," she said. "Is it going to rain? And besides, if you go traipsing up there, bursting with love of your fellow man, it'd be just like Powder to fly in your face. Then you'd forget it soon enough, young fellow. Oh, I know you!"

"No," Mike said. "It isn't going to rain."

"Wind's southeast," Tiz protested.

Mike glanced out at the harbor again. The water, color of lead, shot with stormy silver, rolled in dirtily before an undeniable southeast wind. Its chop caught the bow of the bluff, clumsy, gasoline scow and set her pitching at a crosswise jerk against the pull of her mooring. There weren't many boats out today. Chester Bailey's big seiner, the one they called Mae West, was moored between Mike's boat and the near shore; but she rode high and handsome,

118

and every time her curving bow came up, there was the *Kestrel* just beyond her, steady and clean and white.

"It just doesn't *smell* like rain."

Tiz shrugged.

"You're probably right, though I'm blessed if I see how you do it. Southeast wind means rain to me."

"You've heard of dry easterlies, haven't you?"

"Not from the south."

"Well, keep your eye on this one, then," he told her. "It'll be something new."

"My!" Tiz turned and looked at him levelly. "You sound quite like your own sweet self now. It's kind of pleasant. At least I know *some* things are getting back to normal."

"You know something, Tiz?" Completely serious, he faced her, demanding her attention. "When I got back home here, I felt like there wasn't anything that mattered but me and what I wanted. But the last week or so's showed me something.

"I thought I didn't care what happened to this place or the people in it. Everybody always ready to cut anyone else's throat if there was anything in it for him. But the way folks have thrown together makes you feel kind of good."

Embarrassed, he went over and grabbed his jacket.

"Judast!" he said. "Even Powder. He's part of it. Even people like him. You feel as if everyone was responsible for everyone else. See what I mean?"

"People have to grow up sometime," Tiz said. "If it takes something like a fire to make them do it, why, let it burn."

"Yeah. But I don't fool myself it'll go on. I know as well as you do, as soon as it rains I'll be out again cutting throats with the rest of them."

"All right," Tiz agreed. "Then, while the spirit moves

you and it still hasn't rained, why don't you go up and see Powder? Maybe you could give him a hand."

"That's where I'm bound."

He closed the door, but he hadn't reached the gate before she had it open and was running after him. Hearing her coming, he stopped to wait.

"Thought I'd walk along with you as far as Hanscom's." Tiz gave him a short smile.

Mike glanced cautiously back at the house they had just left. It sat there squarely, its windows blank and shining. But it seemed to him he had caught a movement of the door. If there was somebody else in that house, whoever it was certainly wasn't there without Tiz's knowing about it and why all this mystery?

He glanced secretly at Tiz's clear, untroubled face. She hadn't even noticed his backward glance. Well, he shrugged, it was her business. But he had a hard time to keep from looking again, to assure himself it would not be a shadow that came out that door.

As Mike and Tiz came up the road together, Ginny was out hanging up the first of her washing. She had rigged up a clothesline from the pole to the corner of the charred woodshed. Mike watched her in a kind of hungry silence.

"Give me a shout when you come back by," Tiz said into his absorption.

"Oh, sure." Mike remembered her just in time to meet her amused eyes. He felt himself flush and it didn't escape Tiz. Kindly she looked away.

Enviously he watched her going up the drive, saw her speak to Ginny, who turned and looked beyond Tiz to where Mike was still standing on the sidewalk. She gave him a brief, half-completed wave of her hand and didn't wait to see whether or not he would answer it. That em-

120

bryonic gesture she had made in his direction was much more important than anything Ginny would say to Tiz. She had tried to make it casual and had not succeeded.

Mike was whistling soundlessly but happily between his teeth when he started across the field toward Powder's cellar. The barnyard was half filled with a heap of second-hand lumber and Powder was piling it over with a ferocious, slamming intensity. Powder didn't look up to acknowledge Mike's approach.

"Stubborn so and so," Mike said, too softly for Powder to hear.

He strolled over to the cellar and found himself looking down on Emmy who was scratching around in the ruins with a long-handled clam hoe.

"Hello," Mike said and was astounded to see her jump like a suddenly released spring.

He had seldom seen a face so honed down. She managed a queer, tight, little laugh, summoning it up from some reservoir of convention, as if Mike had demanded it of her.

"You frightened me." She explained the nervous jump away. "I didn't hear you coming."

"Powder's making such a racket I don't see how you could." Mike tried to sound reassuring, but the time for that had passed.

"I was looking to see could I find any of my old iron cooking kettles." She gave the clam hoe a self-conscious shake. "But I guess there ain't anything left."

"That fire was pretty hot when it came across this field."

"You know—" she stared up at him—"I couldn't really think how it would be to come back and find nothing here. I couldn't really believe it till I was standing right where you are now, looking into this cellar. The worst time was before I saw it. When I was really here and really seeing it, instead of imagining, it didn't seem so bad."

The corner of her mouth began to twitch and her hand started upward, unconsciously, to hide it from him. Before the fingers could cover the tic, she was aware of what she was doing and that he would already have noticed it.

"Thirty years living in one house, you get kind of attached to it. I—I didn't realize how I felt. It's kind of like I should think having a leg gone. Like that."

Looking down at her bereft face, Mike could think of nothing to say that would mean anything to her. "I see Powder's got some lumber," he observed awkwardly.

"Powder's awful mad," she said clearly. "I don't suppose he even spoke to you, did he?"

"Matter of fact, no." Mike shook his head. "I wasn't surprised, though. We had a ruckus the other day."

"I heard about it." Her eyes flickered slightly, almost amused. She crossed slowly to the cellar steps and came up to stand beside him, looking across to the lumber pile where Powder was still working.

"He's over that now," she said. "He's mad at me instead. You see, he got it into his head there wasn't any point in putting up a shelter for this winter. He's made up his mind there's going to be another fire and it's no use to do anything about it."

She looked at Mike for disagreement. *I* don't think that's the way to feel. We've got to have a place for the kids this winter. We can't go on living with other folks, can we?"

Answering her demanding eyes, Mike shook his head.

"Well, John—that's my brother up to the Harbor— knew where he could get this lumber. So he went and ordered it and we didn't tell Powder. Now he can't do anything but go ahead and build it."

"That's what I came to talk to him about," Mike said, delighted to have the subject raised with so little effort from him.

Powder came striding brashly across the seared yard to where they were standing. His pale face was puckered with irritation and he looked as pugnacious as an angry rabbit.

"What?" he shouted. "What? What?"

Mike felt a sneaking stir of respect for him.

"Whatta you two standing here whispering about? Hanh?"

Here was Powder, knowing that Mike could have broken his neck with little effort and still his spirit brought him breasting up to them.

"Well?" Powder drew his head back like a striking snake; but without striking. "Well?"

"Climb down, Powder. We weren't talking about you."

"*That's* a damn, black, Arey lie," Powder said and was preparing to say more.

"Powder, wait." Emmy's quiet voice caught her husband's attention and he stopped in midstream to stare at her as if he had just remembered her existence with surprise.

"Well, all right," Mike grabbed at the silence. "We *were* talking about you, Powder; but what I was telling Emmy was—Allen Carter and I was talking just last night, about getting your place put back here. We'd either one of us be glad to help you out. A lot of others, too, for that matter. If you'll let us know." He thought it just as well not to mention Jonesy Dawes.

Powder's anger went down like a pricked balloon.

"Oh, Lord!" he said. "I don't know."

"Glad to," Mike repeated helplessly.

Powder looked ashamed of himself.

"I don't plan on doing anything this fall I can't do

alone." The tone was grudgingly grateful. "Just a shack. I suppose we got to have a roof over our heads come winter." His voice gained volume. "But, by the gods, I ain't putting anything else up here till I see whether or not it's any use to!"

"All right." Mike thought suddenly that if he didn't start back, Tiz would get tired of waiting for him and go home alone. His sudden, urgent fear that she might started him teetering nervously on his toes. But he couldn't just say good-by and go.

"Oh—" He thought with relief of his own bit of news. "Hokey Mitchell says he saw the fellow setting that fire down on the Point yesterday."

Powder spun away from them impatiently.

"Believe what that fool tells you, you're crazier than I thought."

His turning released Mike, who started hastily off across the field.

"Just let us know if you *do* want help," he called over his shoulder.

He heard Emmy say something in a low voice and then Powder yelled after him: "Thanks, anyhow."

"Arrogant, high-stepping, young s.o.b.!" Powder said quietly, making of the word "young" as bitter a condemnation as the two angry words he had linked to it.

"Powder," Emmy protested uselessly, "you shouldn't feel like that. He's just trying to help."

"Help! Coming back like Goddle Mighty coming home. Throwing his weight around. What's he trying to do, take over the town?"

"You might's well get any help you can," she said, des-

perately calm. "We can't do it alone. We haven't got anything to do with."

"What *I'd* like to know," Powder said bitterly, "is where
he's getting it. Buying cars and boats. Throwing around
more money in two months than I see in a year. Probably
Tiz had to mortgage her house so's *he* could start on top.
And she'll lose it, surer'n hell and be in the same fix we
are. Poor Tiz Arey. Out in the cold, just like us." He
thought of something else. "Where'd *he* be, I'd like to
know, if he had the breaks I did? My Lord, Emmy, anyone
else getting it in the neck the way I did would be flat on
their tail now, too."

Recognizing the beginning of the old story, Emmy resigned herself nervously to hearing it through. When
Powder got on this string, she had to let him finish it.

"I could have made more money than anyone around
here ever see. I was a mathematical genius. I was all set.
Then you know what the eye man told me. He said to me:
'Son, if you do anything that involves close work with your
eyes, you'll be blind inside two years.' That's exactly what
he said to me. So I had to give up. Why, look, Emmy, this
place was all we had in the world. And look! There ain't
much left for a lifetime's work. When I think how I worked
to get this place for us!"

For the moment he honestly forgot that he had been
handed the place just for taking care of his father in the
last few years of his life. Powder was the one who had slaved
and pinched pennies. He was the one who had paid off the
mortgage at the bitter rate of twenty dollars a year.

He stood staring across the hundred yards of cleared land
between what had once been the back of his barn and the
edge of the burned woods.

While he had been up there along the Barrett's Harbor road, working like a devil to save somebody else's place, down here in Frenchville they had been letting his place go.

"They could have held it here if they'd really wanted to."

It was perfectly clear to him that nobody had wanted to. Oh, that's just that old shack of Powder Tilton's. He could hear them saying it. Never mind that. Don't take the time to wet that down. Let it go. More important to save Hanscom's house. Wet down the church. Save Tiz Arey's.

You'd have thought they might have done a little for the kids and Emmy, even if they didn't care what happened to him.

"How in God's name's a man going to protect himself when he doesn't know who's against him? There ought to be some way a man could have of getting his own back." He grinned mirthlessly.

"Damn luckly the woodshed didn't go, too, ain't it, Emmy? We'd be living in a tent now, if it had."

"Powder, that's foolishness," she told him soberly. "This has happened to lots of folks. Not only us. Everybody's got to work together now, helping out."

"Yeah!" Powder said sarcastically. He went back to the lumber pile and she heard him mumbling to himself; but she couldn't hear what he said.

As he came quickly up the driveway, Mike's heart was hammering. He must have been walking faster than he thought. The voices came to him like a piece of counterpoint, Tiz's low, Ginny's a few notes higher.

His foot crunched suddenly in the loose, white clamshell

126

of the drive and Ginny spun on him, her face stiffening instantly into the bright, meaningless smile one keeps for an unexpected visitor who turns out to be no one but a chance acquaintance.

"Hi," Mike said airily. "You ready to go, Tiz?"

Then he realized with dismay he had said the one conventional thing that would make it necessary for them to leave as soon as they could.

Stubbornly persisting against his own words, Mike sat down beside Tiz on the step.

"You see Powder?" Tiz asked.

Mike nodded: "Oh, yes. He's still determined the town's going to burn. But he had got to the stage where he's willing to put up a shack."

"Well." Ginny glanced hopefully at the sky. "I'm doing *my* best to make it rain. Usually all I have to do is hang out a few clothes to dry and it rains for the next week."

"The same thing happens when I wash my windows," Tiz said.

Mike felt his toes curl with impatience. There was nothing to say against that bright, impersonal glance which was all Ginny was willing to give him. Her face looked to him as if a smiling mask had covered it and nothing he could say would crack its perfection. Now that he was actually here with them, he found three-cornered conversation completely impossible.

"Uh," he said loudly. With their attention fastened on him as if he had made a world-shaking statement, he *had* to go on and say something. So he blurted out the thing he really wanted to say.

"Ginny, how about going somewhere tonight? Bowling or something?"

127

"I'm so sorry, Mike." Her answer was so quick that he knew she was telling the absolute truth without having to grope for her excuse. "I'm busy tonight."

She glanced at his face with a suspicion of amusement.

"Besides, it'd be pretty hard to bowl by candlelight, wouldn't it?"

"Oh, I forgot."

Silence curled around them like leaden water.

"Well," Mike said desperately. "How about tomorrow night, if the lights are on by then?"

Ginny's eyes fell. She opened her mouth to say something. For a moment nothing came out; then, like a drowning man finding his straw, she said: "I don't like to leave Pa alone too much. I seldom go out two nights in a row."

"Well—" Mike persisted unhappily—"the night after that you probably aren't going to be doing anything, are you?"

"That's pretty far ahead," Ginny said lamely.

"Three days." Mike's voice took on an acerbity that told him he was on the point of losing his temper. He got to his feet and Tiz got up too, her dark eyes thoughtfully curious.

"What you mean is, you don't care to go out with me at all, isn't it?" he inquired icily, knowing that anger was the sound of despair more than the sound of temper.

Once he had said it, Ginny looked a little ashamed of herself, but angry, too. He saw with satisfaction the stubborn set of her mouth. At least, he could still make her mad. She started to give him the hot answer he deserved; but she glanced at Tiz first and couldn't do it.

"I— I— No, that's not it at all," she stuttered lamely.

Caught in a net of constrictive silence, all three of them welcomed the interruption for a different reason. Mike and Tiz both thought the shuffling step in the woodshed behind them was Eddie; Ginny alone knew it was Jasper. He came to the door and stood leaning there looking out at them.

"We've got company, Pa," Ginny said, her voice too loud.

"So I see." Jasper gave them a slight nod. For a second his eyes rested on Mike's face.

"How are you?" The words were hardly a question. He was completely uninterested in how anyone was.

Tiz glanced at him thoughtfully. His eyes, the color of Ginny's, were blank as marbles in his short, round-cornered face, impassive as the stone face of justice.

She had known Jasper as a young man and it seemed impossible to her that he could ever have turned into this walking machine. He had been one of the liveliest young men in town. At twenty-five, engaged to marry Boyce Barker's oldest girl. Within a month of that engagement, Jasper had married; but he had married Rena Hamblen instead. Few people knew that story; but Tiz did. She could remember hearing Rena say: "Jen Barker needn't think she'll ever get him. I'll do anything to stop her." Rena had. Ginny had been the innocent means of her getting him. After that marriage Jasper had been like a man whose every vital urge has been taken away from him. He had got back a touch of his old enthusiasm for life when Eddie was born. He'd wanted a son. Now it must be a bitter thing for him to see what Eddie was becoming. It would be enough to make him lose interest in life and everything that had to do with it.

That wasn't quite right, Tiz decided, seeing the flicker as his eyes hesitated on his daughter's face. There was something left; but, whatever it was, it had nothing to do with anyone but Ginny.

"Well," Mike said idly. He took a pack of cigarets from his pocket and held it out to Tiz and Ginny. Each took one, greeting the chance to move as if it had been a lifeline. He half extended the pack to Jasper.

"No, thank you." Jasper didn't look at the package.

Mike offered Ginny a light but she was watching her father and didn't notice it.

"Light, Ginny?" Mike said.

She glanced at the flame quickly and shook her head.

"I really—I guess I don't want to smoke right now. I'll keep it till later."

She shoved the cigaret into her shirt pocket and Mike lit Tiz's and then his own.

He shook the match out, dropped it, and set his toe carefully on its blackened end. His eyes lit on the unpainted wood of the doorstep. He could feel his jaw drop. For a suspicious instant he wondered if he were beginning to see spots before his eyes. The gray, thirsty, unpainted wood showed five, large, wet spots that hadn't been there before.

Mike's head jerked back so fast he heard his vertebra crack. He stood glaring at the sky.

"My God!" he said. "It's raining!"

"Better come in, Ginny." Jasper's voice was as calm as if it had been raining every day for the past two months. "You'll get wet."

Wordlessly she went past him into the house and Tiz and Mike turned down the drive.

"Raining!" Mike said again as if he had been unable to believe his own words the first time. These few drops of rain had driven everything but relief out of his head. The shoulder of the road looked as if some child had scattered handfuls of beads along it. Each drop, when it hit the ground, instead of sinking in, gained a protective dull coating of dust that let it retain its shape. On the tarred road sur-

130

face, the big, individual drops were rapidly merging into solidity.

When they reached the picket gate, Mike said:

"My judas, Tiz, I hope it rains for three days!"

"I thought you said it wasn't going to rain at all," she gibed.

"I *could* be wrong." He gave her a wide, relieved grin. Stepping in through the gate, he glanced down to see once again that unaccustomed moisture. He saw instead his own shadow lying before him. He stood staring at it despairingly for a moment before he turned and looked at the sky where the low, gray overcast was breaking up rapidly under the freshening southwest breeze, the fair wind. With the first gust of that wind came the smell of smoke—bitter, acrid, and stronger than ever.

By the time they reached the back door, the sun lay brightly across the brown grass and the leaves were blowing briskly past the corner of the house.

It was late when Mike left the house; but for want of something to do he was going out to haul a few traps. He wouldn't have time to haul his whole gang before dark. He had to make a start, though. He hadn't been out since the fire and he was afraid what lobsters there were might be hungry enough to start in on each other. Going so late, he had no idea when he'd get in and he told Tiz not to wait supper for him. He'd stop at the café.

He hauled twenty traps for eighteen counters before he gave it up and headed back for the breakwater.

As he rowed ashore and pulled up his punt, he saw through the beginning dusk a faint light in the leaning, shoddy stand of buildings that housed a sandwich bar and a couple of pool tables. The poolroom was jammed with

131

men and cloudy with cigaret smoke; but nobody was playing pool. They were all clustered around a vital center, the point of which was invisible from the door.

Curiously he shoved his way through the crowd, craning his neck to see what was holding their attention so closely.

Hokey Mitchell was squatting on an upturned nail keg. Only the backs of his knees touched the keg. His shoulders were braced back hard against the edge of the pool table. The rest of him, stiff as a board, touching nothing, stretched between the two points of contact. He was trying to smile; but the terror under it was more obvious than the smile.

Directly in front of Hokey, sitting on another keg and leaning forward more as Hokey pressed away from him, was Jay Stone, his face hard with interest and the attempt to get some sense out of Hokey's babbled mouthings.

"Nobody's going to hurt you," Jay was saying, with the exact, taut, harried patience that couldn't have been more carefully adjusted to set off all Hokey's imaginary horrors.

Forgetting that it was the tone more than the words that mattered to Hokey, Jay let his frustrated impatience get out in tone, not words.

"Nobody's going to do anything bad to you, Hokey," Jay said tightly, restraining himself with an obvious effort from grabbing Hokey's bony shoulders and shaking him like a Doberman with a cat.

Mike saw that the idea of being hurt grasped Hokey as strongly as if Jay's hands were holding him. Hokey looked away from Jay, letting his eyes claw wildly around the circle of waiting faces. The one idea in his head was to get out of this mess he'd got himself into. From where he was standing, Mike could get a good whiff of him. Hokey was giving off an odor that was the concentration of fear.

132

"Who was it?" Jay began again. "Just say who it was, Hokey. What was his name?"

Hokey stared, his eyes turning milky.

"*Name!*" Jay roared suddenly, infuriated at being so near knowledge and unable to prize it out. "*Name,* Hokey."

Hokey let out an animal whimper and clawed defensively at the air in front of him.

"Ah-ah-ah din see face. Ah-ah-ah doan know na—"

"Ah, you're lying." Jay sounded disgusted. "If you saw enough of him to recognize next time, you must know his name."

Jay was forgetting in his excitement that Hokey's mind probably didn't work the way Jay's own would. All he could think of was what Hokey had seen: He had seen the firebug, had recognized him, and was now too frightened to say the name. With a gesture of wide disgust, Jay started to his feet.

Hokey screamed and fell forward on his hands and knees. Startled, Jay sprang back, away from him, and Hokey, head down like a tortured animal, started out through the forest of legs. His sudden advance had the advantage of surprising his inquisitors who had expected no quick action from him. They shoved to let him through without contact. Hokey won to the free space around the door. He climbed laboriously to his feet and shambled out into the open and nobody made a move to stop him.

"Let him go," Jay said wearily. "We won't get any more out of him."

Hokey staggered up the road not turning to look back until he was a good hundred yards away. When he *did* glance back and saw the men standing in the door looking after him, he let out that inhuman, terrified yell again. He

133

looked like a scarecrow, stumbling up the road in the fading light.

"Jay," Mike protested. "That's not how to treat Hokey. You'll never get anything out of him if you scare him to death first."

"Thanks." Jay was frustrated and angry. "I find there's always someone to tell me how I should have done something—after it's too late."

"Okay." Mike gave him a wry grin and Jay flushed slightly.

"Sorry," he said. "Forget it, will you?"

It wasn't the right moment for it; but Mike went rushing into the question as soon as it entered his head.

"Jay, where was By Sawyer during the fire?"

"Why, I don't know." Jay's voice was slow, but the look behind the words was narrow and dangerous. "You still riding that horse?"

"Just tell me this. Did you or didn't you tell him to stay in Barrett's Harbor?"

"Are you nuts? Why would I tell him to do any such fool thing? And if I did, he wouldn't have to do it."

"But you didn't, did you?"

Jay's silence was answer enough.

"Did you see him any time in those three days?" Mike persisted against the danger signals.

"*See* him!" Jay exploded wrathfully. "I don't know *what* I saw." Mike was hitting too close to Jay's own target. Unreasonably that made him angrier.

"I don't like all this underhanded business. I'll tell you just what I tell everyone else. You come to me with facts and then you can talk your head off. Till then, shut up!"

"What would you say if I told you I could prove he was up there?"

134

"I would say—" Jay gave him a glassy stare—"that we weren't running a young ladies' school. Anyone had a right to be wherever he wanted to. Good night." He stumped over to his car, indignant spurts of dust rising behind him.

"Forget it," he repeated, leaning out to say it as he pulled away.

It seemed very strange to Mike to go into Cairns' Café and find it lighted by kerosene. It looked like all the movie versions of dens of iniquity. Actually there wasn't a more respectable place in town. Judging from the noise, everyone was feeling daring and a little wicked. There were three Aladdin lamps on the counter, resurrected from some attic. A smaller lamp stood on each table in the booths along the far wall; but they were little more than an aggravation of darkness.

It was strange to Mike sitting at that counter listening to the familiar voices swirling at him out of the murk and not being able to identify them. Completely separated from his neighbors, he could listen to their voices with detachment. They were troubling voices: loud and hilarious. The people who came here did not habitually use tones that could be heard across the room. There was a tension of near hysteria about the hilarity that set his hackles on end.

If he had come in here on an August evening, he would have expected to meet something very like the sounds he found now. But that was in the summer time and the accents would have been completely different. The people sitting here in the dusk were not summer people out for fun. But they were behaving as if they were. It was as if each one had to insist to his neighbor: Here I am. Notice me so that if anything happens you'll be able to say I was right here.

Mike didn't care for it. He shook his head nervously and looked down at the plate that a nearly disembodied hand had set in front of him. Glancing up he found that Al Cairns himself was waiting on the counter tonight. Al shook his head with a gesture exactly like Mike's.

"Funny," he said, his cigaret-rough voice lowered. "Seems queer in here tonight, don't it?"

"Certainly doesn't sound natural." Mike found that Al's half whisper had been contagious. "Too noisy."

"Yeah. Nobody's doing anything but yelling," Al grated. "Sounds like the middle of summer."

"I was just thinking the same thing. What's wrong, anyhow?"

A not-fully-amused grin split Al's rectangular, slabby face.

"They're all like me," he said. "Afraid of the dark. Afraid of the boogerman."

He put both of his big hands on the counter and leaned forward to look down the length of the low room.

"I've got me a new 'regular,' too."

"That so?" Not really interested, Mike was still willing to listen for the sake of having somebody talk to him.

"Not making much on him, though." Al gave a snorting laugh. "Mr. Perry."

"The minister?"

"He's the only Perry *I* know," Al said. "He's eating here on tick now."

"I thought you only did cash business. If you can trust him, you might trust me."

"You ain't the minister," Al pointed out. He leaned over still farther and lowered his voice again. "Did you hear what the cussed fool did? He said he had proof that the Lord will provide, so he went and give every penny he had to that Nate Baker got burned out up to the north end. I

136

guess he found he got kind of hungry, though, waiting for the provisions to come in. So I'm kind of acting like a stand-in till he gets paid or the Lord gets around to him."

"I'll be condemned," Mike said against the rumbling burr of Al's laughter. "I must of misjudged Hokey."

He told Al about Hokey's radio.

"You'd think he'd direct his giving a little better," Al commented.

"Well—if he really feels that way, he probably gave it to the first one to come along, just to get rid of it."

Al lost interest in the minister's vagaries, not understanding, deciding lightly that everyone was a little crazy right now. Different people showed it in different ways.

"Well, I don't know. This reminds me of the old days, though. It sounds just exactly like the kind of a crowd I used to get during prohibition. I didn't care much for 'em then. I don't like it much now."

"I think they'll be all right as soon as the lights come back on," Mike said. "You'll have to be careful then, Al. Right now nobody could tell whether you wiped the counter or not."

Al took the ribbing easily.

"You better eat with your fingers if you can't see," he suggested. "I made up that plate myself and I'd hate to tell you what I missed after I give it to you."

"No news to me."

"I was expecting the electricity to come on before this. Somebody said they had the line fixed now."

There were four men sitting together in a booth just behind the big pot burner Al put in every winter. Their rising voices penetrated the steady racket.

"Patrol tonight?" one said loudly. "Damned if I will. Need my sleep too much. Rained today, didn't it? Why,

137

you couldn't set a fire in the woods now if you was to try."

"Yeah? Well, I wouldn't advise your trying it." Another took it up furiously. "Not if you want to live in good health and die in bed."

"All right," the first one said triumphantly. "What'd you say if I was to tell you I already did? Right after supper I went out and scraped me up a pile of spruce needles and put a match to it. And it wouldn't burn. I ain't going to lose my sleep tonight."

"Probably forgot your can of kerosene, didn't you?" The third voice was a new one to the discussion and it was just as unpleasant as the words it said.

"Just whatta you mean by that?"

"I mean by that—" the third voice said with careful diction—"anyone would be damn fool enough to pull a stunt like that is probably pretty fond of seeing things burn."

There was a muffled, profane roar, completely out of character with the general noise. Al, who had been stiffening to attention, forgetting that it really *wasn't* the old days after all, reached under the counter where his groping hand found nothing but law-abiding milk bottles. He gave Mike a sheepish look before he slid easily around the counter and headed across the room.

"By the judast! I clearn forgot I didn't keep a shillelagh there any more."

His big, clumsy-looking body moved with deceptive ease across the room and Mike saw him leaning over the table where discussion had rapidly approached something more ugly.

Mike spun his stool around to see what was going to happen and in the instant of his turning, the lights came on. Every switch in the place must have been turned on because the resulting glare was as shocking as a flash of light-ning that kept right on burning. Mike sat blinking, owl-like, against it, feeling as if his eyes were going to drop out of his head and roll across the floor like two glass alleys. When he was able to make out anything at all, he wanted to laugh. The sudden return of light had been like a magic wand that had turned everybody to a lifeless statue of him-self. A silence as profound as the silence of time settled in for an instant over the room. Slowly, sheepishly, people started to move. They began to look around to see who was sitting next to them. And a good many were wondering just what they had been saying so loudly the minute before.

At the booth where Al stood, the four men stared curi-ously at each other, as if they were seeing for the first time in their lives the familiar outlines of each other's faces. Herman Freid, who had been declaring a moment ago that he'd be eternally blanked if he'd take that kind of talk from anyone, let out a jovial roar of laughter, got up, circled Al as if he hadn't been there at all, and lined it for the juke box. He stuffed a quarter into the coin slot, punched at random five numbers across the face of that glowing jewel, and before he was back in his seat the trombone notes were sliding down the silence, golden and unperturbed as maple syrup.

Al came back across the floor.

"See?" he said. "Afraid of the dark."

"Yeah," Mike agreed tightly and grinned; but there was nothing to the grin but a drawing back of his lips. His eyes stayed as cold and unamused as two black coals. Looking down the line of booths now that the light was back, he had discovered in the end one reason why Ginny had refused to go out with him tonight. Three girls had their heads together over the table and Ginny was saying something. Then he saw the other two heads go back, heard the laughter, and gritted his teeth impotently.

It hadn't occurred to Mike that she had turned him down tonight for feminine company. He thought he wouldn't have been quite so put out if she'd been with Byron. When the clear, light laughter reached him the second time, Mike got up and stalked out of the restaurant, letting the door go behind him with a crash. So that was what she had to do that was so important—sit around gossiping with Alice Haines and Mina Billings!

"Hey!" Al said blankly, staring after him. "What ails him for the love of Pete? Never even paid for his supper!"

As Mike sat simmering behind the wheel of his car, he watched the big front window.

He could still hear the juke box.

Makes no difference now what kind of life fate hands me.
I'll get along without you now, that's plain to see.

He watched the three bright faces enviously, knowing that whenever he came anywhere near Ginny he defeated himself through the intensity of his own feelings.

He remembered suddenly that he hadn't paid his check; but he could not go back in now.

He put both hands on the wheel and laid his head down against the bony knuckles. Out of the blackness behind the closed lids the pressure brought swirls of bursting color that fell into kaleidoscopic patterns and faded.

It was pretty childish wanting something you couldn't get so much it gave you a quivering feeling of sick nervousness in the pit of the stomach. You wanted things that hard when you were a kid and nothing else in the world mattered. The moment of desire seemed to stretch out to the horizons of time, and from the middle of that great plain you knew it would never end unless you got it.

Couldn't even pass up a gab fest like that to go out with me, he thought angrily, trying to disregard the cold knowledge that Ginny would grasp at any excuse at all to avoid him.

Lifting his head he looked at her once more, sitting behind that protective shell of plate glass. They had both come full circle and now they were looking at each other hopelessly across a chasm just that many years deeper and wider than it had been the night it first opened between them.

Hell with the whole thing. Resentfully Mike snapped on the ignition, kicked the starter, and shot down the street as far as the neon sign that once more announced across the nights of terror: BEER TO TAKE OUT.

He took four bottles and drove away slowly, wondering where he could go to drink it. He must have thought of the place before his conscious mind recognized the thought, because he was abreast of the familiar side road already. He spun the wheel savagely against too much speed. Squealing, the tires twisted on the tar and chattered unsteadily over the gravel. When the wheels found the firmness of packed dirt again, he was still going too fast. If he'd met a car on this one-laned road where the alders leaned out to brush the canvas top of the Chevy on both sides, one of them would have been forced to take to the woods.

Fortunately he met nobody. The moon was right for parkers; but the weather was not. Tight and nervous and dry as a chip the lovely night lay across the land with danger in its beauty and fear in its secret places. Sullen as he

141

was, Mike felt it and was aware that—even as he told himself firmly he didn't give a hoot—his eyes were alert to find the first traces of ruddy light in that darkness.

He shot the little car out of the woods and halfway across the bumpy field before he stopped. For a second he sat staring at the sea, rolling out there beyond the point of land as sheeny and hammered as a big, silvery tray.

He opened the first bottle of beer.

When he opened the last one his mind had made itself up without his having to direct it one way or the other.

This is what you mean to me, he wanted to say to Ginny. All I ever wanted from you or any woman was just what I could get for nothing.

But—if he said it—she wouldn't care. She would expect that of him and would know he hadn't changed at all.

We used to come here together, Mike told the silvery night. He got out of the car and stood there with his hands clenched on the door. He was shaking as if it were cold and the cold had found him vulnerable.

It's only because I can't have her, he told himself furiously. It's crazy—it's childish.

He could almost remember the way a fifteen-year-old boy felt on a windy, moonlight night with the whole world waiting for him in the dark. He could nearly recapture the exciting lift under the ribs that meant anything could happen and would. Life *had* to be exciting and changing, and new. It couldn't be the same for him as it had been for all the others who were old and settled and indoors. They'd never got what they wanted and disappointment was the same thing as growing old; but when you were fifteen, it was up to you to see that life was more than disappointment. You were a good deal older when you found out it

142

wasn't that easy—older even if it happened in the next moment.

Driving more slowly back up the road, he had time when he saw the headlights coming at him to pull off into the ditch. As he crawled out of it again, the right hind wheel spun, but hardly enough to slow him down.

If we'd had decent weather, he thought, I'd have been mired right up to the hubs there.

In the shadow of the big maple that stood at one corner of Al's Café, he stopped the car. Might as well go in and pay that check while he still remembered it.

Mike saw instantly that Ginny and Mina and Alice were no longer sitting at the table in the corner. He saw Ginny at the door and waited, for the first time not wanting to meet her.

Safely concealed in his shadow, Mike could see that she was talking hurriedly to someone behind her without turning her head. She stared out into the night as if she were talking to herself. His mazed eyes picked out at least four more people, crowded around the door by her refusal to move.

Open the door, Ginny, Mike said to himself. You're holding up progress.

As if she had heard him, Ginny opened the door and came shooting out into the street. She was still moving fast when she drew abreast his car; but she wasn't looking to right or left.

"Ginny, wait!"

Ginny hesitated, still without turning and Mina came running down the sidewalk, her high heels clicking lightly on the cement. Mike, glancing through the window, saw Alice standing at the door with an air of exaggerated impatience. Beside her were three men he had never seen before. He looked them over carefully, their strangely similar dark faces, the bright tweed jackets they wore, the pale slacks. They looked enough alike to be brothers.

"But, Ginny—" Mina was saying—"don't be like that. Don't spoil all the fun. He *likes* you, honey."

"My Lord!" Ginny said in a low, angry voice. "I am flattered. Believe me, I'm deeply flattered. I was terribly worried that he wouldn't."

"Don't be so stuck up!" Judging from the tone there was a rapidly fraying temper in the offing. "Who d'you think you are, anyhow? I suppose you're too good—"

"I'm too good to be picked up in any juke joint!"

One of the three men detached himself from the others and came toward the arguing girls, his heavy shoulders swaying.

"Look, baby," he said in a soft, cajoling voice. "Come along like a good girl. We'll just go find ourselves a little excitement."

"Sorry." Ginny's voice was beginning to tatter. "I'm not interested."

"Ah, you stuck-up bitches make me sick." The male voice roughened under her scorn and began to be nasty. Mike, having seen those shoulders clearly, knew that he would gain nothing but a thorough going-over by getting out to discuss the matter. He leaned forward and switched on the ignition, his foot heavy on the starter. At the roar of the engine, the three people on the sidewalk, stared in surprise at the empty car. Relying on that surprise, Mike stuck his head out the door.

"Ginny," he said. "Here!"

Hearing the voice as a known one and not waiting to put a name to it, Ginny got in. She was barely inside the car

144

before Mike jerked it away from the curb, leaving the other two standing there staring.

"Nice people you know," Mike said lightly.

She didn't answer him; and, thinking to give her time to calm down, he drove slowly down Main Street. He passed the junction that would have taken them home and kept on going to the next side road that led past Job Hanna's house to the sea. With Job's house, the last of the town was behind them and ahead only the spruces, darkly ominous, and beyond them the water.

He parked under the first dimness of the trees and switched the lights off carefully. To his slightly fuddled brain everything he did had great significance and it was important that he should finish one thing completely before starting another. With his fingers on the key he sat feeling the even throb of the old engine through his arm before he turned the ignition off and let it die.

Ginny reached out and her cold fingers closed over his. In silence they sat there holding hands, staring straight before them.

Mike was deeply conscious of her hand. His nervous fingers explored each articulated joint, each fingernail, as if he were blind and must recognize this hand again by touch the next time he found it.

He was drowning in a relaxed peacefulness like water which would hold him beyond the time when he should have moved. Even his own voice sounded as if it came through a hollow cave of water.

"It's so beautiful here," he said quietly. "Looking at it, you don't really believe anything could happen to change it."

"I wish—"

"What?" he said quickly, feeling that whatever she had been going to say and had thought better of would have been deeply important.

"I was trying to think how to say how it is. The way you feel about the people and things that make your own life —when there's a chance you might lose that particular set of people and place. Everything seems twice as important. You feel as if you had to be awfully careful what you say or do so you won't destroy anything yourself."

He heard the self-derisory, little laugh that swallowed her last word.

"You don't have to laugh at yourself for feeling like that," he told her roughly. "Everyone feels the same way. Oh, maybe they don't say, but they feel it."

He hesitated a minute, wondering whether to say what he felt himself, anxious to say it in such a way that she would not laugh at him, too.

"The way we live around here ordinarily, you get to feeling as if there was a wall between you and everyone you know. Something solid and hard to see through. But when anything happens, the wall gets thinner and thinner and you begin to feel as if there might be a chance of its giving way."

"Yes." Her agreement came quickly, followed as quickly by her protest. "But you aren't sure you really want it to. It kind of scares you to think the wall *might* give. You have to have something to hide behind."

Her fingers moved nervously in his, tried to escape his grasp, and gave up at the first sign of his resistance.

"No," she said. "Let go."

"I don't think I want to."

"You've got to do better than that."

146

"Well, then, I know damn well I don't want to."

Ginny laughed softly and the sound echoed around the walls of that resounding cave until Mike heard it like a distant thrumming of low wind blowing.

Her hand was a human contact in whirling, dangerous darkness. He knew there was no wall between them. There was nothing. Moving with a carefully premeditated decision, Mike took her hand in his left one and put his freed arm around her shoulders. The pressure he exerted was a mere suggestion, not enough to be completely responsible for the ease with which she turned to him.

He felt rather than heard her lips say his name, felt them move against his own in that short, known word. Her fingers barely touched the short hair on the back of his head. He heard her make a faint, remembered sound far back in her throat and he wished for a strong second, to die right where he sat, to die with her in his arms freely, easily, rightly, like this

Not to die, then—but live forever.

She turned her head a little away and, with a quick betraying intake of breath, turned it back again and found him waiting.

Mike didn't know how much later it was when she said in that breathless, exciting whisper he knew so well: "Mike, we've got to stop this!"

"I don't see why; but if you say so."

"Oh, Mike! Damn you anyway."

"Anything—anything you want—only—"

"No, wait." Her retreat was definite this time.

"Look," he began stumblingly, thinking that maybe this was the time to tell her. "I worked hard to get back here, Ginny, because this place and the people here belong to me. I mean, I belong here, I guess. Everyone has his place and even if he's not in it, he knows he should be. This place is yours and mine."

He felt her stiffen and this time, when she moved to pull her hand away, he let it go.

"That's fine for you," she said, her voice sounding distant and muffled. "But you're a man. Everything you need is right here for you. You know where you're going and how to get there. But, my Lord, look! Look—I wish you could be me for just one day. If you're a woman and not married, you're on the make. If you're married, you've settled down to stodge away the rest of your life! There isn't anything—"

"Oh, judast! Just because a couple of drugstore cowboys tried to pick you up— Why, if I saw you sitting in a joint like that, you'd look awful good to me, Ginny. I think I'd try the same thing."

"Oh, it's not that! Don't think that was important enough to— No, it goes a lot deeper than that and I couldn't ever make you see how it is because we will always look at things opposite. We *have* to. I'll bet Tiz would know what I mean. *She's* been contending with it all her life."

Mike was momentarily silent, remembering the static birds flying forever around Tiz's kitchen walls.

"Who *were* those guys?" he asked. "You ever see them before?"

"Somebody said Ralph Swain had put a crew of men in that old camp on the Bobtown road." Gratefully she took up his question. "All I could think of, they were some of his men."

Mike sat digesting that in silence. So Ralph had gone right ahead with his project in spite of Jay. There wasn't anything that could be done about it. But Mike knew, if he'd been a stranger on the Peninsula right now, he wouldn't have gone around calling attention to his presence. Not until it rained, anyway.

Neither of them heard the car coming down the road from town. The back window blossomed suddenly into light and a door slammed. The cab of the Chevy was pinned down under the glare of the torch thrust through the open window.

"Oh, sorry Mike!" The flashlight was withdrawn abruptly.

"That you, Anse?"

"Well, yes." Ansel Barker sounded as if he wished he hadn't had the light at all. "We got orders to look at every car we find parked around."

"That's all right." Mike climbed slowly out of the Chevy, preferring to talk standing up.

The light was pointed at the ground now; but when Mike got out, Anse couldn't help giving him a quick glance.

"You better go along, Mike. Jay told us not to pass up anything. We have to flush all you birds, see?"

"I know!" Mike said impatiently. "I've been riding patrol, too. I'm not going to give you any trouble."

"No, I know you won't. And it'd probably be all right to leave you here; but once you go making exceptions—"

"Sure, sure." The only thing Mike wanted was to have Anse go along and let him get out of here and take Ginny home.

"You can tell the lady I didn't even see who she was," Anse said abruptly. "She don't have to worry."

"Okay."

"Uh—I'll go down to the end of the road," Anse explained heavily. "When I come back, I hope you'll be gone."

Mike glanced at the car parked behind him. Another

149

figure, tall and shadowy, stood waiting beside its door.

"Who's that?" He jerked his head.

"Charley Kelly."

"Okay," Mike said again, flatly. "I'm on my way."

He sat waiting as they started up and pulled by him. Ginny was stiffly silent and Mike was swearing to himself. They'd been getting along so well; but it had all been so tenuous it needed only a third person to make it uncomfortable again. He didn't glance at her as his fingers found the switch and flipped the key. He was staring after the taillights of the patrol car.

He never knew what made him look into the underbrush to the right of the road. But he did look and he saw with quickened attention the vague, white spot that seemed to waver slightly as he watched. Mike's mind narrowed down to an aware point, focused on that white thing that shouldn't have been there just as it moved.

The bushes parted enough to let through a frantically scrambling body. Against the lights, Mike saw human arms and legs moving as fast as a man could move. The figure hurtled across the road and apparently dived head first into the underbrush on the other side.

He leaned on the horn, savagely. Instantly the taillights ahead bloomed as Anse shoved on the brakes. Mike snapped on his own lights and half fell out of the car. Ginny cried out something to him as he went; but he heard only her voice.

"Anse, turn your spotlight over there."

"Where, where?"

"Where I'm pointing, dammit. I saw him."

The instant before the light went on seemed hours to Mike. He was breathless. Anse's light searched the dead-silent woods and the little rise that went up naked and ledgy on the other side of the narrow swale. Charley got out and came around to stand beside Mike. In the under-brush nothing moved, nothing betrayed.

"Don't see nothing," Charley muttered.

"Well, he's there. He crossed the road just after you pulled away. He hasn't had time to get out of that pucker brush. I'd have seen him if he went up that rise."

"Pete sake, Mike, you're seeing things," Charley said; but the words were something to convince himself, not to say that Mike was lying.

"I know what I saw. I saw a man come out of that ditch there and cross the road between the two cars. If the cussed fool had stayed where he was, I wouldn't have. He must have gone crazy when we were all standing here talking. He couldn't wait till we'd gone."

"All right." Anse shifted in his seat, reaching over the back to fumble in the darkness behind him. His arm came up stiff with the shotgun gripped firmly in his big fist. Looking at that set square jaw, Mike felt his own blood slow in his veins.

"Judast!" he said. "What if he ain't the one, Anse?"

"If he's where you say he is," Anse said coldly, "he knows he ought not to be there or he'd give us a hail."

"I'll get him out," Charley said heavily.

He took the gun from Anse and walked over to the shoulder of the road. Anse got out and followed him, with Mike at his elbow. The excitement that grew in the other two was contagious. For a second he thought: Who will it be? But that went under in a flood of anger. If this was the so-and-so who'd been trying to burn them out, he deserved anything he would get.

"I don't believe he's there," Charley whispered. "He must've got away without you seeing him go, Mike."

Stubbornly Mike shook his head. The three men paced the road shoulder staring into the breast-high stand of steeple bush and young alders. In each of them there was an obvious reluctance to set foot into that dangerously waiting darkness, to get out of sight of the others. They came back together again and stood listening.

"He's there," Mike insisted. "It's too quiet for him not to be."

"I'll flush him," Anse said, his voice a thread of sound.

"You got that gun, Charley?" Anse spoke loudly this time for the benefit of the man who cowered out of their sight. Loudly—and Mike remembered the hunting owl that screeches across the moonlit field to frighten into motion anything defenseless that may be hiding there.

"Yeah." Charley's voice was just as audible. "I sure have."

Anse made one more turn up the road and back. Ten yards away from them he stopped and yelled: "There he is, the son of a bitch. Shoot, Charley! Shoot!"

Charley pointed the shotgun into the air and the blast of it shattered the night.

Instantly something came to thrashing life in the undergrowth. A frantic body wrenched its way into the open and started hopelessly up the little rise of ledgy ground toward the shelter of the taller trees behind it. Clear in the moonlight, he ran like a kangaroo rat, with long, despairing leaps.

"Let him have it," Anse roared.

Charley lifted the gun, took careful aim, and lowered it. "My God! I can't do it."

Anse snatched the shotgun and it seemed to Mike he hardly took time to aim before the second charge let go. The man running desperately in the moonlight went down without a sound as if a big hand had reached out and pushed him over onto his face. Before they broke and ran, too, the

152

three men on the road stood staring at each other with moon-blanched faces.

"You got him," Charley said as blankly as if he hadn't expected any such result.

"Yes, and if I aimed right, he won't do much running for a couple of weeks," Anse agreed grimly. "I bet I nearly took his leg off."

Arms high to protect their faces against the slashing tips of the pucker brush, they forced their way in through to the solid ledge. Ahead of them they could hear a voiceless scrabbling as if an animal lay wounded on the rocks.

Almost reluctantly they came up with him. He lay, face down, his fingers clawing in the thin, ash-white soil, one leg still making the motion of running, trying to pull him away from them. The other leg, his right one, dragged use-lessly.

Anse reached down and flipped him over. At the touch every trace of resistance went out of the small body. He let himself be turned over and lay there panting, his narrow-chinned, high-browed face wet with sweat in the cold light, his eyes as senseless and scared as an animal's would have been. In shocked surprise they stood looking down at that familiar face, each of them seeing it for the first time as the face of his fear.

"I never thought it was *him*," Charley said in a tone as detached as if this were something he'd been reading about in the newspaper.

"So *you're* the one." Anse was pale with fury.

Mike went down on his knees beside the pain-stiffened, unknowing figure.

"Jonesy," he said. "Can you hear me?"

At the moment Jonesy Dawes couldn't hear anything, his consciousness was set so firmly against the searing pain

153

in his leg. He tried to speak and Charley and Anse, anxious to hear it too, knelt beside Mike, waiting for the first thing Jonesy would say.

Mike was thinking: It sounds just like gargling, the queer noise in the back of his throat.

"Oh, my loving Lord!" Jonesy wailed. "What'll I tell Mother!"

Mike said very clearly, to pierce that shell of pain and apprehension: "Jonesy, why did you do it?"

"I never. I never," Jonesy sobbed. The sweat on his face was mixed now with tears. "I didn't do anything. I was minding my own business. You've broke my leg!"

Anse rolled up the tattered pants leg and looked thoughtfully at the blood-drenched calf of Jonesy's leg. He put one hand behind the knee and probed. Jonesy's foot jerked.

"It ain't broke," Anse said. "All's you've got is a load of bird shot; but by judast, if I had my way it'd been a rifle slug instead."

Jonesy opened his eyes and for the first time there was a cold sane look in them.

"I never set your damned fire," he said. "But now I wisht to God I had!"

Doubt thrust a cold finger simultaneously into three minds. There was an honesty that was completely horrifying in Jonesy's quiet voice, in his pain-shot eyes.

"Well, if you didn't," Anse said against his own doubt, "you've got some explaining to do."

"Why in God's name did you run?" Mike asked.

"Look! If you was out here alone and three crazy men with a gun started after you, *you'd* run."

"Yeah, I sure would!" Uneasily Mike met Charley's uncomfortable glare.

154

"All right," Anse said, intentionally brutal. "Talk fast. Jonesy."

"No."

"This is not a picnic," Anse said. "You're in a harder spot than you've ever been before in *your* life. If we was to take you into town and tell how we'd found you, I wouldn't guarantee what would happen." He stopped long enough to let Jonesy think that one over. "By the Lord, I've got half a mind to let you stay here and bleed to death!"

Jonesy's breath hissed suddenly between his teeth.

"Charley, I've known you all my life. You won't let him do it. Will you? Will you?" When Charley didn't answer, Jonesy said on a dying fall of breath: "Mike—"

Mike turned his eyes away from the prone body.

"It's my own business," Jonesy yelled.

"Any man caught running around in the woods right now on his own business is in a pretty hard spot." Anse's voice was more convincingly implacable than his words.

"I been up to Polly Hanna's," Jonesy said, his voice as automatic as if it came from a metal larynx. "We been going together now for fifteen years. I can't— My mother— We couldn't let anyone know because of Mother—"

The grating voice died away and the three men standing above him purposely didn't meet each other's eyes.

"Well," Mike said. "We could take him home. If it's true—What I mean is, if he *has* been setting fires, he won't do it again for a while anyhow. If he hasn't, it may happen again while he's laid up."

"That's all right with me," Charley said gruffly.

"Let's go ask Polly," Anse suggested deliberately.

"Oh, no!" Jonesy tried to sit up and made it after a struggle. "Please. Please!"

155

"Hell with that," Charley said.

Jonesy's poor confession had given each of them a sudden vision of Polly Hanna's clean, worn, bony face. And none of them could have faced her, knowing this about her, where nobody had suspected such a thing before.

Fifteen years, Mike was thinking soddenly. Fifteen years of sneaking around corners and being afraid all because of an old woman who'd make life miserable if she knew. But, judast, how could it be any more miserable? No wonder Job Hanna's only daughter had that worn-thin look around her deep eyes!

But is it true? his mind asked coldly.

Well, even if it wasn't, Jonesy wouldn't be doing much running around for a week or so. After that, they could watch him. Mike wasn't at all satisfied with their quarry. He was beginning to feel pretty much ashamed and Charley, judging from his attitude, was feeling the same way. You couldn't know what Anse was thinking.

Anse handed the shotgun to Mike and, stooping, thrust his great arms under Jonesy and picked him up easily. The going was rough and Jonesy kept letting out an inadvertent grunt of pain whenever Anse's foot went into a hole or hit a high place. Anse laid his load carefully in the back seat of the big sedan.

"You'll have to tell people you were cleaning your gun and it went off," he advised straightly. "Unless you want what happened to get out."

He hesitated and then added sharply: "But don't think we won't be watching you. You won't make a move from now on that one of us ain't watching you. Don't forget that!"

Mike, feeling as if he had been clouted over the head, went back to his own car and got in. Driving back toward

156

town, he could feel Ginny in the darkness beside him as tense and stiff as a thinking robot.

"I'm sorry you had to sit through that," he said numbly.

"It wasn't pretty. It wasn't hardly human." Her voice was a thin thread of impersonal sound. "I don't think people are human when they're scared."

He didn't speak to her again until he stopped the car at the foot of her drive. When he turned to face her, Mike knew she was sitting there tautly, afraid he wasn't going to finish the evening as abruptly as this. He thought of the most important thing of all he had had to tell her, the "I love you," the simple truth. But it was too late to do it.

"I guess I better not drive in," he said, keeping his voice as normal as he could make it through the recurring waves of weariness. "Good night, dear. I'll see you."

As if his own body were a projection of hers, Mike felt her relieved surprise. Standing there looking in at him, as invisible to him as he must have been to her, she said with a new, half-astounded gentleness, "Thanks a lot, Mike. You came along at just the right minute tonight."

"I hope I'll always be able to." Mike heard his own sententious words with a little quiver of tired amusement. Once-more-into-the-breach Arey, he thought; but thankfully didn't say it.

When he went into Tiz's warm kitchen, he was thinking: Poor old Jonesy! Fifteen years!

At nine o'clock in the morning Tiz came out that kitchen door. She was going down to see Polly, as she had promised to do; but going to see Polly was simply an excuse to move. Tension with Tiz, instead of lessening when nothing happened, grew stronger and she needed an excuse to get out of doors. Polly would do as well as any.

She walked at great speed so that anyone who saw her must necessarily suppose that she had reason for being out and away at this hour in the morning instead of doing housework. Forcefully, as if much depended upon her coming, Tiz went up Job Hanna's drive.

Job was standing in the door, his thick, clipped, white beard obscuring whatever expression there might have been around his mouth, his blue eyes hot and smiling. Job Hanna was the only person in the whole town of Frenchville who addressed Tiz by her Christian name and she saw him so seldom that she heard that name with surprise.

"Lord, Elizabeth!" he said. "Did you ever in all your borned days see such a spell of cussed good weather?"

Tiz restrained the impulse to glance over her shoulder.

"No," she said tartly. "I never did. And if it goes on much longer, I doubt if I'll live to see another such spell."

Job lowered his eyes just a fraction from the point in the middle of her forehead which he usually addressed and met her straight glance with another as straight.

"All of us feel the same, I don't doubt. I can't settle down to do anything. I ain't worth the powder to blow me to hell, really I ain't. Everything's sort of landed full weight on poor Poll and Lord knows, *she's* in no shape to take over. This morning, especially!"

"What's wrong with her that's not with the rest of us?" She might have known, Tiz thought with a wry, inward grin, there'd be something wrong with Polly.

"We had a little excitement here last night," Job said slowly. His face, above the beard, turned a harsh, dusky red and his angry glance moved vaguely away from her, leaving Tiz feeling like a woman constructed out of thin air through which he could see so easily that it wasn't worth his while to look.

158

"I better let her tell you," he said. "She's out gathering eggs now. I'm glad you come, Elizabeth. Maybe a little good sense talked from somebody else can make that stubborn girl of mine see the light of day." He permitted himself a slight, unamused smile.

"I been at her till I'm near as crazy as she is myself and *I* can't beat no sense into her silly head. I suppose she's persisted in her ways so long she can't let go without a fight."

Having said what he'd had it in mind to say to her, Job turned abruptly away. Tiz saw him go without surprise. Job always had in mind something else he had to go and attend to once one chore was over, so when he'd had his say, he went to do the other thing.

Tiz found Polly sitting on the doorstep of the hen house in the sun, crying into a large basket of eggs. Her grief was grotesque to watch. At the sound of steps, Polly stiffened and the sobbing stopped.

"Leave me alone, Pa," Polly said, her voice ragged and jerking.

"It's me, Polly," Tiz said easily. "What's the trouble?"

Polly took one startled, pink-eyed glance, gave a short, cut-off scream, and threw her apron over her head.

"Don't look at me, Tiz, for the Lord sake! I'm a mess."

"There, there." Tiz sat down beside her and began patting her shoulder soothingly. "Calm down and try and tell me what's happened. I couldn't get it out of your father. All he'd say was that you'd had a little excitement last night."

"Little excitement!" Indignation and sorrow proceeded in equalized waves from the mound of cotton over Polly's head. "They shot Jones last night! Right down here in front of the house!"

159

Tiz felt for a minute as if somebody had hit her hard in the stomach. Completely incapable of speech, she sat staring at that shapeless mass of cloth.

"*Shot* him!" she said finally in a strangled whisper. "Is—is he—?"

"No, he isn't dead." Unable to express herself fully in the hot tent of her apron, Polly flung it away from her and met Tiz's horrified stare bravely, her eyes worn with crying, blinking against the strong sunlight. "I heard it, Tiz! They shot more than once. I went down to see what was happening and I was just in time to see them loading him into the car. They shot his legs. But he wasn't doing anything, Tiz. He'd just been up here to see me and he was going home and I guess he got scared when he saw the patrol car and run. And they shot him!"

Tiz was too astounded to speak. She simply could not believe that the men riding patrol—men she had known all her life—could be shoved into a state of such concentrated hatred and fear as to shoot a man before they found out who he was and what he was doing. She sat there foolishly opening her mouth and then, finding nothing to say, closing it again.

"I'm surprised you didn't know already," Polly said accusingly. Her voice broke and hiccupped. "Mike was there. I saw him and his girl. *They* weren't being shot at. *They* just got sent home. It was Jones that got shot. And for not doing as much as *they* were either!"

"Mike!" Tiz repeated stupidly, still unable to take it in. She had heard Mike come upstairs last night, had heard him go along the hall slowly, breathing with hard, long inhalations, like a steady sighing. She had thought he was only tired. Now she realized what had been the matter with him. And he hadn't told her and didn't intend to!

"Pa says," Polly began bitterly, "it's a sign. He says I ought to forget Jonesy. He says I've wasted my life on him and he's nothing but a—a—jellyfish. He says Jonesy hasn't got the gumption to get away from his mother and never will and I'd be better off to forget about him."

"Well," Tiz said heartlessly, "wouldn't you?"

"Tiz, I love him!"

At the unbelievable words, spoken in a quiet, decisive tone she had never heard from this woman before, Tiz gave her a straight glance. Polly's long face was undeniably illuminated. That strange light gave her a look of great and ingrained dignity and, recognizing the power of an emotion that could do that for Polly, Tiz gave in without a cavil.

"In that case," she said in a low, careful voice, "maybe it's time you revalued your life. Maybe this is the time to do it, when you're all torn up with something else anyhow."

"What do you mean?" Polly sounded as if she were afraid to hear what Tiz was going to say to her and Tiz was doing a lot of soul-searching, too. Reluctantly she said, in that same careful tone:

"Go away with him. If you don't now, you never will."

"I know it." Polly's voice had faded. "I could go. I've had my clothes packed ever since the fire."

"You won't, will you?" Tiz watched her curiously. "You aren't even considering it, are you?"

"I don't dare."

The three words jerked out raggedly, as if Polly hadn't really wanted to say them.

"I don't dare. There's his mother. I'm afraid Jonesy will say he can't leave his mother and then, of course, I'd never be able to face him again."

"If he won't—" Tiz made her voice as cold as small

stones falling into the dust in front of them—"why, I think you'd better take your father's way out. If he won't, then you don't really want him anyhow. Isn't that what you're trying to say?"

"I suppose so." Polly stared unhappily at her lax hands, drooping bonelessly over her knees. "But he'll say the old lady can't take care of herself. That she needs somebody."

"Look." Tiz's ice-water voice fell across Polly's shrinking ears. "You know as well as I do that Jonesy's mother is capable of doing a lot more than she does; but she certainly won't do it as long as *he's* there to do it for her. And if she needs more, she is also able to hire it done. She's had Jonesy too long, if he won't leave her now. And if that's the way of it, *you* certainly don't want him because you'd never be anything but another mother to him. And that's not what you want."

"No. That's not what I want." In spite of the blush, Polly's eyes met Tiz's with a full admission.

"Oh Lord, Tiz! You make it sound so right. I'm sure it would be, for you. I've often wished I could be like you. You do what you want to and that's that. I wish I was like you!"

"Oh!" Tiz said blankly. It was her turn now, and to Polly's astounded eyes the dusky red flowing up behind her dark skin was nearly as embarrassing as it was to Tiz. "Oh, my God!" she said and, getting up from the step, went striding off down the drive without a backward look.

Polly sat watching her in astonishment so deep she couldn't make a sound with her paralyzed tongue.

It had never occurred to her before that Tiz wouldn't take kindly to having anybody want to be like her. She still couldn't think that was why Tiz had got up as if she'd

162

been stung and gone off like that without a word except that unbelievable "Oh, my God."

When she came into the house alone, her father said curiously, "Where is Elizabeth?"

Polly didn't even hear him. She set the eggs down carefully on the table and went up the back stairs to the bare bedroom over the kitchen. Once there, she sat on the edge of her thin-mattressed bed for a long time, staring at the blank wall opposite and not even seeing it.

PART THREE

Small-craft warnings from Cape Cod to East-port for increasing southwesterly winds.

⟍

THE FIRST thing Trooper Amory thought of afterward was the way he must look. Second was the dismayed accept-ance of his dizziness. When he leaned forward to glance at his puttees, scratched and blackened and only distantly re-lated to the shining leather casings he had wrapped around his shins a few hours ago, he was shocked. His deep, personal vanity made appearance important to him and he knew his blue-gray uniform suited him well. At the moment he looked like nothing under the sun.

He straightened and took two uncertain steps, putting his hand out for support and finding none. After a second the dizziness passed. He walked slowly over to the fire truck, taking his time, looking carefully at the soot-blackened men who stood there, picked out of anonymity by the circling spotlight. The flashing red light over the cab was blinding against his weary eyes. The engine throbbed in a regular, low, deep beat which sounded to him like the beating of a gigantic heart. It was the red, living heart of life here at the center of this doomed land; and when that beating stopped, if it did, life on the Peninsula would stop too.

"Amory, you look like the devil himself." Mike's voice

164

gave a personality to one of the dim figures clustered around the huge truck.

"Feel like him, I'm sure." Amory managed a grin. "I realize I'm no fireman."

"Trouble is," Allen Carter snapped, "none of us are. Not enough, anyways."

"Allen, you're doing all right. Just keep on the way you are and no man here will complain."

"I don't doubt that," Allen said shortly. "The first crack I hear and by God, there'll be war. But we don't know enough. Things like this tonight, they're different. A kid could have handled this. But, Amory, if it don't rain soon, we'll have something on our hands that a kid can't handle, no, nor anyone short of the devil himself."

"Who was it reported this?"

"Powder Tilton's wife." Allen's voice was strained. "She was just getting ready for bed when she looked out the window. She said she saw it start and not a minute later the flames was shooting up like out of a blowtorch."

Amory nodded.

"That patch of blackberry bushes were as dry as anything I've seen yet." There were a couple of dry leaves clinging to the rough cloth of his sleeve. He picked them off and held them out to the light and they went to dust in his fingers. "Looka that!"

Allen shook his head.

"What I can't figure—" Amory went on slowly—"is why even a crazy man would set a fire out here. If he wanted to burn the town out, Lord knows, he couldn't do it this way. Why, once that blackberry jungle went up, there isn't really fuel enough to carry fire. He must have known all you'd had to do really is sit and wait and it'd burn itself out."

"Maybe he feels like I do," Allen said somberly. "I feel like the air itself is dry enough to burn."

"Any fire right now has a nuisance value," Mike said slowly, trying to think how to say what he meant. "And any fire *could* be dangerous. *Is,* in fact. You can't tell what the damn stuff will do in a drought like this one. But you can be sure that even a match flame will keep people hared up."

"I think you got it right there," Amory agreed. Wearily he turned away. "Well, it's out, anyway."

He had left his car in Powder Tilton's yard and had run the fifty yards to the fire. Going back, he felt as if that fifty yards had stretched to three times fifty. He was so tired he wasn't even aware for a moment that somebody walked beside him. When he did hear the sound of steps and realized there was more noise than he could have made alone, he glanced around quickly, recognizing Powder more by his general outline than by any visible detail.

"The thing of it is," he said, continuing what he'd been saying before as if Powder must know what he meant, "they'll work just as hard to put out a little bonfire like that one as they would on any fire. Right now. Everyone's nervous, you see. It keeps them tired. It takes just as much energy. And when everyone's shot and half crazy, then's when he'll start the real trouble."

"All's I hope is," Powder said shrilly, "I never lay *my* hands on the low son of a sea cook. I'll tear him to bloody ribbons. So help me, I'll kill him!"

Amory looked thoughtfully at Powder's scarecrow shoulders in the moonlight. If Powder ever came up with the firebug, Amory wouldn't have taken any bets on which one would be torn to ribbons.

Emmy Tilton heard them coming up the drive and
166

she pulled the woodshed door open to peer blindly out at them.

"That you, Powder?" she called shrilly, nervously, into the night.

"Of course it's me."

Powder scuttled for the door and Amory, not quite sure why he did so, followed right behind him. When his big body came into the distorted rectangle of light, Emmy gasped, started to close the door, and thought better of it.

"What d'you *want?*" Her voice ended on a hysterical high note.

"Nothing much," Amory said gently, his eyes on her distracted face. "It's all right, Mrs. Tilton. Just wanted to thank you for being right on the job, that's all."

"Did *you* report that fire?" Powder asked. He turned his head and looked at his wife's pale face with a surprised, intent interest.

Amory happened to be looking down at her hand on the thumb latch and he saw its fingers jerk convulsively. It didn't seem to Amory that such a direct question, answerable by a single syllable, should have taken such concentration; but Emmy couldn't seem to make her tongue form the word.

She stood staring at the two men, her eyes withdrawn and inward looking, considering the question. Her mind was running frantically. Not over the answer to that question, but the answers to subsequent questions.

It would be no lie to say simply: Yes, I reported it.

Then they would logically ask: Did you see it start? She could answer that honestly: Yes, I did.

Finally, coming up against the stone wall of truth, she hestitated, wondering how to answer the last, the crucial question: Did you see who set it?

Anxiously she groped back through the past hour to the moment when the first flame had touched the first dead leaf. That flame, cupped between her own trembling hands, fascinated her own downward-staring eyes. She reached the moment of horror when the flame's voice changed from a hiss to a crackle and she had stood staring at it, thinking: God forgive me because I *know* what I'm doing.

When the question came, would she be able to answer it at all? If she couldn't, would her silence be more suspicious than a yes or a no?

Powder's frankly horrified eyes were on her.

"Why, I was sitting right in front of the firehouse when it started," he said heavily. "I was talking to—"

His voice hesitated. He turned and gave her a curious look.

"The whistle nearly scared the tar out of me," he finished lamely. "And *you* reported it."

"Yes," she said stiffly, and answered the next question before it had been asked, anxious to get it over and know once and for all what she would say. "I saw it start."

"Well, how did you report it?"

"I ran up to Hanscom's and phoned the firehouse."

"Oh, yes," Powder said in the voice of one politely interested. "But didn't you see someone around down there? Didn't you see the man who set it?"

She was looking at Amōry, not Powder, when she shook her head.

"All I saw was the fire before I started to run. I didn't wait to see anything else." Relief was as bracing as cool water. She had seen no man. She had been able to tell the God's own truth.

"Look," Powder said. His head seemed to sink into a hollow between his shoulders. He stood glowering down at
168

her. "I was the one stood to lose by that fire tonight. It couldn't do anything but come this way and clear out this palace we're living in, Emmy. Whoever's doing it's got a grudge against me. And my judast!—" his voice started to go up—"you couldn't even wait a minute to see who he was! Let him go to try again! My own wife! You don't care what happens to me any more than anyone else in this town does. I believe you'd like to see me dead, wouldn't you? Hanh? Wouldn't you, Emmy?"

She started to back away from him.

"Powder, please," she said softly, her eyes frozen by his stare.

"Oh, shut up!" Powder screamed. He set one hand flat against her throat and pushed. It wasn't much of a shove; but it took her off balance and she staggered back away from him. The edge of the one, straight chair caught her just behind the knees and she sat down hard. She began to whimper, deep in her throat.

"I oughta—" Powder started savagely.

Amory took a step forward and put his hand on Powder's arm. He held his instinctive distaste under enough to be able to do it easily.

"All right, Powder," he said. "You're tired like the rest of us. Go to bed. Get a night's sleep."

Powder spun on him and remembered, apparently for the first time, that the blue uniform meant something. He swallowed the hot words.

"Yeah," he said with forced quiet. "Yeah, I guess you're right, Amory."

He went over to the water bucket and stood lipping down a dipper full of water. Emmy's eyes followed each movement he made with a disinterested intensity. She looked like a woman watching an exciting movie, bemused with vicarious tension, aware that it had nothing to do with her.

Amory's foot scraped heavily on the uneven floor, startling him and making Emmy jump.

"Please go," she said softly, looking at him with the same disinterested desperation. "It's all right now."

"Well," he said uneasily. "If you're sure—"

"I'm not going to lay a finger on her," Powder said. He didn't turn his head as Amory let himself out the door, bending beneath the low lintel.

As his steps faded, Powder said, wtihout turning to, look at Emmy: "I'm a smart man, but I'm wasted. My life doesn't amount to a hannah cook. They all look at me the same way. It's my looks. Just because of my looks, they all treat me like an idiot. I can't help it, can I, how I look? I'm an educated man, Emmy, and I don't have to thank anyone for it. I did it all myself and if I had it to do over again, I wouldn't bother. When you look as funny as I do, you can't get anywhere."

He went over to the mirror and stood there, staring into his own almost colorless, faintly pink eyes. Watching him, Emmy felt for him something that she hadn't for years now. Recognizing the stab of quick pity, she said softly: "Powder, *I* know you're smart. *I* believe in you. I'd do things for you I wouldn't touch for anyone else, Powder."

"You believe in me, don't you, Emmy?" He repeated her words, tenderly. Then his face twisted and he roared: "Because you have to."

The four walls of the shed reverberated around her under the force of the slammed door and she was alone and shaking with nervousness.

Amory felt his way across the lumber-cluttered yard to his car. As he was climbing into the driver's seat, he felt

170

dizzy again. He waited, for a minute, staring out the windshield; but nothing happened.

There was a light burning in Tiz's kitchen and he could see the shadow of her moving around. If I know her, he thought, she's making coffee. Maybe if he had a cup of coffee it would get him home. He certainly was feeling queer.

He backed the car down to her gate and got out. For a second he stood there waiting before he left the safety of the big sedan and went heavily up the walk.

She didn't seem surprised to see him when she opened the door, but he fancied she looked at him closely when she stood aside to let him in.

"I thought you'd probably be up there," she said quietly. "I thought I saw your car in Tilton's yard when I came back to the house."

"I was there all right." He sat down heavily and leaned forward to look ruefully down at himself. It seemed to make him feel a little better, too, leaning forward like that. The smell of coffee was thick and rich in the room. He put his head on his fists and stayed quiet. Then he remembered that he hadn't taken off his cap. When he did, letting the light fall directly on his face, Tiz stiffened.

"Amory, is—are you all right?"

"Just tired." He shook his head. Quickly he realized that was a mistake and stopped doing it. "I thought you'd be making coffee for Mike and maybe I could have some."

She went hastily across to the pantry and got a cup and saucer, putting it on the table at his elbow. He knew she was watching him sharply, but he couldn't seem to make himself care enough to look back at her. His head felt stuffed with cotton batting and if he tried to say anything his tongue would be thick, too. She started to pour his coffee and he turned to it hopefully.

The instant the smell of it strengthened in his nostrils he began to feel sick. Horrified, he started to his feet. The sudden motion was too much for him. His legs buckled and he kept right on going. There was no feeling of impact when he hit the floor. He fell with his arms stiffened so that he went only to his hands and knees. Unable to move, his head hanging, he knew it was finally going to happen. Confusedly he was thinking how he must look to her; desperately he was thinking: Thank God she's not a screaming woman! He could hear her voice saying something indistinguishable. He could feel her hands strong at his shoulders and he tried to tell her not to touch him; but only a strangled, animal sound came out. With a gush of relief that woolly pressure in his head was gone. His eyes cleared slowly and, looking down, he saw with conscious horror the great splash of blood against the clean, scrubbed boards.

"Oh, my God!" he said. "Tiz, I'm so sorry." He tried to get up; but he found her hand stiff on the back of his neck.

"Don't move," she said sharply.

"All over the floor."

"Never mind the floor," Tiz said distinctly. "Just let it go for a minute. You'll feel better."

She moved quickly across the kitchen and when she was back beside him, he felt something wet and icy cold at the nape of his neck. His head was clearing quickly; but the puddle still grew beneath him. He felt if only he didn't have to move, it would be all right. Her hand was firm and steady under his forehead. He reached up cautiously to his face and pulled his hand down, shining and red.

"What?" he said numbly.

172

"It's all right. Just a nosebleed."

"Oh." He managed to hoist himself to his feet. "Feel better," he said. He took the cloth from her hand and held it to his nose. "Maybe it'd stop if I could lie down a minute."

He stumbled across to the couch and went down on it like a sack of sand. Tiz pulled the pillows from under his head and stuffed them instead beneath his knees. He thought disconnectedly, I've got my shoes on. In a sort of dream he could hear Tiz moving around and decided she was probably cleaning up the mess he'd made all over her floor. He heard the door open; but he couldn't open his eyes. There was a startled silence, then Mike's voice said: "For pete sake, what did you hit him with?"

"Sssh!" Tiz hissed. "I think he's asleep and I should say it had been a long time since he had been."

Amory wasn't even able to show them he wasn't. He could feel himself floating on a cloud and it was soft and comfortable as he had always imagined clouds would be. The last thought in his conscious mind was that his car stood outside her gate and would be there for everyone to see.

The next thing he felt was a deep well-being. He was comfortable and warm and just waking up from the first sleep he'd had for what seemed like weeks. All I needed was sleep, he thought peacefully and put out his hand without opening his eyes to the bedside table where he always left his cigarets.

The table wasn't there. Completely awake, he lay with his eyes shut and one arm stiffly extended. Nothing. Cautiously he moved his hand, trying to find something solid in what was apparently a vacuum. Slowly he drew his hand back and patted curiously at his chest. There was a wool blanket over him and that was right; but under the

173

blanket his exploring fingers found uniform buttons and his Sam Browne belt.

Lord amighty, he thought. I must have got into bed with my clothes on! Shoes, too. He could feel them. He was just reaching out again to see if there wasn't something, anything, solid around the bed when somebody started to laugh.

"If you'd open your eyes you might find out where you were."

"I'm dead!" he said. "I always knew the first thing I'd hear in heaven would be your voice."

"Amory, don't be such a fool! Open your eyes."

"I don't want to. I'm afraid you'd disappear."

"I won't."

"I'm dreaming!"

"Well, you're not."

"I often dream I hear you first thing in the morning."

"Clyde," she said. "If you don't open your eyes I'll let you have a glass of ice water."

"It'd be worth it if you'd call me that again. You never called me Clyde before."

"First thing in the morning, indeed!" Tiz ignored his answer. "What time d'you think it is?"

"Half-past heaven," Amory said.

He opened his eyes just in time. She was standing above him with the glass poised, and the western windows were brilliant with sunlight. He sat up with a jerk and stared at the nearly setting sun.

"Be damned!" he said.

Tiz lowered the glass and leaned over to look at him.

"How do you feel?"

Instantly Amory remembered everything that had happened to him. He remembered above all the figure he must

174

have cut on his hands and knees there in the middle of her kitchen floor with the blood pouring from his nose.

"I—I don't know what you must think," he began sheepishly.

"Well, I certainly don't think you did it on purpose, although there isn't much I'd put past you." Tiz laid her hand competently and impersonally on his forehead, reducing him by the gesture to a child again.

Firmly he removed the hand and swung his feet to the floor.

"All right, Doctor Arey. The patient has fully recovered and there's no need for further treatment."

"I think you really should see a doctor, Cl—Amory."

"Look, Tiz. If I hadn't been so tired last night, I could have told you. I've been having those nosebleeds since I was a kid. It's just something that happens when I get tired. I should have known better than to come in here feeling the way I did."

"In a way, I'm glad you came." Her eyes were something completely new to him. "It really did me good to see you when you needed help from somebody else."

He grinned ruefully.

"I wish I'd found that out about you years ago, Tiz. Believe me, I'd have made out I was weak as a kitten whenever I came within fifty feet of you if it would have made all that difference."

"It wouldn't have made any difference," she protested uncertainly.

"I'm not so sure. You called me Clyde once and started to do it again. Don't you think you could make yourself do it as a general thing?"

He got to his feet and stood looking at her, waiting for her answer. In a moment she would have been forced by the weight of silence alone to say something. But as she opened her mouth there was a sound outside the door and she turned to it with relief. Amory sighed and said something under his breath.

When Mike came in he gave the sofa a quick glance and, finding Amory on his feet, grinned at him widely.

"I'm glad to see you're up," he said. "I was beginning to think I ought to sprinkle a little salt on you so's you'd keep."

"What's worrying me is that car." Tiz's face was ruefully amused. "Nobody would think much of it, just sitting there all night. But to have it sit there all day, too—why, that's really immoral."

"Maybe I better take steps to make an honest woman out of you."

"We'll wait and see if it's necessary before we do anything rash." Easily she met his pleasantry with another; but she refused to meet the look behind it.

"Hopeless!" Amory said to Mike. He gave Tiz a quick glance to see how she was taking her ribbing and her eyes said: That's far enough. Quickly he changed the subject.

"Anything happen today, Mike?"

"Nothing new. Everyone's nervous as cats. I am myself. Just waiting. Anyhow, we eliminated one suspect last night."

"You had one, then?"

"Jonesy Dawes," Mike said uneasily.

At the sound of that name, Tiz glanced at him secretly. She hadn't yet had an opportnuity to face him with her knowledge. But she saw his uneasiness and hoped Amory couldn't see it as clearly.

"Oh, yes. I heard Jonesy nearly blew his leg off the night

176

before last. I didn't know you had any idea he was setting the fires, though."

"Well, I don't know's we really did." Mike was wishing actively that he'd never mentioned Jonesy. Amory was too sharp. Two and two made five in his mind too easily. "Just one of those things. Anyhow, Jonesy wasn't in any shape to go wandering around last night."

"Who shot him?"

Tiz let out a startled thread of sound and Mike made a strangled noise deep in his throat. He didn't dare look at Tiz knowing her capacity for finding out what he didn't want her to know and aware that somehow she knew as much as he did.

"Who shot Jonesy?"

"I don't know what you're talking about! He shot himself, cleaning his gun."

"If Jonesy, after forty years, is still fool enough to clean a loaded gun, you can depend on it, his mother wouldn't let him. Jonesy didn't shoot himself. Who did?"

"Are you asking me that as a police officer?"

Tiz was frozen in the middle of the floor, staring from one darkly angry face to the other.

"You bet I am, son!"

"Then, I don't know. All I know is what Jonesy says. If you think there's any more to it than that, you better go see him yourself."

"I don't know's it'd do any good." Amory was really thinking out loud. "Whoever did it has got him so scared he'll swear on a stack of Bibles he did it himself. But don't think I don't know you boys down here riding patrol are doing it the rough way. Just keep that in mind the next time you feel like a little target practice!"

177

Mike said nothing.

"And another thing. Did you ever stop to think you might have a *couple* of nuts floating around down here? That fire last night was set where it would be seen immediately; it wasn't set in a place where it would cover ground fast. It wasn't like the first one at all. Almost like the feller set it wanted to be sure it *would* be seen before it had a chance to do any real damage. The first one you had was set to do as much as it could. Don't really seem to me like the same man set both of them."

"All right," Mike said. "I didn't set the fire, either."

"I didn't say you shot Jonesy," Amory said from the door. He glanced at Tiz. "Thanks for everything. If you ever want your floor scrubbed, don't hesitate to call on me, will you?"

Going down the walk to his car in the late, warm, afternoon sunlight, Amory rubbed a hand along his jaw. It felt the way a porcupine looks. What a devil of a way to repay Tiz's hospitality, jumping on young Mike like that!

The afterglow from the sunset was still brilliant in the narrow main street as he drove through town. Frenchville had always been unprepossessing in a solid way, its public buildings blocky and uncompromising and ugly. But, lying passively in the path of doom, it took on a wistful softness, like something remembered instead of seen. It felt to Amory as if the stiff-backed, waiting horror of the people who lived here had transferred itself to things as inanimate as buildings, to the elms that stood high-arched above the gray street.

When the center of town was behind him and the houses getting farther apart, Amory trod down on the accelerator. The winding road led up into the scorched hills and the sooner they were behind him, the better he'd feel. It made him nervous, too, being down there on that slope of land above the sea with only one road out and that a road that had already been closed off once with fire. It was easy enough to understand how people felt and why they were all as taut as fiddle strings.

Topping the hill, he glanced hopefully at the west. There lay the islands as sharp as paper cut-out pasted against a pane of glass. The western sky, almost colorless, but hopelessly clear as if the air were nothing at all, belled upward behind the distant land lying blue and impassive along the horizon.

As soon as the door had closed behind Amory, Tiz turned on Mike.

"Now you can tell me just what happened the night before last. What ails you fellows anyhow, shooting that poor, little rabbit? And who *did* shoot him? Did you?"

Mike raised his eyebrows and shrugged his shoulders, a gesture that told Tiz as if he had said the words: I'm lying. She saw that he intended to carry on the lie in the face of her knowledge and knew that if he had done the actual shooting he would have said so.

"I think something's gone to his head," Mike said blankly.

"I know Amory and he's not the type to say a thing like that unless he knows pretty well what he's talking about. Besides, I know better myself."

"If you know something why didn't you tell him?"

Tiz made a sharp, clicking noise with her tongue and turned her back on him.

"All right," she said impatiently before she realized that the sound behind her was Mike closing the door. She went over to the window and watched him wander aimlessly

179

across the yard. His hands were thrust into his pockets and he was staring at the ground. She saw his back stiffen, and he looked like a man who, glancing down, sees the earth open under his feet, revealing great, shadowy depths of mystery.

"What the devil ails him?" she asked herself anxiously, trying to see what he stared at there beneath his feet. As Mike turned suddenly and ran for the front gate, she realized that he had heard something, not seen it.

"Oh, Lord!" she said, remembering the last time somebody had called to him from the gate. That had been the day of the fire on Hardwood Point, and the speed with which Mike covered ground now was very similar to the dash he had made then.

Hastily she went through the dining room to the front window, fully expecting to see him climbing into a car and roaring away down the road. But Mike was just standing quietly at the gate talking to Ginny.

Quickly, feeling nosy and overcurious, Tiz moved away from the glass. One more glance from the safer obscurity of the room and she knew she didn't have to worry about their having seen her.

She went back to the kitchen, thinking that if she never had to see any other person she would feel as if she could never grow old. One of the few things that made her know she was getting along, too, was when a familiar face looked suddenly and startlingly young to her. Ginny was twenty-five and Mike a year older and she had thought, seeing them standing at the gate together: How *young* they look!

When she glanced out again there was nobody there. Looking down the road, she saw them nearly at Hanscom's driveway. They were walking slowly and Ginny seemed to be doing the talking.

"I was so ashamed when I heard," Ginny said. "I don't know what to do about him, Mike. I'm afraid he'll kill himself."

"I don't see why *you* were ashamed." Mike shrugged. "It's not your fault. Nothing you can help."

"I know; but I don't like the idea of you riding patrol alone. I didn't know Eddie was supposed to go with you."

"As far as I know, Eddie doesn't either," Mike said flatly. "I didn't bother to tell him. Didn't know as it'd do any good."

"You might be able to shame him into sobering up. Can't you get mad at him or something? Can't you help me?"

"This ought to go down on the books as a famous first occasion." Mike gave her a straight, glinting look. Against her raised brows but unspoken question, he added: "You never asked me to *help* you do anything before."

He saw by her sudden startled acceptance of his words that she, too, realized the occasion. But she was trying to see why it existed.

"I don't know as I ever felt before that you'd be the one to help."

Watching her, Mike thought: Once I would have cut off my right hand to help you. Once he would have said that and meant it; but now he would never say and mean anything so flamboyant. Now he would have preferred to say: I would keep my right hand to do something for you.

"I'll do what I can, Ginny," he said soberly. "I don't know that it'll be much."

He didn't miss the quick, surprised look she gave him; but he didn't acknowledge it either. It wouldn't do her any harm to be surprised. Let her find out for herself that she

181

was not the only person who could change. Let her do a little thinking about him.

When he had said to her so easily: I've changed, Ginny; he'd said it because it seemed the thing to say at the moment. But he *had* changed. Right at this minute he wanted her more than he ever had, wanted to touch her, to hold her. But the instinctive desire to snatch at what he wanted was gone. What he could get by snatching meant nothing at all. A thing that had to be forced would be unsteady and shaky and nothing to call a foundation. By holding back at the final moment the night before last, when all his instincts and desires had been pulling away from forbearance, he had established more confidence between them than he could have done in hours of wordy protestation.

"What're you *thinking*, Mike? You look so ugly!"

Mike flushed, finding he'd been standing there staring at her in complete silence. Instead of answering her question, he said hastily:

"Where is Eddie now?"

"I left him sitting in the kitchen. I suppose he's still there."

"Haven't you got something you could do?" At the door Mike hesitated. "Let me talk to him alone for a minute, will you?"

She sat down quietly on the doorstep, leaving Mike to go alone through the shed. He didn't bother to knock at the closed kitchen door.

Eddie sat in a chair at the table with his arms sprawled out across the oilcloth and his head down between them. There was a betraying tightness about his shoulders. He knew somebody had come in; but he had no intention of admitting the fact, either to himself or to whoever was standing behind him.

182

Mike glanced around the room. It had been years since he'd set foot inside this house and in those years not so much as a chair had changed. The wide pine floor boards still thrust their uneven spines up through the checked linoleum in worn lines. The huge, black Clarion still had its polished nickel grin and there was a cracking fire in it right now—its heat alone was enough to tell Mike it was neither coal nor oil. The pitcher pump still stood guard over the black iron sink in the corner. And, opposite it, beside the dining-room door stood, the anachronism—the gently humming, gleaming refrigerator, a refugee from another century.

Eddie was getting restive with the quiet. Mike saw his lax right hand twitch. He grinned slightly. He would have outwaited Eddie if the room hadn't been so hot. The doors and windows were closed against the warm October evening and that stove was throwing off a heat he wouldn't have believed possible. He took a step toward the table and Eddie said in a weak, muffled voice:

"I don't want any supper, Ginny."

"I don't care if you never eat again," Mike said icily.

Eddie snapped upright in his chair; but he didn't turn his head. Instead he clasped it in both his hands as tenderly as if his skull were made of eggshell.

"What in hell d'*you* want?"

"I had a little time to waste," Mike said, giving the last word its full importance and more. "Thought I'd come over to see if you were still alive."

Eddie's voice had thickened noticeably. He still didn't look around. Mike saw his head begin to nod slightly.

"I don't want to talk to anyone."

"Then suppose you listen."

"Doan wanna listen neither."

"You'll listen and like it. I been riding patrol now for nearly a week alone because you were supposed to go with me and you've been sitting here soaking your fool head off. I'm getting sick and tired of it, see?"

"That's tough," Eddie mumbled.

"You bet your life it's tough. No more fun for me than it would be for anyone else. I get nervous too. I've got to go on tonight at twelve o'clock and you're going with me, drunk or sober."

"Oh, no!" Eddie said. Once the word was out, he kept it going like an unfading echo: "No. No. No."

Anger grew hot in Mike's face. He thudded across the kitchen. To his astonishment Eddie's shoulder was taut as a fiddlestring under his fingers. There was none of the drunken relaxation he had expected. More in surprise than anger, he shoved Eddie's head back. Eddie was having trouble with his mouth. It hung open a little and his underlip moved uselessly toward another repetition of the "no." He seemed to have lost all control of his face; the features were swollen and unrelated—except the eyes, which were bright and clear and alarmed and not drunken.

Astonished and a little sick, Mike stared down at him for a long, stiff minute.

"You're no more drunk than I am," he said clearly.

"Why don't you mind your own business?" Eddie said hopelessly. Mike could feel under his hand the hysteria in the tight, young body. It grew in waves, each one stronger than before. "Why don't people leave me alone!" He gritted his teeth after the last word; but before he could stop it a high, whimpering hiccup got away from him.

Unwilling to understand, Mike stood scowling at him.

"Well, you aren't," he insisted.

184

"Get the hell out of here and let me alone," Eddie said clearly. He put his head down on his hands again.

"You might as well know," he said into Mike's intolerable silence. "I'm scared. I'm just plain scared. I ain't had anything to drink since before the big one. I'm scared."

"Okay." Mike turned away. "I'd just as soon ride patrol with a souse. But I'm blessed if I'll do it with a coward. Just sit right here, Eddie, and we'll take care of you along with the women and children."

"You hero," Eddie said bitterly. "Makes you feel good, don't it! Makes you feel like a *big* guy! Well, let me tell you something. If you'd seen as much fire as *I* did that night, *you* wouldn't go hunting for it, neither."

"I suppose you think I didn't?" Mike inquired icily. "I wasn't sitting on my tail waiting for it to come and get me."

"No. And you weren't lying in a culvert in six inches of water listening to it go over you like a goddamn express train, either."

"Don't give me that!"

"It's the God's truth." Thinking about it, Eddie's eyes began to water. He wasn't really crying; he made no sound and seemed unaware of the tears running down his face. "There was a gang of us up by Hio Lake when the fire came up over that hill. You know how shallow that cussed pond is. Only one end of it deep enough to get into over your head. I was scared. I thought I was running for the deep end. When I see that slough culvert the C.C.C.'s made, I knew I was done to. The fire was all around me and not enough water to cover me hardly if I laid down. So I did the only thing I could think of. I dived into that hole and I was in there when the fire went over."

"You *couldn't* a been. You'd have been boiled like a lobster!"

"Well, by judast, I *was!* There was a mess of that slimy, green weed growing in the water. I got all I could and covered my head and face with it. I rolled over and over in the water, trying to keep wet. My clothes would dry off near as fast as I could roll. It was like inside of a pressure cooker. About five minutes there, I could a swore the water itself was burning."

"I guess you got a right to be scared," Mike said, looking away from Eddie's tears in embarrassment.

"You're damn tooting, I have!" Eddie said loudly. "I see anyone light a match, I feel just like somebody hit me in the belly with a board."

"Why in God's name didn't you tell somebody?"

"I couldn't even think about it to myself. I couldn't! If it'd taken that fire five minutes longer to burn across that slough, I wouldn't a been able to. I'd a been there yet."

He looked down at his hands and seeing the tears that had fallen on them, put his fingers up to his face in surprise.

"Judast!" he said. "Bawling like a baby!"

"Why—" Mike felt as if he were trying to talk at somebody on the other side of a wide river. Eddie was the few minutes difference between being alive and being dead. His escape had moved him away from humanity. "I could tell folks for you. Lord, anyone could understand why you're scared."

"My old man wouldn't," Eddie said stiffly. "I'd rather have him think I was on a bat. I don't want nobody told."

"Skip the patrol," Mike said. "I can take care of it. Nothing ever happens, anyway."

He waited a minute to see if Eddie had anything more to say, but Eddie was silent.

At the door Mike didn't glance back, just shut it softly behind him. Ginny was waiting for him on the doorstep and he saw her out of the duskiness.

She looked at him questioningly and Mike shook his head.

"I'm sorry, Ginny. There isn't anything to do but wait until he decides to sober up."

"What did—? I heard Eddie talking to you. What did he say that took so long?"

"Oh, he was just—" Mike began glibly, sure the lie would come to him now he needed it. When it didn't, he was left hanging, wondering what to tell her.

"Mike Arey, you can't lie to me! Now you tell me what's wrong with my brother or I'll haul you right in there and have it out with him here and now."

"Walk down to the road with me," Mike said. "I can't tell you here. Eddie'll hear me."

"He won't hear anything," Ginny said hotly. "He's in no condition to." But she turned, unwillingly, and started down the drive beside him.

"He's not drunk," Mike said slowly and then told her, in short words that came hard because he had just told Eddie he wouldn't do what he was doing. "I don't get it," he finished. "He doesn't want anyone to know he's scared because of his old—because of your father. It has something to do with your father. *I* don't know."

Furious with himself for having told her, he made again that wide, uncomfortable gesture that had betrayed his lie. He couldn't understand; but Ginny's face, angry and tight, told him she did.

"That old man will ruin us both," she said miserably. "The trouble is, he expects too much of Eddie and not enough of me."

187

Mike waited, not understanding, thinking that she would go on with it. She was standing there wanting to tell him something; but she didn't trust him enough yet. Or perhaps distrusted herself too much to say whatever it would have been.

He glanced up, looking past her, and his eyes met squarely those of her father. The old man was coming up from the shore and he wore heavy rubber boots, but although he was only ten feet away from them, neither Mike nor Ginny had heard a sound of his approach.

"Hello, Jasper," Mike said.

"I always find you two talking as if you had great secrets," Jasper said amiably. "Can you tear yourself away, Ginny? There's a little something I'd like to have you do for me."

Blankly Mike watched her walk away from him. Neither Jasper nor Ginny glanced back to see what he was doing.

When she was sure they were out of earshot, Ginny said furiously:

"Pa, you've got to stop doing that to me. You make me feel about two years old. What'll he *think!*"

"I don't rightly care what he thinks. It just don't seem right to me that you should always be huddling off into the corner with him, that's all."

Ginny was shaking with rage.

"That's the end," she said quickly. "I'm not going to stand it any longer. It's only taken you two weeks to do something to me that nobody else could do in twenty-five years. I'm—"

"Twenty-five years or fifty," Jasper said. "You're still my daughter and as long as I can help it, you're not going to make a little fool of yourself."

"I can't have any friends. I can't call my soul my own."

"That makes twice I've caught you with him," Jasper said inexorably.

"*Caught* me!"

"You know perfectly well what I mean. If you don't watch your step, young lady, nobody's going to want to marry you, much less By Sawyer. And think how you'd look if he threw you over now!"

"There's going to be some throwing over," Ginny said warmly. "But By's not going to have the chance to do it. You both behave as if I were a piece of property, something to own. Well, I'm not. I'm human. I'm my own."

"Not any longer. When you told By you'd marry him, then you gave yourself to him and you're his."

"So that's how you feel! That's why you sat there the night before last and let him—" She couldn't say it. Staring at him with horrified eyes, she saw clearly that he denied her any identity of her own. "And he feels the same way. Well, I'm through."

"If you do anything so foolish as to let him get away from you," Jasper said, "I will disown you."

"Good," Ginny said tightly. They were standing there on the doorstep, trying angrily to look each other down and neither one would look away. Jasper smiled slightly.

"It'll be a different matter," he said, "when it comes right down to it. Don't think I don't know how you used to carry on with Mike Arey! You were lucky you could get an upstanding, young fellow like By to put up with you after all that."

"Well, By can stop doing me any favors. Mind, Pa, I mean it. I'm through with him and you, too. You can tell him so."

"Tell him yourself, if you want to do anything so foolish. I won't have anything to do with it. You're your mother's daughter, all right. No pride and no wonder. You come by

189

it honest. Laying your female traps for a young fellow don't want you. Letting Mike Arey think he can come back and find you sitting here waiting for him with open arms. Don't think *he'll* marry you, girl. He won't! Then you'll come worrying back to me and maybe I'll take you in out of the goodness of my heart."

Ginny stood there, her astonished eyes on the door that had closed gently between them, wondering what he'd meant. What did her mother have to do with this? I wish she was alive, Ginny thought wearily. I need someone. Eddie would help; but he's no good now. If only Pa would leave us both alone.

Tiz heard the voice softly calling her name, but at first it was so low, so soft, she thought it was inside her own head. The calling persisted, over and over, in a gentle, monotonous, wearing repetition:

"Elizabeth. Elizabeth Arey. Elizabeth Arey."

After her first moment of doubt, she knew who was calling her and why.

Then she *did!* Tiz thought softly. I didn't think either one of them would have the guts.

Job Hanna was still calling her and she contemplated for a moment the easiest way of not going to the door at all. She didn't want to talk to him, especially not now when she knew so well why he had come. But his patient, soft, enraged voice hauled her toward the door.

She stood with her hand on the knob, feeling with a sharp sense of impending breakage the safe, worn porcelain of the knob in her hand.

With that desperate voice still calling, Tiz looked out. Job was standing halfway up the the walk, staring at the door and he had seen the first, tentative turn of the knob.

His eyes met hers with an implacable distrust, powerful through its gentleness.

"Eliza—" he said, and stopped.

"Hello, Job. Did you want to see me?" Now, that's a silly thing to say, Tiz's mind remarked coolly. You don't think he'd be standing there yelling if he didn't.

"Yes." Horrified at his own presence here and even more so at hers, Job couldn't seem to get the words out without prompting.

"Won't—well, don't you want to come in?"

Job looked at the house as if he felt it alive and waiting, as if he thought once his foot had stepped inside that door, something would reach out and muffle him.

"Thank you, Elizabeth. I'll stay here."

Tiz started down the walk toward him. You never really trusted me, did you, she was thinking, watching the hard-to-identify expression that flitted across the visible portion of the old man's face. She was wondering parenthetically what he would look like without that beard. She had never seen him clean-shaven; but looking at him closely now, she thought his face would be a masculine duplicate of Polly's —long and equine and uncertain. Maybe that was why he wore a beard. Maybe it gave him more confidence to face the world with his visible weakness hidden behind an impenetrable screen.

"What do you want?" She was only a few feet away from him when she stopped.

Job took a backward step, almost as if he believed she would be able to exert some devilish power over him, too, if he let her get close enough.

"My girl's gone, Elizabeth."

Tiz said nothing and her silence was admission enough.

"You knew it." His voice went up half a note. He was

191

boiling with anger; but it seemed to have little about it that was personal and that made her feel guilty where there was no guilt.

"No. Not until you told me."

"You ain't very surprised."

Before she could answer that, Mike opened the gate and came up to the house through the growing dusk. He nodded to Job and gave Tiz a clear, curious, surprised glance. When he went into the house he slammed the door behind him; but Tiz saw to her dismay that he opened it again, just a crack, enough to be able to hear their voices.

"Here's this here." Job held out to her in a gnarled and shaking hand a crumpled piece of cheap, white paper. Tiz glanced at it, and recognized as Polly's the sprawling, poorly formed letters.

"Take it and read it," Job said softly. "In there she tells about how you told her to go. Tells all about how you led her on."

"Well, no." Tiz shook her head. "I won't read it. I know pretty well what she would say; but what do you want me to do about it?"

"It was all because of you, Elizabeth Arey, she ever thought of such a thing! Neither my Poll nor that jelly-fish of a Jonesy Dawes would ever of had the gumption to do a thing like this, running off this way, by themselves."

To her relief, Tiz heard the beginning of animosity toward her in his voice. He would be much easier to face if if he would only be angry with her and not stand there with that unseeing, wounded glare.

"I think it's time they did something definite." She heard her own voice say it. "I'm glad they did."

"There ain't either one of them fitting to take care of theirselves," Job said bitterly. "Might's well turn two babies out into the world and say: 'Go ahead. You're on your own.' Why—" Now his voice was one of deep personal hurt. "Poll took my car and I didn't even know she could drive! Where've they gone? Where are they, Elizabeth?"

"I'm sorry." Tiz let out a little of her own anger into the words. "I haven't got them up my sleeve, Job."

The attack she had been expecting and had hardened herself to meet came now with breathless suddenness.

"Women like you—" Job said, his voice taking on a Cassandra note—"are a menace to society. Good girls like my Poll see you living the way you do, Elizabeth Arey, and the Lord Himself only knows what kind of shenanigans go on in this house, and it leads them on to all kinds of misdoing. My Poll wouldn't no more have gone off with a man like this if you hadn't talked her into it. No. No, it's not decent. The way you are."

"I suppose you mean I should let myself starve or go on the town rather than earn my own way."

"Women are made to depend on men." Sententiously implacable, forgetting that Polly had just illustrated this fact to his dismay, Job droned her down. "You take the bread out of a good man's mouth, you take work away from a man. I knew the minute I first saw you talking to my Poll you'd make trouble for her. Women like you are never satisfied with debasing yourself, you have to drag somebody else down with you to make you think it's right."

"All right," Tiz said levelly. "Now you've got it out of your system. You've had an excuse to say what you've been thinking. And you get! I don't want to see your face here again."

"I'm going," the old man said with a final, stinging attempt to pierce Tiz's half-amused armor of anger. "I don't

193

want to be seen talking to you. I don't want anyone to know I'd stoop to it."

She was furious as she stood watching him go piously down the walk. At the gate he spat on the neatly raked lawn and left the picket swinging helplessly unlatched behind him.

Tiz felt as if her face had frozen. I let myself in for that, she thought; but it's always shocking to find out that somebody you know has never liked you.

She had forgotten Mike, and when she opened the door and found him waiting for her she knew her face said something she didn't want anyone else to see. She half turned to go out again; but Mike put his hand on her arm and pulled her into the room.

"Come on in, Tiz," he said softly. "It's all right."

Gentleness from him where she had expected flip derision broke Tiz's angry reserve as if it had been nothing but flesh and blood and will power after all. The words, if they came, would mean nothing to Mike. *He* would have no way of knowing that it wasn't easy for her to pour out the hours of bolstering-up, of giving away security, of reassurance to people like Polly Hanna. He wouldn't know what she was talking about.

"They *want* so much," she said. "My Lord, Mike, it isn't there! It's all on the surface. If I let them have what they want, it'd be like giving away my skin. I'd bleed to death." She laughed dryly. "You make friends and then you find out they all *want* something. *I* thought I had it to give them, too; but I was wrong. It isn't true. I only look like something I'm not."

Out of a deep disquiet, Mike blurted: "You really *are* like other people, aren't you? You're human, too."

The flashing, furious face she turned on him drove him

194

back as if she had set both hands against his chest and pushed hard.

"What d'you mean by that? Of course I'm human! I'd like to find something to depend on, too. But, no! Everyone comes sniveling to me—to me, and I haven't got anything left."

She looked directly at him and didn't even see his face. "I don't ask anything from anybody," she said, her voice normal again, but puzzled. "I live here and mind my own business and I live a decent life. I have never intentionally done harm to anyone. What kind of a life would you have to live before people would feel they couldn't come at you? What would you have to do?"

She looked at Mike for an answer.

Knowing how they talked about her and what they said, Mike had no answer to give. All he could have said was: You have to look like them, too. You can't be different, not and be let alone.

"Tiz," he said suddenly, remembering the day he had found Jonesy talking to her here in the kitchen, remembering the strange inward-pressing feel of the room. "The other day—when Jonesy was here—Polly was, too, wasn't she?"

Tiz's answering look of amused assent was so easy that she might never have said any of the things they would both try to forget. "When she heard you coming that morning, she ran for the door; but she was so excited she got the wrong one. She thought she was going out the cellar door. All the time you were sitting there eating your breakfast, Polly was shut in the broom closet. I didn't know but what she might smother in there."

"I knew there was something going on." Mike was triumphant. "You can sense kind of when somebody's gone out of a room like that just before you come in. But why did she run?"

Tiz shrugged.

"Tell me why she did anything. I guess she'd been hiding so long she just did it without thinking. You always scared the poor thing to death, anyhow. But I thought I'd never get you out of the house that day."

Mike sat watching her get his supper for him. She didn't seem like the same woman who had been doing this same thing for him nearly all his life. She had shown him that he was living with a buried, unrelated stranger, not the Aunt Tiz who had always been ready to pass out confidence as materially as she would have handed him a slice of bread when he was hungry.

Years of bolstering up other people's faltering self-possession must take it out of anyone, he thought. You give and give without taking anything in, and sooner or later it's all gone.

He ate supper acutely conscious of the quick, secretive glances she kept stealing at him. Once or twice he was as strongly aware of her impulse to speak as if it were something stirring in him as well as in her. He tried to show her that it had been forgotten, remembering how she had often given him confidence through just being there, and trying consciously now to give it back to her in the same way.

"My judas, though," he burst out finally. "Just think of it! Fifteen years that business has been going on and they wouldn't have been any further if Jonesy hadn't got shot —if it hadn't been for the fire and everything happening. Tiz, it's really pitiful."

"That's the word," she agreed. "And when Jonesy did get shot, it kind of drove her crazy—or sane, however you want to look at it. Said she couldn't stand it any longer and what could she do. I told her in her place I'd go tell Jonesy either to come away with me or never let me see him again. And, by the Lord harry, Jonesy went—even though he had to go on one leg."

"What d'you suppose will happen to his old lady?"

"Well, as long as Jonesy has been around, Mrs. Dawes couldn't so much as lift a finger. But when he wasn't there she never had much trouble. I think you'll find she's not so much of an invalid as she, or anyone else, thought she was."

"Mike shook his head.

"My Lord, Tiz, how do you get into these messes? Where do you pick up all your lame ducks?"

"I don't know, blessed if I do. Everyone brings their little bundle of troubles and lays it right in my lap."

"Well, you better take a rest for a while. The next one you see coming, you better say no."

"I'll practice up on saying no," she told him. "Do you have to ride patrol tonight?"

Recognizing the question as a means of getting rid of him, Mike nodded and got up.

"Yeah. Guess I'll take a nap. I start out at twelve."

He took the alarm clock upstairs with him. He wasn't thinking about Jonesy when he lay waiting for sleep. He was thinking about Tiz. If I've got anything to spare myself, he thought, it's hers. If I can give her anything—

The night shattered before noise, and Mike sat up straight on his bed, jerked out of sleep by the sound which was gone by the time he was fully awake. He sat there in the dark, his eyes wide, his head turned in the attitude of listening.

Was it a siren? A shout?

He looked at the luminous dial of the clock on his dresser, seeing the hands pointing to eleven-thirty, and knew he had waked just in time to hear the last fading bell of the alarm.

He swung his feet to the floor and groped for his shoes. His nerves still crinkled even after he knew what had brought him up out of sleep.

Outside his window, the night crouched, waiting and hushed. He was aware of night as he would have been aware of a great, velvety, dangerous animal. In the dark all the normal, little fears grew out of proportion and he felt like a mouse permitted to run free for a few minutes between the momentarily clawless, furry forepaws of a big cat.

The southwest wind rustled the thin leaves gently and blew softly and unceasingly, brushing across distant cove after cove of dark trees, acre after acre of thirsty ground, porous and dry, where even as he sat here some madman might be lighting the torch, or some crazy kid flipping out his cigaret butt.

He heard the stirring of the wind as something hateful and to be feared. This had always been a country of great winds, open to weather from the east and south. The Peninsula thrust itself into the south like the bow of a vessel breasting blue sea; like the back of an unbelievable animal pushing up out of millennial ocean. It lay with its nose on forepaws and the glistening water had honed its edges down to shining bone. Mike had seen the shore drowned and pounded and beaten by the weather. He had seen the snarling storms rip across this ridge of land in an annihilating flood as if the weather becoming personal wanted to wipe out every trace of man, to erase forever the forbidden foot.

198

To the north now, and for as long as he would ever live to hear it, the wind would never have the same sound again. There was nothing left to interrupt it, no needled branches to make the hushing sound of wind through trees. Only the ruined hills with the great, brawling tumble of air moving without hindrance from the east and north.

Sitting there on the edge of his bed in the moment before he could bring himself to move, Mike understood thoroughly how Eddie felt. Everyone felt the same way; but with much less reason than Eddie had. When the familiar becomes strange and the friend turns killer, man, who is always suspicious, finds his fear justified and proved.

He got up, feeling twice his age and cold with suspicion of what might come upon him out of the night, and went stumbling down the stairs to the kitchen. It was light and warm there and the smell of coffee made him feel better.

"I heard your clock run down." Tiz was filling his thermos bottle. "I was just coming up to wake you."

Mike mumbled something and went to the sink to splash cold water on his face. He wanted to say to her: I'm glad you're here. He didn't because he never had and didn't know how. If he said it, without precedent, Tiz would have been reminded of how she had betrayed herself—would think perhaps: Here is another want; and once more she would be uncertain and inadequate.

Trying to look casual, Mike went over to the gun rack and took down his light carbine. He stood it quietly beside the door knowing that she watched every move he made. He had never taken a gun with him before; but tonight, thinking of those long, dark roads where he would soon be driving alone, he wanted something to give authority to his presence there.

"Do you think you'd better?" Tiz said easily.

"If I didn't, I wouldn't."

"All right. Only for the love of God, be careful what you do with it, Mike."

She hesitated and then added: "I wish you'd take the shotgun instead."

"I want to be able to hit what I aim for," Mike told her smoothly. "Be a good chance to pick up a little venison."

Her silence said clearly that she didn't accept that.

"Look." against that accusation he felt he had to justify himself. "I've been over this pretty careful, Tiz. And I get nervous, too. It's lonesome, riding that patrol alone. I'm no hero." He hesitated slightly before the lie. "I've taken that carbine other nights, only you just didn't see me do it. I don't intend to use it; I just want to know it's there if I have to."

"It's your business, Mike. Would you—I could come with you if you want company."

"No!" He lit his first cigaret and stood in the door for a minute looking at her, the gun neat and murderous in the crook of his elbow. Coffee and tobacco and warmth had restored him completely and the grin he gave her was unrestrained. "Don't worry, Tiz. Nothing's going to happen."

"I believe you really enjoy this." She gave him a curious, calculating look.

"Well, I suppose I do—in a way. It's exciting, too. Kind of different, though, hunting a man. Go on to bed," he said over his shoulder. "I'll be back· at four."

He went stumbling out across the uneven yard to the car and groped his way into the driver's seat before he saw that somebody was already there waiting. His breath caught in a muffled gasp and he switched on the lights.

Eddie's face was pale, his forehead gleaming with betraying sweat.

"Happy surprise!" he croaked.

After the circling lights had flashed across the wall and vanished, Tiz sat trying to hold onto the sound of the engine, feeling that it was the sound of safety and as long as she had it with her she would be all right. The feeling faded with the lights and she was alone in the house with nothing at all left but her own living breath between her and whatever it was she needed protection from.

The room felt crammed with apprehension, like too much rice put to boil in a kettle and at last lifting the lid and boiling over. The worst thing was being unable to see. Here she sat, surrounded by four walls, cut off effectively from the horizon where destruction, if it came, would be spelled out in flaming letters on the blue, windy night.

"I've *got* to be able to see," she said aloud and went out, not locking the door behind her.

Her undirected feet stumbled over the rough, bare ground of the spring flower bed. She blinked her flashlight on the bed. After the tulips and the daffodils were gone, Tiz never found any other flowers worthy of taking their place and all summer long the drying stems stood there until they rotted and fell. She thought with envy of the bulbs lying warm and safe, shut away from every contact by the blanket of dry earth above them. It would be wonderful to be able to crawl into a hole somewhere whenever anything happened to threaten you, crawl in and pull the insulating dirt over you and stay there until everything was over.

How could I have gone away and left them? she thought.

If I had to leave again, I'd dig every one of them up and take them with me. Nothing else. Just the tulips.

The undamaged south drew her irresistibly. To the north, along Main Street, there would be strangeness and she wanted the familiar and the known tonight. Too, the wind galing from the south was their wind of danger.

She had no idea how far she had come from home and couldn't remember taking the turn toward the sea again. When she found herself abreast Anse Barker's big, dark house, she was amazed that she had had time to get that far.

That meadow, she thought coldly, looking across the heavy, moon-silvered, dry heads of nodding grass, hasn't been mowed in years. Anse spent most of his time roaming the woods with a gun over his shoulder or a fishing rod under his arm. He had no time to waste on mowing. The old fog under that deceptive expanse of grass would be ankle deep and once you let a fire start in that— It was nearly one o'clock when she passed the house, looming dark and quiet on its little rise, and went down the road to the bridge that crossed a dry brook bed. The night was noisy around her with the growing wind and the lashing of the young spruce boughs.

She stopped on the bridge and stood looking down toward the ocean. The intermittent sound of water on the shore came to her strongly with the wind behind it. The night was so peaceful and so false like her own life. On the surface the appearance of peace and under it the true, bubbling chaos.

She saw the flash of light in the swale at the woods' edge below her and a little to the left. It didn't come again and she looked away and beyond it before she realized what she had seen. There was no reason for a light to show down there in the swale. There were no houses, there was nothing between her and the southwest shore but another sea of dead, dry, knee-high grass and thick-growing spruces.

She clutched at the bridge rail with cold hands. Her mouth was dry and she couldn't even raise enough spit to swallow, though her throat clicked ineffectually with the effort.

The first flood of fear ebbed a little and she knew the light must be legitimate. It was simply impossible that it should be anything else.

Not pausing to give herself time to think because then she'd never do it, Tiz climbed hastily down the banking into the swale and made her way along it toward the first dark trees, her own flashlight clutched in her hand. She was already so sure it was all right that she nearly called out, longing for the sound of another voice to answer hers, anxious for the voice of the patrol to reassure her.

She wasn't sure exactly where the light had shone and when she saw it again it was only fifteen feet away from her ,and its character had changed. The first light had been a flashlight. This one was unmistakably a match.

Tiz let out a strangled yell and ran—toward the light, not away. She was in time to see a stooped figure straighten, hesitate. She saw the white blur of a face. Somebody crashed away from her into the sheltering darkness of the trees.

Before she really had time to be afraid and while she could still hear feet in the underbrush, the stab of her flashlight had found its focus. She stood staring down at the circle of light and what was pinned in it. There on the dry ground lay the innocent looking, little tepee of grass and twigs and broken brush, shining wetly in the light. The air around her was permeated with the pungent smell of kerosene before the wind carried it away.

Her mind said icily: You nearly caught him. Instantly Tiz was bathed in a flood of cold. It was hard to know the hunter from the hunted. It was hard not to think: He nearly caught you. If what she was feeling now was fear, she had never before known what it meant to be afraid. If the madman had known she was nothing but a woman, she wouldn't be standing here. Likely she'd be lying under a brush heap somewhere with her head bashed in and the released fire coming at her before the southwest wind.

Her first impulse was to turn and run back across the field to the road, to Anse's, to safety and away from the smell and the feel of her danger. In that second of longing for somebody else to share this danger and thus dispel it by half, Tiz realized completely and for the first time what it was to need company, to long for somebody else, no matter who. Here before her was the evidence and somewhere in the dark, dangerous woods was the man; and she was only a woman after all and without physical backing for this kind of bravery.

The wavering of that circle of light told her her hands were shaking. She was shaking all over. Her flesh felt as if it clothed something as fluid as water and not the solid, upholding bone.

The sound of running feet had stopped. It seemed to Tiz that it had been a very long time since she'd heard anything but the sodden pound of her own heart. Off in the woods somewhere, a twig snapped.

Tiz jumped and dropped the flashlight and it went out. She fell to her hands and knees and went squattering around in the dry leaves trying to find it. Her teeth were clenched tightly against the possible revealing sound of her fear.

The twig snapped again, closer. Tiz's hand touched the

204

light and knocked it away from her. Gasping, she went after it and had its comforting solidity firm in her fist when the voice said:

"All right, you son of a bitch, I've got you this time!"

The voice was a familiar one and the words were hardly what she had been expecting. She sat there, spraddled out on the ground, too weak with relief to get up. She did manage to light her flashlight and, in competition with the powerful lantern in the man's hand, it neutralized the glare enough so that her eyes could make out the tall, skinny figure behind that great light.

"For God sake! It's Tiz Arey!"

"Lord, Powder!" Tiz's voice was stronger than she had expected it to be. "I'm glad it's you!"

"I don't see why! Whatta you trying to do? Burn the town up?"

For the first time it occurred to Tiz how she would look to anyone else, caught here in the tinder-dry woods with the evidence right beside her.

"No," she said quickly. "You've got it all wrong. *I* nearly caught *him*. I was walking along the road right up there when I saw his light. I came down in here thinking it might be the patrol, though if I'd had any sense, I'd have known better. I caught him just lighting a match."

Nobody, looking at her white face, could have doubted what she was saying, much less the man who held that lantern trained on her. It seemed to Tiz she must have been terribly convincing. He accepted her words without a flicker of hesitation.

"Did you—see who he was?"

"No, I did not." She was angry now with frustration. "He was back to me and I was so damn scared I forgot to turn on my light. He was off into the woods before I had a chance to get a look at him."

"Are you sure?" The softly casual voice insisted.

"Good Lord, d'you think I'd lie to you about anything like that! If I'd seen who he was, I'd be yelling it at the top of my lungs."

The light traveled with impassive stolidity from her face to the fire that had been so carefully laid, to the tin that had held the kerosene, and back to her face again. Powder sighed heavily.

"Well," he said, "you'd better get home. I'm cussed if I see why you were out running around alone this time of night anyhow. You're apt to get yourself into real trouble, Tiz. Why, it's Sunday morning."

"Do you think we'd better go and leave this? What if he come back and finishes the job?"

"He won't. See? He won't have any way of knowing who you were or if you were alone. He wouldn't dare I shouldn't think. He might run into almost anything, coming back."

That made sense to Tiz. She hesitated for a minute, contemplating that long road home through darkness, realizing more than ever the need of humankind for its own company. Even company as poor as this would be better than nothing.

"We—you—we might as well walk along together," she suggested, unable to bring herself to say to him: I'm scared. Don't leave me here alone.

"I'll walk along with you if you'll come now. I'm tired myself. All this watching, a lot of foolishness really. Never catch him this way. I got to get some sleep."

Hardly thinking what she did, Tiz picked up the can and the light was instantly on her again.

"What you taking that for?"

"Oh, I don't know. You always think there might be something you could find out. If only—I didn't know but I'd give it to Jay."

"All right." He held out his hand. "Give it here. I'll see it gets to him tonight."

She surrendered it doubtfully. "Be sure it doesn't get smudged."

"If he'd had any brains—" Powder's voice was coldly sensible—"he'd a used gloves. Anyway, there won't be any prints on it but yours and mine—and his."

Tiz knew all that and knew the futility of trying to identify those prints; but she couldn't relinquish the idea that there might be something. Sooner or later there would *have* to be something!

She strode across the field in bitter silence, kicking herself mentally for not having caught a glimpse of the man's face when she had been nearly as close to him as she was now to her protector.

Powder was wondering how he could get rid of the can. He didn't really believe there was much in that fingerprint talk. You couldn't just go around with a fingerprint saying: Does this belong to you? But there was enough uncertainty in his mind to make him nervous. He was wondering, too, whether he had underestimated Tiz. Woman were notoriously dumb; but this one was different. Maybe he should have knocked her on the head when he'd had the chance. Fire would have destroyed all evidence of anything else— his mind balked at the word "murder."

He had already struck once tonight. Had had to. That had been like striking down something that wasn't quite human. The first one had flinched away from him and made no resistance at all; but Tiz would fight like a tiger

207

and he was not sure he could handle her. He put out his hand cautiously and felt for her shoulder. Under the light, unexpected touch, Tiz swerved away from him like a skittish colt.

"Don't do that!" she said sharply, but without personal animus. "I'm nervous enough already."

In another minute, at this rate, they would be on Main Street. Harshly aware that this was his last chance for safety, Powder hesitated and slowed his pace. The instinct for self-preservation surged up in him strongly. A moment's pressure at the right spot on that throat and he would be safe. He looked with impassive sorrow at her tall, dark, striding figure.

Tiz hadn't slowed when he did and she was several paces ahead of him.

"You coming?" she said over her shoulder and he saw her grow sharper, clearer, as she passed into the first, safe circle of light from the street lamps.

His hands relaxed. Well, that was his sign. It was too late and he was just as glad of it. He caught up with her and walked in silence by her side until she turned left again.

"I'm going on down and see Jay," he said to her back. "I think he better know about this right away."

"Yes." Tiz stopped and looked at him. "If he wants to know any more, tell him I'll still be up. If he comes over I'll tell him anything more I can."

"You better stay in the house nights, too, Tiz." The familiar voice was tired. "It's no time for women to be running around alone. Anything might happen to you."

Tiz gave a nervous, little snort of unamused laughter.

"I'll take your advice, I guess."

208

He stood watching her walk away from him before he went on down the deserted street toward Jay Stone's house. He'd have to tell him. If he didn't, Tiz would. He would be in a worse spot if he didn't tell Jay now.

PART FOUR

*Southwesterly winds, increasing in velocity
and shifting to gentle north and northeast
early tomorrow morning.*

AFTER HIS first look at Eddie's shadowed face, Mike
looked away again, fast. It was enough to make him wonder
if his own courage existed now or would exist in a tight
spot. Eddie didn't even look human to him.

As Mike started the car, Eddie began to gather himself
together into the impulse necessary for speech. Before he
managed it, they were pulling out of the yard. He said in
a voice as ragged as an old pillowcase that had been flapping
on the line through a three-day northwester: "You didn't
expect to find me here."

"No," Mike agreed.

Eddie sounded as if he was clenching his teeth and trying to talk through the barrier.

"I didn't either."

"Look, Eddie." Mike let the car roll to a stop before he
turned the corner and sat with his hands on the wheel, looking straight ahead, "Eddie, do you think you'd better
come?"

"Yeah. God knows I don't want to. But I'd better."

His voice was creaking.

"I—I didn't know you'd been riding alone. Ginny said I couldn't hide behind you any longer. She said if I let you go alone again—"

It was deeply important for Mike to know what else she had said.

"What *did* she say?"

"Well—" Eddie mumbled and let the word die aggravatingly.

They sat in infertile silence with the quietly dark Main Street lying before them and beyond that the long, lonely roads where they would go searching for their enemy.

Mike started to ask again. Before the words got out he decided against it. Shoving the quaking car into low, he roared around the corner and down the long stretch of macadam toward the town hall.

They were a little late and whoever had preceded them had been a little early. The two Indian pumps stood on the sidewalk in front of the big entrance door like some strange mushroom growths that had come out of the arid concrete. Mike got out, feeling as if his feet were touching foam rubber instead of cement, and shoved the pumps into the open rumble seat.

When he got into the car again, Eddie had relapsed into his corner. In the first half hour of that patrol, Mike was revising a few of his ideas. Eddie had been so scared this afternoon that it made him actively sick. Yet here he was, doing the thing he had been afraid to do with all the strength of a bowl of jelly; but doing it!

If a man had never been afraid of anything, it wasn't courage that kept him going. Mike had never bothered to wonder what courage was. But, sitting beside the silent, quaking Eddie, he decided that Eddie's courage which involved a conscious effort, was more important than the

211

courage which said brashly: Hell, I'll do it! Don't know what it means to be scared!

Eddie didn't look like a brave man and he didn't act like one. In that first half hour Mike had to stop the car twice while Eddie got out to go behind a bush. In the second half hour, while they were on the return end of their first circuit, Mike began to have the curious sensation that he was alone in the car. But this loneliness with Eddie sitting there beside him was deeper and more nerve racking than the loneliness he had known when he was riding patrol by himself.

"I'm worried about her, you know," Eddie said suddenly.

Mike's brain groped for the meaning of that and he saw that Eddie was still talking about his sister. His strained mind, all this time, had been groping around after something he wanted to say and had just now reached it.

"About *Ginny?*" Mike let a little of his astonishment get out in the words. It seemed to him that Eddie had enough to do, keeping his own ragged soul in some sort of shape, without worrying about Ginny. "What for?"

"I know." Eddie answered the surprise first. "I'm a mess to be worried about someone else. That's what you mean, isn't it? And I don't know why I bother to tell *you* about it, either, only you're making things harder for her."

"What are you talking about?"

"Well, I mean, if you'd leave her alone— After all, Mike, you had your chance. Now, if you could leave her alone, she'd be better off."

"Look." Mike was furious. "Either come out and say what you mean, or shut up. I don't see what business it is of yours, anyhow."

212

"I suppose I like her," Eddie said slowly. "She's my sister. I suppose I've got a right to like her. And I don't enjoy seeing her miserable when there's no need."

"But *I'm* not bothering her, Eddie." His voice rose a little with the lie. "Why, I haven't seen her more than a couple of times since I've been home. Not that I wouldn't like to."

What ails you? he was thinking. Spilling out like that to him! What's the matter with you? But his voice went on in spite of him: "I like Ginny a lot."

"Well, if you do, leave her alone. You're just making matters worse." Eddie wanted to let it go at that; but Mike couldn't.

"You've got to tell me what you mean," he said hardly. "You can't say that much and stop or, by the Lord harry, I'll have your tongue right out by the roots."

"It was all right before Marm died," Eddie said softly. "Then she had somebody on her side. But it's different now. The old man, he's hard on her. See? He won't trust her. Mike, you wouldn't believe the way he talks to her. And you see, he's made up his mind she's going to marry Byron Sawyer."

"*He's* made up *his* mind," Mike repeated. "What about Ginny? What about her making up her mind?"

"Well, that's just it. She was all right till you showed up. After that, really. It's just the last few days—since the fire— she don't seem to know whether she's coming or going. It makes it kind of uncomfortable, living there."

"Like what?" Mike couldn't keep the ice out of his voice and Eddie stole a quick glance at his set face.

"Well, that night Jonesy Dawes was shot. She was with you, wasn't she?"

"What of it?"

"I *thought* that was your car!" Eddie said triumphantly. "When she come in, Pa was waiting for her. He always asks her now where she's been and who she was with. Ginny was standing in the door, see? Not quite in the room. She said she'd been out with Byron. I guess it was the first thing she could think of. Then all hell broke loose, because By was sitting there, too, just inside the door where she didn't see him at first.

"He got up and grabbed her by the wrist and started talking to her, kind of low and ugly. I couldn't hear what he was saying. I said to the old man, 'You got to make him stop that.' Pa just looked at me that way he looks lately. He said, 'Somebody's got to take her whorish ways out of her. It better be Byron.'

"I don't know what happened after that. I couldn't stand it. I went up and went to bed. But they were at it, hammer and tongs, half the night. Every time I woke up, I'd hear them going it down there."

"He just sat there and let that big ape maul her!" Mike wasn't asking a question and Eddie let his silence confirm the statement. Mike realized that his fingers were so tight on the wheel they had cramped into position. Carefully he loosened his right hand and moved the fingers stiffly. The anger that lay like a lump of clear, green ice just over his stomach was new to him. There was none of the flashing, red, quickly over, blind fury he had known so often. This was a thing that was going to last a long time and that he intended to do something about.

As they coasted into Main Street, Mike was staring into the cone of light from the headlights, not thinking, just driving the car. He heard the sudden, surprised sound Eddie made and his own eyes swiveled around the edges of the sky,

214

looking for whatever Eddie saw. There was nothing but night.

"What the devil ails you?" he said harshly.

Eddie gestured.

"Something's happened." His voice bubbled unpleasantly in his throat. "Look."

Letting his gaze be directed by that gesture, Mike saw two men standing on the sidewalk in front of the brightly lighted doctor's office and was amazed that he hadn't seen them before. That light in the dark street was like a shriek in church.

"Pete sake!" he said, in stifled surprise and swung the car in to the curb. As soon as he stopped, Jay pulled the door open and looked in at them, his face white and tired in the thin light.

"Mike, that you?"

"What's wrong, Jay?"

"Well, the damndest thing. Byron here picked Hokey Mitchell up from the side of the road half an hour ago. He was pretty bad off and By thought a hit-and-run driver'd got him. But Hokey came to enough to say somebody'd slugged him. By brought him in to the Doc and then he come and routed me out."

"If he's hurt bad you shouldn't have moved him," Mike said stiffly.

"Judas!" Byron stared bitterly in at him. "That's what everyone's been telling me. But what could I do? The Doc won't come out on a call at night if you claim you're dying. I didn't think I could get him out there for Hokey. Thought it'd be quicker to bring him in."

"We've been all over that," Jay said impatiently. "And it's done now and we can't change it. What I'm wondering is whether Hokey's crazy enough to make up a story like

215

that. He'd say almost anything; but would he say somebody slugged him if it was a car hit him? And if somebody
did hit him, why did they do it?"

For a sick second, Mike's glance met Jay's steady, knowing eyes. He said angrily: "Oh, my judas priest!" and struck
his forehead hard with the heel of his hand. "It's my fault.
It's my fault!"

"What?" Jay said.

"Well, look. Hokey told me that story first. You know,
how he saw the guy starting that fire on the Point. I told .
him to come to you with it. I never figured there was much
in it. I never thought to tell him to get you alone. Look,
Jay, somebody heard him tell you that yarn. Somebody
who had good reason to know Hokey might have seen him."
And any fool would have known better, Mike thought,
than to move him, unless he wanted to be sure that Hokey
died. But that didn't make sense, though, because Byron
had had an opportunity to see to it that Hokey stopped
talking without going to all this trouble.

"I don't know how we could have foreseen this," Jay
said slowly; but his mind was going over the things he
might have done, slowly, steadily. The retina of his eye
still held the image of Hokey lying on the table, looking like
an old pile of rags. He saw the limp, dirty hand swinging
slowly against the shining chrome.

"It's my fault," Mike repeated blankly.

"All right!" Jay's patience slipped a little. "Stop blaming
yourself. If you want to put it that way, it's everyone's fault!
But, my God, how's a man going to know these things?
We've never had to do with anything like this before. It's
nobody's fault. We're just waiting around till he comes to.
See if he knows who did it."

216

Sensing Jay's impatience and realizing there was nothing personal in it, Mike held his ragged temper. Once you get yourself worked up to a certain temperature of emotion, anything beside the point unleashes a substitute anger that is really a safety valve.

"I'll stick around a minute or two," Mike said. "I'd kind of like to know before I do any more running around."

"He was pretty bad hurt." Jay offered little hope that Hokey would ever tell who had slugged him. "He didn't look good to me."

He faltered and then said numbly: "You—you're on patrol, aren't you?"

"You know darned well we are," Mike snapped. Recognizing Jay's question as the vocal expression of his need to keep the silence at bay, he added more easily: "Just finished the first round. Haven't set eyes on a soul the whole way. Everything's quiet as—death, except for this blessed wind." The hesitation before that word canceled out the carelessness with which he finally said it, and it left them all numbly thinking of Hokey, waiting for it in the shining office.

The wind, funneling down between the buildings, set a whirligig of yellow leaves squttering along the gutter. Mike's eyes, drawn irresistibly by the rustling motion, followed them until they were beyond range of the lights. His stare, starting back to Jay, picked up instead another motion, across the street and nearly safe in shadow, but coming closer.

"Somebody's coming," he said softly.

Jay found that motion, too, and he straightened up as if it would help him see more clearly.

"Hey," he roared and all movement ceased just as the

217

man who made it came into the dim farthest range of Mike's headlights. He was nothing but a tall, thin not-known figure, too far away to be anyone they recognized.

"Hey, you, come here!" Jay yelled again.

Powder had been legging it along at a good jog and so busy thinking that he couldn't realize that hail was meant for him. The second one left no doubt in his mind. Transfixed by the light, he stared wildly down the street. He remembered the can he was still holding in his hand and with a quick, reflex gesture he couldn't have prevented to save his life, gave it a jerky toss behind him. He heard it land lightly in the crackling leaves windrowed along Mary Babcock's dahlia bed.

Damn her! he was thinking. Damn that Tiz! She must have gone right home and called Jay. Did she think I wasn't going to tell him? I should have shut her up while I had the chance. She must've called him. He wouldn't be standing around out here this time of night, for any other reason.

"Powder!" Jay called. "Come over here!"

Moving like a man whose joints were activated by wire, Powder stepped off the curb and started across the street.

"Did Tiz Arey call you?" he said quickly, thinking to get right to the root of things and find out where he stood. Instantly he saw his mistake mirrored in their astounded silence. He thought: When'll I learn to keep my big mouth shut!

"What about Tiz?" Mike said.

"Why should she call me?" Jay's question was all mixed up with Mike's.

"I—I—" Powder groped. "Well, when I see you all standing around here, I thought sure she must've called you."

"What about?"

"She nearly caught the firebug," Powder said quickly. Astonishment held his audience gaping. He was beginning to be relieved himself. Maybe this was going to turn out all right. Maybe it was the best thing could have happened. It was kind of enjoyable, too, being the center of attention.

"Yes," he went on, letting his voice begin to sound excited. "I come across her down by Anse's place with the cussedest story I ever heard. Said she nearly caught the feller we're looking for. Said she nearly walked right up to him. Showed me the place where he was building a fire and everything."

"But I left her at home!" Mike protested, unable to believe his ears. "She was going right to bed!"

"That's as may be," Powder said importantly. "She certainly wasn't in bed when I saw her last. There was all the stuff handy to start real trouble, too. I didn't know what to do, really. I walked back home with her. She was kind of scared, seemed to be. Didn't want to go home alone. I figured the sensible thing to do was get her home and then come and find you. Kind of stood to reason, the guy wouldn't come back, being scared off like that. So I come right to find you, Jay. When I see you all standing around here, why, I thought sure she must've called you."

He became aware that he was doing all the talking and doing it fast.

"Everything at once," Jay said bitterly. His shoulders drooped slightly. "No, that's all news to me, Powder. I was standing here waiting to see what was going to happen to Hokey."

"Hokey?" Powder croaked and stopped there, this time because he was incapable of asking the question. It seemed

219

to him that his heart had ceased to beat for a space long enough to make him think it wasn't going to start again ever. When it did, he had to breathe hard to catch up with it.

"Yeah. Poor old devil. Byron picked him up out of the gutter. Thought it was a hit-and-run. Guy wouldn't even know it hardly, hitting that poor old bag of bones. But Hokey come to for a minute. Said somebody slugged him."

"Who?" Powder sounded breathy. "Did he say who done it? My God, what'd anyone want to slug that poor half-wit for?"

"He didn't say who. We're waiting for the Doc to bring him around. Thinking, you know, he might be able to tell us."

Powder felt as if his body were suspended on a thread as fine as spider web across a chasm as deep and flaming as hell itself. I'm getting careless, he thought. I'm getting foolish! God won't be that good to me twice in one night. Why didn't I make sure he was dead!

The door of the office opened and the doctor stood there in the rectangle of light, looking out at the white faces jerked suddenly toward him. He beckoned to Jay with a curious, half-defiant, half-reluctant movement of his hand.

"Go talk to him, will you, By?" Jay's shoulders slumped even more. "Go listen to what he's got to say. I can't. I guess I know what he wants."

"How d'*you* know?" Byron hesitated just long enough for Jay's answer.

"I know," Jay said wearily. "*You* go. He'll tell you."

Byron vanished into the lighted office past the doctor's stiff figure. The door closed with a soft implacability that somehow supported Jay's acceptance.

"Well, that's that," Jay said sadly. Then: "Guess I'll go up and talk to Tiz a minute."

"I'll go, too," Mike said harshly, thinking maybe she would need him.

"No." Jay shook his head. "You finish your patrol. That's most important now."

Byron burst out of the office and came running down the sidewalk to tell them importantly what they already knew.

"Hokey's dead," he said.

"Where *you* going?" Jay asked coldly as Powder swung into step with him.

"Home." Powder stared blankly. "Right on your way. Mind if I walk along with you?"

Jay grunted; but Powder didn't find it necessary to resent that. Hokey's death had been a sign to him. The Lord was on his side. He'd let Hokey die slowly as a personal warning to Powder to be careful.

Powder glanced around him at the windy night, thinking: I'm safe. Tiz don't really know anything. I'm calling the turns now. The Lord wouldn't let anything go wrong. I'm the Lord's big hammer. And Hokey's dead.

It was such a lovely night, so peaceful, with the soft wind pouring like a flood of sound and smell out of the southwest, over the miles of choppy water. Fair wind, dry as bone, dry as dust—

They passed the quiet, dark, sleeping houses, went silently through the deserted, moonlit street. And in each one of these houses the sleepers turned uneasily in the night, hearing the wind blow while they slept, listening with ears that never relaxed, for the sound of their danger. At intervals, through the beautiful darkness, somebody would wake, rise on his elbow, and stare wide-eyed at nothing listening to hear what raucous voice had called him in the night.

Hearing nothing now, he would settle back to lie awake and listen still—but tonight there would be nothing to hear.

Powder wanted to yell out to him: Go back to sleep. Take this night while you've got the chance. Nothing will come and get you tonight. But get ready. There's more nights coming. This wind will blow till doomsday. Get ready.

This night had been a clear sign to him that it wasn't supposed to happen all at once, not yet. He had been over-eager. He'd thought the time had come. The Lord had shown him that He didn't intend it like that. Slow and teasing and implacable, that was the way. Then, when the right moment came, when they were thinking they'd got away and he had forgotten them—pounce!

Every window in Tiz's house blazed with light.

"My judast priest," Jay said softly. "Don't it look awful to come around a corner in the dark and see a house lit up like that at one o'clock in the morning?"

"You'd think somebody was dying," Powder said before he remembered Hokey.

"Brother! You're about as happy as the undertaker."

Jay hardly seemed to notice that Powder passed his own drive without hesitating and came along with him.

It might be just as well to hear what Tiz would tell Jay. Might as well know what he had to face.

Jay's knuckles against the door cut the silence inside like a knife slicing cheese. Tiz's steps came quickly across the room and stopped. The door didn't open. She stood on one side and Jay and Powder on the other, frozen and listening, before Jay happened to think she would naturally be nervous about opening the door to an anonymous knock.

"It's Jay Stone, Tiz," he said carefully. "It's all right."

222

She didn't answer, but instantly the bolt slid back and she opened the door.

"Powder told you," she said flatly before she noticed Powder's pale face peering past Jay's solid shoulder. "Come on in." She stood back away from the door and they filed solemnly past her into the kitchen.

"Everything's happening at once," Powder said importantly. He marched briskly over and sat down in the chair near the stove, dragging their glances after him. Jay gave him a stiff, restraining glare.

"I'll handle it, Powder, if you don't mind." He wanted to hear Tiz's story before this business about Hokey could stir her up all over again. "Okay, Tiz," Jay said calmly. "Let's have it."

"Well, I don't know, Jay." She was still too tense to quiet down and she went fidgeting around the room. "Powder knows as much as I do, really. I was walking along the road there by Anse's and I looked down toward the water and saw a light where there shouldn't have been one."

Seeing her struggle to go on, Jay tried to calm her.

"What were you doing out that time of night, anyhow?"

"Because I'm nervous. I knew I couldn't sleep. I thought if I went out and took a walk, I'd get tired. You know—" She let it go with a shrug. Jay, looking closely at her dark, strained face, saw that she was telling him the truth such as it was. She was so close to the point of breaking that even his gentle questions seemed brutal.

"Well," he said soothingly. "Just try to remember what happened exactly—everything—and try to tell me about it. Don't leave out a thing, no matter how foolish it may seem. This guy is smart. The only hope we have of catching him is through some careless, little mistake he may make. I

223

don't believe he'll make a big one. You see—" he went groping through his mind for the idea—"they say, with people like that, maybe crazy, they're even smarter than the sane ones. There's a sort of crazy cunning that nobody who isn't crazy, too, can understand."

"It all happened so fast!" Tiz put the palm of one hand flat against her forehead as if she expected the bone to bulge outward under whatever inner pressure she felt there.

"Don't try too hard," Jay suggested mildly. "I don't want you to dream up something that didn't happen just because you think I'd like to hear it."

Tiz laughed suddenly and the tension in the room broke like a rubber band snapping.

"Jay, I'm not an infant, you know. You talk to me as if you thought I was two years old."

Jay grinned with answering relief.

"I'm sorry, Tiz. I get so used to talking like that, I do it to everyone. Now, how about it? What did you see?"

"Nothing," she said bitterly. She hadn't seen the man's face or anything that might identify him; she hadn't seen anything that would give them the slightest help. "That's the plain, unvarnished truth. I was so damned scared, Jay, I didn't see a thing."

"We get stopped cold at every turn." Wearily Jay spread his competent hands and stared at them as if he had held possibility in those stubby, strong fingers and had felt it crumble to dust and sift away.

"I had another kerosene can to add to the collection," Tiz said, looking suddenly at Powder. "What'd you do with that can?"

Powder's face was as blank as a newly plastered wall.

"Judas!" He held his own hands out in front of him and looked foolishly from one to the other. "I don't know. I

224

had it, last I knew and then, when Jay yelled at me, I *didn't* have it."

"It's all right," Jay said into the quiet. "It wouldn't have done us any good any more than the other one. You can't identify a fingerprint when you don't have anything to check it against. Like trying to say whose footprint when you don't have any idea who's been walking there."

The pause lengthened out and Powder moved his feet uneasily.

"Well." Jay turned to go. "Might's well go along, I guess, Powder. But I'm telling you, Tiz, you're a darn lucky woman that Powder came along tonight when he did. If I was you, I'd stay home nights. From now on." He hesitated with something else obviously on his tongue to say. Not sure whether or not to say it. Not wanting to frighten her any more than he needed to. With most women, he wouldn't have gone on and put words to his thought; with Tiz, somehow, it was different. In quick, hard syllables, he told her about Hokey Mitchell.

"This baby we're fooling around with," he said, "isn't fooling around with us. He means business and evidently he won't stop at anything. And he hasn't any way of knowing you didn't see who he was, Tiz."

She finished the warning in her own mind and said clearly: "You think he might try to do *me* harm?"

"What would *you* do if you thought your safety depended on somebody else's word, like that? Look at Hokey.'"

"Oh," Tiz said. "Yes, I see."

Jay heard her shoot the bolt home again behind him as soon as the door closed. It made a rusty, unused sound. He nodded with satisfaction. Sensible woman, that Tiz. Scared stiff, as who wouldn't be; but not so scared she couldn't still be sensible.

As he walked away, Jay thought with a flash of surprise of the obvious solution. Suspicious as he was, it hadn't entered his head that Tiz had been caught in an extremely compromising position. Any other person he could think of, found as she had been, would have been doomed right there. But the suspicion when he mentally tried to hang it on Tiz evaporated like fog before a brisk northwest wind. It was ridiculous to doubt her word and he couldn't do it. Even Powder—who was abnormally suspicious of everyone —seemed to have no question in his mind but what Tiz had been telling the truth.

No. That story was the truth as far as Tiz knew. It would be a good thing, Jay thought, remembering her level eyes, to have an honor so shining and impervious that suspicion slid off it like rain off a tin roof.

Usually the slightest noise in the night woke Emmy Tilton; but tonight when she opened her eyes at the first sound of the thumb latch, she was already awake. She had heard Powder go out quietly, trying not to rouse her, unaware that she lay listening to him move softly around and afraid to let him know she heard.

After he had gone, she could only wait for the inevitable sound of the siren. She was nearly crazy, waiting, by the time she heard him return and knew that one more night was over without that brazen voice of danger screeching actually as she so often heard it inside her own head.

She didn't want to know where he was or what he was doing. She didn't want him to know she had been aware of his absence. She somehow had to cut herself off physically from whatever was happening to him and from what he was trying to do to everyone else.

The door swung inward carelessly—he wasn't even trying to be quiet now—and when it did, Emmy shut her eyes tight.

Powder came in as noisily as if it were broad daylight and the most ordinary thing in the world for him to be coming home. He lit the lamp on the table, went over to the little chunk stove, and started building a fire. When he had it going and the drafts adjusted, he came to stand looking down at her. She lay trying to persuade herself she was asleep. He had lost all power to frighten her long ago. He could still hurt her; but she wasn't frightened any more. Except now.

"Emmy," Powder said softly. "I want company. You aren't much in that line; but you're better than nothing, so open your eyes again."

She lay as stiffly silent as a log.

"Emmy." Powder put his hand on her shoulder and gave it a gentle shake. "*I* know you're not asleep. Open your eyes."

She opened them so wide he could see a circle of white all the way round the darkened iris. He was leaning low over the bed and his face, seen at that angle and so close when she had not expected it, was distorted and unfamiliar.

Once he was sure she was paying attention he started pacing slowly around the cramped, little room. He had his hands clasped behind his back and was looking carefully at the crude studs across which she had started to tack pasteboard cartons to keep out the coming winter's cold.

"I wanted to talk about our home, Emmy," Powder said, not looking at her. "You really must take pride in it, since you keep it so beautifully. Just look at it! It has always been my ambition to live in a palace like this. And to see that everybody else does, too!"

227

He spun on her with fierce suddenness and she shrank before his glare, as concentrated as a blow.

"Do you understand that?" he said and his voice was a smooth, soft sound that sent chills up and down her spine as if somebody had run rough fingers through her hair the wrong way.

"I would like to see everybody else in this town living the way we do, Emmy. It's so pleasant. To work all your life and then to end it in a palace like this! Why did it happen to me? What did I ever do to deserve all this?" He made a wide, enveloping gesture that took in the frowzy bunk, the unsteady table, the whole room, and her with it.

"I tried before," he said. "I went down on Hardwood Point one afternoon and tried to make it so all our loving neighbors would be able to enjoy the same kind of luxury I have. But I wasn't quite good enough."

"No." Emmy's own bleating voice made her jump. She lay there flat on her back watching him with wide, horrified eyes. "No, Powder! I don't want to hear!"

"Oh, you see what I'm getting at, do you? Well, let me congratulate you on having such fine perception. You were beginning to make me think I'd have to use force to tell you this. But I might have known I was mistaken. Anyone as intelligent as you are; Emmy, surely you can tell a *T* when it's crossed for you. I am lucky to have such an intelligent woman for a wife."

He took a faster turn around the room. Watching him, she thought blankly: I'm glad the kids aren't here. I'm glad.

"I nearly did it tonight," he told her brightly. "If it hadn't been for that nosy bitch of a Tiz Arey, I would have. Everything was right."

228

He went over to the mirror and looked at his face carefully.

"No, it just isn't a murderer's face," he said softly. "I had her right here." Emmy's eyes froze on the graphic circle of his hands. "Right here," he told her firmly. "I should have done it then; but I couldn't. That trusting face looking at me. You soft—"

As the horrifying names he called himself poured over her, Emmy covered her ears with her hands.

He reached over and pulled her hands away.

"Old Hokey was different," he said. "I finished him off tonight because he was talking too much; but he was nothing but an idiot. It wasn't like killing a human being." He smiled.

"I'll do it yet," he told her. "You just keep your eyes open, Emmy. Get ready to run. Because it's going to be a thorough job. No halfway about it."

She was incapable of coherent speech. She knew all these things he had been telling. But one. She hadn't known he would kill. He had killed and was cursing himself because he hadn't killed again. This was what he had become and she remembered with a chill what she had done herself to throw suspicion away from him. She had done a thing almost as bad as what Powder himself was doing, hoping against hope to hold him until it rained and he would be himself again.

But he had stepped beyond the mark she had set up for him. He had killed—with the hands he had just used to touch her!

The gasp she let out was hardly human and Powder looked at her in astonishment.

"Emmy! What's the matter with you?" His eyes narrowed intently on her sodden face. "You aren't very surprised by all this, are you?" he asked flatly. "How long've you known?"

Helplessly she shook her head.

"There's one thing was puzzling me," Powder said, holding her gaze steadily. "That fire down in the field the other night, Emmy. The one you saw start."

Emmy made another sound like the first one and hearing it, he grinned toothily.

"We-ell! I wasn't sure you cared that much what happened to me. You set that fire, Emmy. Didn't you, Emmy? You knew where I was when you did it. You did it so's to take any suspicion away from me. How did you know it was necessary? Well, it don't matter now. I certainly didn't realize what a good wife I had! I underestimated you, Emmy!"

"You're crazy! Powder, you're crazy!" Too late she remembered that the last thing to tell a crazy man was that he was crazy; but Powder's expression only turned to innocent bewilderment.

"I'm not anything of the sort! Sometimes I used to think I was going; but I know now I'm not. No, look, Emmy. It's only fair this way, see? Why, if some of these fellers *do* have their houses burned over them, why, they won't be starting out any worse off than we are. Matter of fact, it'll even things up a little." The quiet voice went on, reasonably calling the roll of their neighbors.

"Look at Jasper Hanscom! Look at Tiz Arey! And Job Hanna!" When the names were there in the room with them, Powder proceeded to characterize them all in short, indecent words. "And there ain't a one of them," he finished, "hasn't had a knife into me ever since I can remember. Why, there's not one of them ever turned their hand

230

over for me. Not one of them would! Now's my chance. The Lord has shown me that He needs an instrument for His vengeance. You can't expect Him to take care of the evening-up all by Himself. I thought for a while that's the way it would be. But they were too smart for Him. He needs help."

Emmy sat up in bed, clasped her head in her hands, and began to rock back and forth in wordless dismay. He *was*—he was crazy as he could be; but what was there to do? All she could possibly do was go and tell Jay Stone what Powder had said.

She felt as if, once she looked directly at him, his madness would break into the open like sand through the bottom of a boiling spring. Who would help her? Whom could she tell?

As if he read her thoughts, Powder came and stood over her.

"Emmy," he said reasonably. "You're in it, too. What they do to me, they'll do to you, too. You mustn't breathe a word to anyone. You see, most people would be silly enough to think I *was* crazy. I don't know what they'd do. Only you and I know now I'm not. We've got to keep it a secret. The Lord has picked me out and there isn't a single, solitary thing I can do now but go ahead with it. But the way people feel, they might even lynch me. You either got to keep quiet about it or I've got to make you."

She saw his logic easily and understood.

"Besides—" his voice narrowed to a single thought—"stop and think what would happen to the kids—*without you!* They'd get awful hungry, Emmy, and I can assure you that none of your lovely neighbors would give them so much as a crust of bread."

"I'm sure you're wrong, Powder." She made one more

231

fruitless plea. "Mike Arey came over here the other day to say he'd help you out."

"Yes." Powder smiled. There was no amusement behind it; but there was hatred. "He came over; but you didn't see him coming again to really *do* anything, did you?"

"All you've got to do is tell him you need help," she begged. "He said, just let him know."

"What he'd like to see is me come crawling to him for help—then there wouldn't be anything he wouldn't do. Providing I crawled first. Well, it's too late. I'm not going to crawl to that black bastard or any of his like. It's too late for them to come buttering me up. Ten years ago, or two months ago—but not now. No. I've gone too far to stop now." He took the words out of her mind: "It's too late."

He stared at her unseeingly, an impersonal sadness and determination giving him an expression of dignity he had never had before.

"The people who're willing to do good on their own terms and in their own good time are always too late."

He went out into the darkness, closing the batten door softly, leaving the long sound of the words dying in the silence. Leaving her shaken and afraid and sure she was mad herself.

That man, she thought, is the father of my children. They've got his blood in them and I've got to let them grow up and be—whatever they will.

The café was quiet at seven that night when Mike went in. All day he had been feeling as if time itself were closing in on him. He had an oppressive sense of being crowded, as if everything important enough to do should be done and completed at once while there was still time.

When he had come unsuspectingly to Tiz's ever-open door at four that morning, turned the familiar knob, and met the resistance of the bolt, it was the small thing that pointed up climax for him. Standing there, hearing Tiz get up slowly from the kitchen couch, hearing the creaking of those worn springs released from her weight, hearing her come across to the door—all those familiar things heard for the first time through·this new barrier made Mike know surely that he would never hear them again with the same half ear. He had been doing all the things that were expected of him, with hardly a tremor. He had been feeling, ostrich-like, that really it was a kind of game they played.

Her quiet voice asking: "Who's there?" brought him understanding. She could quite easily accept the possibility that danger might be knocking for admittance, and it would be all the more terrible because it would be clothed in familiarity. She could expect the answer to come from another known voice, not his. Yet she had the guts to come over to the door and ask of that imminent danger the most pertinent fact, its identity.

"It's me," he said. Then added his name, feeling that disembodied sense of embarrassed nonexistence it gave him to speak his own name aloud: "Mike."

After she let him in, she slipped the bolt again.

For a long time they sat in the kitchen talking in quiet, strained voices. Finally, unable to bear the hashing-over any longer, Mike got up and headed for the stairs. At the door he turned to look back at her. The gray light in the room was strengthening rapidly into daylight and it lay unkindly on her weariness, on her realization that another day lay before her to be lived through with a new companion. Fear was something Tiz had had little to do with and she accepted it resentfully.

"You see, I can't get it out of my head that I really killed that poor, old devil," Mike said stiffly, thinking of Hokey. "If I'd taken the trouble—told him to be careful—seen that he *was* careful about talking, he might still be alive."

"It's easy enough to have hindsight." Tiz wasn't helping him much. "But you can't say that, really." The help came. "He might have told anyone, you don't know. In fact, you know he did. He told Jay down at the shore where anyone could have heard him. And you don't know how many others he told before or after that."

"I suppose—" Mike said the conventional words as if they had never been said before. "I suppose he's better off."

"*Nobody's* better off dead," Tiz disagreed with impersonal anger. "Not even Hokey."

Mike spent the morning dozing fitfully, never sinking far enough into oblivion to be sure he slept. The afternoon he spent lounging around in the front room with a book. Half the time he read, following each word heavily with his eyes and unable to put a meaning into the finally achieved sentence. The rest of the time he sat and stared, logily, inertly, knowing now that he was like everyone else, frightened and unfit for anything but to sit and wait. He knew he would be able to act when it happened and there would be somebody else with authority to tell him what to do. Until then, he couldn't do anything but wait.

After supper, unable to contemplate an evening spent the way his afternoon had been, he told Tiz to lock the door behind him and went rapidly down the street to the bright neon sign that hung over the door of Al Cairns' place.

Others had had the same idea. The café was well filled. The quiet was oppressive as if everyone else felt as Mike did, stunned into stillness and waiting. In spite of that,

234

with the heavy, plate glass door closed behind him, he felt as if he had stepped from danger into safety.

In the corner booth next to the window, where the three girls had been sitting the last time he'd been in here, Mr. Perry, the minister, was quietly drinking a cup of black coffee. As Mike watched, he lifted the cup and the unsteady shaking of his hand deposited a dollop of liquid down his coat front. Fussily he pulled the gleaming handkerchief from his suit pocket and dabbed at the wet stain. He still didn't have his glasses and his eyes looked queer and strained.

Al was sitting quietly behind the cash register with the morning paper spread out before him. The headline, black and square and attention-demanding, said coldly: STATE DECLARED DISASTER AREA.

Al wasn't reading that story. He knew about that. He had found something on one of the inside pages that held his attention more closely.

Mike went quickly down the length of the counter to stand behind Ginny who sat there staring unseeingly at her cup. Whatever she was thinking about held her attention completely; and, before she noticed him, he stood there long enough to see the way the small, golden hairs grew against the warm, brown skin low on the back of her neck; he saw the way her ears lay flat against her head and the sun-bleached light and dark of her hair.

He felt there should have been something about her to show she had been living through the things Eddie had told him about just this morning. Tiz and Hokey, between them, had driven all conscious thoughts of Ginny right out of his mind. Looking down at her, Mike found he had been carrying the memory of her in some warmer, closer part of him.

235

His cold anger and his necessity to defend her against whatever was happening to her had gained in strength for having been in abeyance.

She reached her cigaret out to the ash tray and, with the motion half completed, became aware that somebody stood behind her. Mike saw her hand waver and stiffen and stay there, half extended. She didn't turn her head, but somehow she recognized him.

Raising his eyes, he met her glance in the mirrored wall behind the counter.

"Hello, Ginny. Mind if I sit down?"

"If you want to." Her voice sounded tight and strained and he recognized it as a tone so usual with her now that he had come to accept it as normal.

As he settled onto the stool beside her, Ginny turned to face him with a tense, defensive turning of her shoulders, not her head alone. The door opened and closed and though she did not look up she could not control the quick tremor of nervousness in her betraying hands. They had been above the counter. She looked down at them dispassionately and put them out of sight as deliberately as she would have hidden anything else she didn't want him to see.

"What's the matter?" Mike turned to stare; but whoever had come in had already sat down. "You expecting somebody?"

"Yes."

"Perhaps I'm interrupting."

"Well, not yet, apparently."

"Before he comes, there are a few things I want to talk to you about." Mike met her questioning glance with another so steady that she looked nervously away.

"Mike—" Al shuffled down the aisle behind the counter and slapped his newspaper down in front of them. "Sweet

236

loving peter!" he said. "Did you see this here thing in the paper?" He switched the folded sheet around so they could see the picture his stubby forefinger underlined.

"Lookit here. Says this lady hasn't washed her face for twenty years. Did you ever hear of anything like that?"

He ruminated a moment.

"She certainly don't *look* too dirty and this story under the picture says she's a lady. My judast, though, you find any woman around here hasn't washed her face for that long, you wouldn't call her a lady, would you?"

"No, Al, I wouldn't," Mike said. "Now, beat it."

"Hanh?" Al stared.

"Just go away is what I mean, unless you want to stand there and listen to me tell Ginny I love her!"

"No kidding!" Al's big, coffin-shaped face broke into a wide grin. "Well, I'd sure like to hear how it's done. I never could manage it; but I guess the ladies don't like an audience, do they? Sorry, boy."

He gathered up the paper, shaking his head admiringly, and moved slowly away. He settled down behind the register again; but he was watching.

Ginny stared after him hopelessly, thinking: Please, God, make him come back. Don't let him leave us here alone. Because Mike was going to say to her the one thing that would shake her resolution.

I don't want to be owned, she thought, like a car or a house, and that's how By wants me. But I don't want what Mike has to offer, either. I'm sort of halfway between them.

Mike and Byron and Jasper, among them, had worked her resolution to the point where she was ready to tell By just that. That she didn't want to be owned. But, if she had to expend any of that resolution on Mike, there wouldn't be enough left to stand against By.

I can't keep saying no all my life, she thought desperately. If Mike would only let me alone. I don't want to be just something for him to sleep with, either.

Ginny's face was dusky and furious. To his horror, Mike saw her underlip quiver uncontrollably.

"You're so kind, Mike!" Her voice shook. "You really enjoy making me look ridiculous, don't you."

Instantly he was ashamed of himself.

"My God!" he said angrily. "I—Ginny, that was a cheap trick! It wasn't the way I wanted to tell you. Let me forget it, will you, and start again? Ginny—"

Instead of answering him, she glanced around at the low-ceilinged room. Somebody had just put a nickle in the juke box and punched the same old button and the same, old, sweet music filled the café like whipped cream flowing out of a pastry bag.

"This is almost the way I dreamed it would be," she said, and laughed, her eyes hotly resentful. "Listen! There's the soft music. But I wouldn't call these lights low. You have to have the lights low, Mike. It just doesn't count when they're as bright as this. It isn't traditional."

"None of it is, I guess." The hurt had gone deeper than he had ever dreamed it could. "It's harder to lie under bright lights than it is under soft ones."

"I'm not so sure," she said.

"Dear, listen to me just a minute." He nearly put out his hand to take hers; but thought better of it. Don't touch her. Just tell her. Maybe he could make her believe it.

"Ginny, listen! I love you. I— You really haven't any reason to believe me and I know it. That's why I want to tell you here. If we'd been alone, I know I'd have made a pass at you and you'd think this was more of the same old stuff. But it's not."

238

He stopped then, looking at her face. Ginny had never seen him look so much as if he meant what he said. It did her good to see him shaken and wanting something terribly —something he wouldn't get. She didn't have to fall for that line again. She knew better.

"Do you know that this is the first time you ever told me that?"

"Is it?" Surprised in spite of himself, he thought hard. "It's the first time I've meant it, Ginny. I didn't realize— You mean, even before? I never told you that?"

She shook her head, not trusting her voice to be steady if she spoke. Under his narrow, intent stare, she thrust both shaking hands through her hair and Mike saw on her right forearm the proof of Eddie's unbelievable story.

Her coat sleeve came down over the four dark spots; but not before he had grabbed her hand. Shoving the sleeve back, he stared down at the marks which could have been nothing but the prints of four fingers closing ungently around her arm. Over the bared wrist their eyes met briefly. Ginny's lips moved into a smile; but her eyes were as deadly sober as his.

Mike let her wrist go as if he had seen something shameful.

"Damn his soul!" he said tightly. "I'll kill him."

"It goes away." Ginny touched one of the spots with a curious finger. She accepted stilly his knowledge of what they were. "That's been there before and nobody's done anything about it."

"I've got to have the right to do something," Mike said, his eyes furiously doing battle with hers. "Ginny, listen." He felt as if he were trying to say something in English to somebody who could neither speak nor understand the language.

239

"Marry me, Ginny. Forget about him. Marry me."

She looked at him as if he had gone up in a shower of sparks. She had accepted Jasper's estimate of him, had known him so well herself, that the possibility of those words from Mike had never occurred to her.

"I mean every word of it, Ginny! Will you?"

"Will she what?" Byron's voice said lightly, but the hand that closed on Mike's shoulder wasn't light. It made him see how Ginny came to carry the marks of those fingers so legibly on her wrist. He reached out and picked the hand off his arm as if it were something highly distasteful and stood up to face Byron.

"The next time I propose to Ginny, I'm going to charge admission. It'd be well worth my while. I was just asking her to marry me, if it's any of your business."

"No, she won't." Byron was still smiling. His teeth looked very large and white and the light in his yellow eyes was not amused.

"Byron," Mike said patiently. "I'm terribly sorry. I didn't know you cared. You should have gotten to me sooner. But, you see, you're not the one I'm asking to marry me. I'm asking Ginny."

"Mike!" Ginny said. "Please. By! People—everybody's looking at us."

For all the effect she had on them, she might not have spoken at all. Al, watching, laid down his paper and moved back toward them, carefully careless about it.

"What the hell're you talking about?" Byron stared.

"Oh, skip it."

"I don't care about having you hanging around my girl every time I turn my back."

"Well, don't turn your back. Keep right on looking. I'm getting used to an audience."

"I can't make it clear to you by talking, so if you'll step outside, I might be able to *show* you what I mean," Byron suggested.

And that was probably the Lord's truth, Mike reflected. By was half a head taller than he was and had a good fifteen pound advantage in weight.

"Haven't you heard it's not polite to walk out on a lady?"

"I always heard it wasn't very polite to force unwelcome company on her, too."

"Then, why don't you leave peaceably?" Mike grinned, tantalizingly, watching the dark blood surge up By's shiningly blond face. He saw By's tall body settle for the blow and knew it was coming.

"All right," Byron said tightly. "If you want it here."

The only warning was a slight shifting of By's weight; but that was enough. Mike got his forearm up just in time to take the full force of that first punch. For a minute he honestly thought his arm was broken; but during Byron's momentary hesitation of surprise he found it wasn't. That pause was going to be his only chance and he took it fast, hearing Ginny's voice saying something, hearing Al's yell. He landed with his right under By's left eye and with his left at the corner of By's wide-lipped, smiling mouth. He had just time to see with satisfaction the trickle of brilliant blood that appeared, startlingly, against that fair skin before Byron's follow-up punch got him under the point of the jaw.

As if from a distant and detached vantage point, Mike felt the fist. He thought he was falling slowly until his head hit something with a solid, dull clunk and even his distant vantage point suddenly got so far away he could see nothing.

He wasn't really out. He sat there groggily on the floor between two stools with the counter at his back the only

241

thing holding him up. He couldn't seem to make his legs stiff enough to carry him. He looked up thoughtfully and saw Al's astonished face peering down at him.

"She didn't want to listen, hanh?" Al said.

Mike got up feeling like a kitten that's been thoroughly shaken by an Airedale.

"Where'd he go?"

"He went out right after she did," Al said hopefully.

Mike stumbled over to the door and pulled it open. The wind, cool and bracing as water, hit him in the face. He shook his head hard, trying to clear away the blur behind his eyes. I must have hit the counter, he thought numbly. Then he saw them standing there on the sidewalk. Byron had Ginny's wrist and was leaning toward her talking in a quick, low voice. He didn't see Mike coming and Mike, taking full and ungentlemanly advantage of his chance, didn't say: "By!" until the wild haymaker was well on its way.

Byron turned his head quickly to receive full benefit of it. Mike felt with a surge of bloody satisfaction the firm resistance of By's chin against his fist. Even then By didn't go down; but he wavered uncertainly before he came back for more.

Mike was never sure what happened in the next few seconds. He knew only that it was painful and too fast to follow and when it was over, he and Byron were sitting on the sidewalk staring helplessly at each other, both of them incapable of motion.

"You—you animals!" Ginny said bitterly. "If I never see either of you again, it'll be too soon!"

Mike was barely able to see her walk firmly away, leaving them there. The circle of curious, shocked, admiring faces

242

around them heaved a little and Mr. Perry shoved his way through before the circle closed again.

"She's right," he said loudly. "You're no better than animals. Here you young men have lived through the working of a modern miracle and all you can do to show your reverence is fight over a woman! Sex and money," he shouted suddenly, turning to face his attentive audience.

"Sex and money are the demons of our civilization. Forget the one. Give the other away. Turn to God, not Mammon, while you have a chance! The Lord has tried us sorely and seen fit to give us one more chance. I beg of you that you do not throw it away as these two poor creatures have started to do. Be careful! Take care! Go softly with Him lest He see fit to take away from you the chance He has seen fit to give."

His voice stopped and the sucking wind filled the hole it left in the night. In the voiceless quiet, Mike thought at first that the sound he heard was inside his own head; but one startled look as those faces, instantly withdrawn and listening, told him they heard it, too.

The fire whistle was muttering into life and a moment later its high shriek had filled every inch of space between the earth and the betraying, rainless, windy sky.

The Frenchville men who lived and fought through the next two days and nights felt as if they had just dropped out of the world—somewhere else things were going on as they normally did; but not here. Mike Arey, after a while, got to have a peculiar picture in his mind. He could see the map of New England just as it had been in his geography book when he'd gone to school. But on his mental map, this state had lost its foundations and sunk below the

243

others, leaving a hole with that familiar shape. And anyone could have walked to the edge, stood on the border,
and looked straight down to see it there, hot and dry and
spotted with fire. There would be a hot wind coming up
out of the pit and ashes and cinders and smoke. It would
be like looking down into a real hell.

Everything stood still in a vacuum of heat, of dry, un-
ceasing wind, of the smell of smoke and the presence of
fire. The radio told them they were wrong, they were not
forgotten; but they felt forgotten. The radio said that
people were thinking of them and praying for them.

It was comforting for a second; but before the blistering
wind, thoughts and prayers lost what significance they might
once have had and all that mattered were pumpers and
engines and deep wells and, above all, man power.

For two days and two nights the southwest wind blew
without a letup, without one second's stop. And all up and
down the western shore the calls kept coming in.

The first call came at eight o'clock in the evening. Jack
Nelson, who was officially on duty, was sitting inside the
open, sliding door of the firehouse, his chair tipped back
against the wall. He was holding a western story magazine
open on his knee, but he wasn't reading it. He was listening to the voices of the men who were sitting on the liar's
bench outside the door. The cavernous firehouse was quiet
and the great, red truck sat gleaming and potent with
hushed power. The voices came to Jack as a low humming
sound. He could have joined in the talk without straining
himself; but he didn't feel like talking and he could understand the long silences that fell and lay heavily over the
others. They couldn't seem to keep away from the firehouse
and he could understand that, too. Everyone wanted to

244

be where he could get right into the beginning of things. Jack was saying to himself: Please God, don't let there be a beginning, when the telephone on the wall three feet from his head let out its shrill, uninhibited screech. The noise pierced his ears as sharp as the point of a fine knife, as cold as an icicle.

He nearly fell off his chair and his stumbling momentum carried him to the phone. As he took it off the hook, he was numbly aware that the conversation outside had stopped and the men sitting there had got up at the sound of the phone and were standing in the door waiting.

"Fire station," he croaked.

"This is Alice Cowles. We can see fire over back of Bobby Bartlett's barn. My Howard's just going across the field now. Bobby's out there. In that little stand of hard wood. Send—"

Jack didn't wait for her to finish. He was relaying the message on to Allen Carter almost faster than he heard it. Before Alice had got to: "Send the fire truck," the big pumper was shivering into life under Allen's frantic foot. As it roared out the door, the men who were waiting, piled on any which way, grabbing with ready hands at the stanchions when they whirled past.

The fire truck moaned its peremptory way down Main Street, gathering a string of cars behind it, as if it towed them on a cable. Allen swung into Bobby Bartlett's driveway so fast the heavy truck chattered on the turn. Mrs. Bartlett was standing in the kitchen door in the rectangle of light, waving them on with her apron. Allen caught a glimpse of her out of the corner of his eye and all he could think of was a woman trying to shoo a flock of hens out of her way. He twisted the truck through the narrow lane between the house and the barn before he saw anything but

245

the glow against the sky. When he finally saw the fire itself, even when relief coiled through him, he found it a horrifying sight. The darkness magnified the flames and he had seen enough of fires to discount about half of what his eyes told him.

It was low yet, burning steadily through the grove of young Getchell birches, confined so far to grass and dead leaves and brush. If luck was with them, they'd have it out in minutes.

Across the grove, on the upwind side of the flames, he could see Bobby and Howard Cowles. Howard was working like a demon. He had what looked like a wet gunny sack and he was swinging it wildly, bringing his arms far back over his head, slamming the sack down, using twice the energy and achieving half the intended result. Bobby was being a little more sensible. But even as Allen looked at him, Howard's frantic hysteria began to communicate itself to Bobby, and Allen could see him degenerate into jerky, undirected slashing against the clean flames coming at him.

Bobby cooled down, though, as soon as the flash of the turning, red light on the truck told him they were no longer alone.

Allen's estimate of a few minutes had been made on his experience with normal conditions. It had never occurred to him that a grass fire could be so stubborn. At first he thought they'd be able to handle it as they would have any brush blaze, with Indian pumps and main force. Fifteen minutes of backbreaking work showed him his mistake. Inch by reluctant inch, the fire was pushing them back toward the waiting woods.

"Get that pumper down to the shore! Get the hose out!"

Allen grabbed at a couple of sweating men and shoved them toward the truck. "Hurry!"

Damn fool, he thought. Why didn't you do that in the beginning? But he couldn't remember when he had to lay out his hose for a grass fire!

Inside five minutes the hose line was laid across the field. The pumper's deep-throated, roaring force started pushing the cold salt water up the rise.

Out of the corner of his eye, Allen had watched the truck's lumbering process down the field, wondering how much her springs and axles would take. He saw with relief they'd had the sense to use a fog nozzle on the hose.

Even with that unlimited supply of water at their backs, the crew put in an hour of good solid work in the birch grove before any of them dared to call a halt even for breathing.

Usually the first thing a man does when he's been working hard and steadily and stops to rest is light a cigaret. Not one of the twenty men in that grove so much as scratched a match. In the light from the car headlights, Allen could see their faces shining with sweat, blackened with flying soot, and scared. There was no other word for it. It shouldn't have taken twenty men an hour to put out a simple grass fire, one that size!

"You any idea how it started, Bobby?" Allen said, finally getting his breath back.

"By God, no! I haven't! First thing I knew, I looked out the window and there it was. I yelled to my old lady; but we ain't got a telephone. She started screeching out the door and Howard heard her. Hadn't been for that, I don't know what would have happened."

"Funny." Allen scraped his toe thoughtfully through the

247

deep-burned grass and the black scuffed away, leaving bare, singed earth.

He didn't say aloud what they were all thinking. He knew they were thinking it.

"Been a bottle, piece of glass, something like that," Bobby offered, "you'd think it would of started in the heat of the day."

"Might have smoldered a long time." Allen was thinking aloud now. "What you burn in the kitchen stove, Bob?"

"Wood." Bobby bristled defensively. "My chimney don't throw no sparks! Don't go trying to tell me I started that with my own chimney. Why, look, Allen, no sparks would carry that far. It'd a been nearer the house, been anything like that."

"Yeah." Allen agreed reluctantly. "I guess you're right, Bob. Well, it's out now; but you and Howard between you better keep an eye open tonight. Come out and take a look around every hour or so."

He thought it would be better not to conjecture about how the fire had started. The mood of the men around him was an ugly one, and he could feel it as solid and biting as the smell of smoke. If this fire meant what he thought it did and what they thought it did, they were going to need every ounce of energy left in their bodies and they couldn't afford to waste as much as they would once the angry talk started.

He could be wrong. He turned and started for the truck, hauling some of them with him like sheep after the wether. Maybe it was just one of those freak things that happen. Any other year, any other circumstances, he wouldn't think anything of it. Almost anything might have started this fire. Fire did queer things, smoldered sometimes for hours before there was enough of it to see.

248

It was only now—

The second call came five hours later, in the early morning:

"There's a fire close to the shore at the back of my field. Not very big yet. If you hurry—"

During the next day there were two more.

"Bill Knowles' kid just come in. Says there's a blaze on the Bobtown Road, about a mile to the south of Ralph Swain's cutting. Hurry."

"This is Fred Baker. There's smoke coming down in my pasture. Just over the top of my red cow."

After the second alarm, when they came wearily back to the station, Allen couldn't deny to himself what was happening. After the third, he couldn't deny it to anyone else. This was the showdown. Something had happened to push their enemy right off over the edge of sanity and he had gone sliding down the abyss into the darkness. Much more of this and, Allen was sure, he'd have everyone else down there with him.

After the fourth alarm, Allen made up his mind that it was going on until the end this time, until the triumph. And he knew, too, that flesh and blood would give under the strain. Sooner or later the alarm would come and they would find themselves incapable of answering it. Until that happened, there was nothing to do but wait, grabbing every available minute for sleep.

If we can only get help from somewhere, anywhere, Jay was thinking frantically. His hand on the telephone receiver had sweat so that the hard, black rubber kept slipping out of his grasp like a piece of macaroni. He put in a call for the fire chief in Sanger. A woman answered the phone. To Jay's sensitive ears she sounded as if she were crying.

249

"Lemme speak to Roger, will you?" he snapped.

"He's not home. Who is it?"

"Not home!" Jay hadn't even stopped to think his call wouldn't get the man he wanted. "Goddammit, he's *got* to be. This is Jay Stone, down to Frenchville. We need help bad down here. Can he send his truck?"

"Oh, Mr. Stone!" She took a quick, gasping, tearful breath. "It's so awful. I know."

"Well, where *is* he?" Angrily, fuming at the wasted time, Jay tried to cut her off.

"He's out on a fire," she told him quickly, recognizing that desperation. "He can't come. He's been out on a brush fire for the last two hours. He's—"

Jay hung up there. There were only two trucks in the whole town of Sanger. They weren't much better off than Frenchville. He'd been crazy to waste his time anyhow. Roger Brown wouldn't feel much like bringing a truck way down here, twelve miles deeper into the Peninsula and leaving the whole northern end of it only half covered. He couldn't do it!

Barrett's Harbor had more equipment than any other town he could think of, near enough to do any good. The telephone rocked on its base under the force of his hand on the crank.

He got Dave Johnson in Barrett's Harbor and Dave's voice was so sane it felt like a good bucketful of cold water down over Jay's head.

"Dave," he said. "Jay Stone. Look, can you let us have some apparatus down here? We're going crazy! I think we've got a nut on the loose. Three fires in the last eight hours or so."

"Jay—I don't know. I don't dare to let the Harbor get too spread out."

250

"Look, Dave! I know there's two tank trucks up there besides your pumper. We're down here with one truck and it's on the hop every minute. So far we've been lucky. One call at a time. But if we get two at once, or the pumper lets go on us, we're done for. Dave, for God sake!"

"All right." The decision had been made while Jay was still pleading. "One of the tank trucks'll be down, Jay. Just as quick as they can make it. You got a crew?"

"Yeah; but you better send a couple of guys know how to use it. Thanks, Dave."

"Judast, Jay, I didn't know before what a fire was really like, did you?"

"No," Jay said shortly. "But I've sure found out!"

He hung up and instantly called the Coast Guard station. They had a small portable pumper there; he'd seen it work. They were sorry, they couldn't let him have sole call on it; but if he got into a tight spot and called them, they'd send it right over with a crew to work on it. They didn't have much hose and it could only handle inch and a half. Jay wasn't sure how much inch-and-a-half hose Allen had, or how much he could free for use with another pump.

He sat staring at the telephone blankly, not sure what to do next. It rang as he was looking at it and he was so startled at the idea of anyone calling him that he sat frozen for a second before he could bring himself to answer it. Over the wire Allen's voice was strained and metallic.

"Jay," he said. "For God sake, can't you get us something to back this truck up? One truck isn't going to do us any good if we get two fires at once."

"It's all right," Jay said, dragging up out of a deep well of unsuspected confidence enough to spare some for Allen. "Dave Johnson's sending us down a tank truck from the Harbor."

"Better than nothing, I suppose," Allen said grudgingly. "Them tankers only hold eight hundred gallons or so, though. When that's gone, it's gone, ain't it?"

"I suppose so. I don't see what else to do. He didn't dare let us have his pumper. Don't blame him."

"No." Allen started to hang up and thought of something else. "You tried the rangers?"

"Yeah. They're flipping around like mosquitoes in a wet June. Look, Allen, keep an eye out if you possibly can. See if you can't find out who isn't around when the alarm comes in."

"I suppose you think I ain't got anything else to do but play detective, hanh?"

"Allen," Jay said patiently, "we've got to find out who's doing it. That's all! If we don't get him, he's going to have the whole Peninsula cleaned off like the palm of your hand."

"Well, *you* watch," Allen said, nastily, tattered with nervous exhaustion. "I'll fight the fires. *You* watch."

"Okay." Jay hung up before he said something he didn't want to. It woud be easy, he thought wearily, to pick a fight with yourself right now and easier than that to do it with somebody else.

The phone exploded again, instantly, and Allen's voice, a little calmer now, said: "Jay, will you for the love of God see if you can't do something about the traffic down through here? Every time that whistle goes off, there's a string of cars, bumper to bumper, goes past. It's about all we can do to get the truck through them. It's slowing us down something awful."

"Well, what'll I do?"

"I don't care *what* you do as long as it's something! Call out the national guard. Get us some martial law. It'd be better than this mess. The damn fools keeps running over the hose. I've lost three fifty-foot lengths already because some damned half-witted ass keeps running over it. *I* can't tend to the traffic and be a detective and do everything else, too, can I?"

The broken connection hummed in Jay's ear.

The only man he could think of now was Clyde Amory. He called him and couldn't get him the first time. During the next five hours, he tried four times and finally caught Amory at home. Amory listened, said yes, yes, he'd do what he could. Yes, right away.

Jay had to take it for granted that Amory had said yes because he couldn't seem to understand the actual words crackling over the wire. Something was happening to his hearing, he thought; but Amory must have said yes. Under the circumstances, he couldn't have said anything else.

Jay sat staring blankly at the three shining tins sitting alone on the dusty top of his desk. There they were, the trademark of madness. The first one from Hardwood Point. The second one he himself had discovered just where Powder had let it go the night Hokey was killed. The third one had come from a ditch alongside the Bobtown road near Ralph Swain's pulp camp. Jay felt that their shining sides should have told him something. If he could make his brain work to get it. On the first can there would be the prints of every man on that hose crew. The only man who hadn't touched that first can was Powder Tilton, and he'd been down on the shore with the pumper. On the second can, there would be only four sets of prints: his own, Tiz Arey's, Powder's, and one other. But on the can that had come from the Bobtown cutting, there should be only his and the enemy's. If there was some way to eliminate, some means. His head felt tight and uncomfortable and he thought angrily: Ralph Swain put that crew in there, too. By Judas, I wish there was a way to get him for that.

The fire whistle blew and Jay tumbled down over the stairs, seeing, as he came out the door, the hateful smoke coming up over in the direction of Fred Baker's place.

Sometime in the middle of that day, Tiz Arey took over the telephone in the fire station, letting Jack go. Somebody else, thank God, had thought about food. Sandwiches and coffee, sandwiches and coffee—more sandwiches. Allen thought heavily that if he was exposed to much more heat and smoke he'd be just about ready for some starving god to slap him between a couple of gigantic slices of bread; he'd be done to exactly the right turn.

It seemed queer to him and doubly horrifying that a call never came until they were back at the station. As if *he*, whoever he was, could watch them with an all-seeing eye, could wait until the lovely lassitude of relaxation had begun before he touched off another brush pile. It was like a cat and a mouse. He was playing with them.

The telephone rang six times in the course of that forty-eight hours. Six times and not once was there a false alarm.

Tiz sat tensely inside the door with her eyes glued to the impersonal black stalk of the phone, as if she expected to see the sound before she heard it, her hands ready to grab, her voice to say: "They'll be there."

And they were there; though after it was over none of them could ever figure out how they had done it. After the first twenty-four hours, none of them was quite sure why. It was only a sort of dogged, gritty stubbornness that kept them going—they didn't really care whether or not they

254

got there in time—it was only a thing of reflex and habit by then.

After the first two or three calls, when they brought the truck back they put it away, thinking: *If* there's another, we can get there. But when the calls kept coming, they began to think: *When* the next one comes— And they left the truck outside, backed into the parking space and ready to go in either direction.

Late in the afternoon, the Barrett's Harbor tank truck with four men aboard turned in to the parking space before the firehouse and the effect of its being there was like that of fresh blood pumped through anemic veins. Confidence lay like a sheeny gloss over its red enamel and gold leaf. Its men were fresh and optimistic. They looked like white angels talking to grimy imps of hells.

There would be a period of as much as two or three hours when nothing happened. In those times, Tiz could look out the fly-specked window and see the men draped over the trucks and lying on the sunburned grass in the shade. They didn't look alive the way they lay there in the sun, relaxed but angular, as if, once fallen, they hadn't moved again. But the minute the phone rang, they were on their feet and looking at her, knowing what she would tell them and barely waiting to hear where it was before they started to move.

They had their toughest battles when it was necessary to lay the hoses across the road. All through the daylight hours the cars of sightseers, bumper to bumper, came slowly down the Peninsula road, the tires pounding across the hose lines, splintering the two by fours, which were the only protection they had. And the grimy, sweating men on the nozzle presently found themselves holding a worthless piece of metal while out at the road—where the tough-

255

fibered canvas had finally given way under that remorseless pounding—the lovely, sparkling water went shooting uselessly into the crackling, dust-laden air.

The sightseers brought their cameras with them, expensive, beautiful instruments, and the men stood with the soot settling on their smoothly polished shoes, taking pictures of these less than men, taking pictures of the death of a countryside.

Finally, after the frantic appeal from Jay, Clyde Amory took his big sedan up to the road junction and parked it across the paved surface so that there was no room for the big, wide-shouldered cars to get through without going into the ditch and scratching their enamel on the snatching pucker brush.

He had several acrid arguments, but his uniform gave him a backing of official power that worked and the traffic thinned out, leaving the noisy and pitifully small red trucks to race alone up and down the dusty Peninsula roads, unaccompanied by the kite tails of curiosity.

At one-forty-eight on the second morning, the southwest wind died as completely as if it had been shut off at a tap somewhere out in the darkness that hung over the sea. The Frenchville fire truck was coming fast up the long, dirt road from the tip end of the Point where John Babbidge's house had stood alone and lonesome facing into the east, and now stood there no longer. It was the first house they had lost. And Allen, sick and discouraged, was wondering thinly: How many more? He knew they had accomplished the impossible long ago and had been gnawing away at the insurmountable for the last twenty-four hours.

As the wind ceased, the truck drew in to the firehouse and the men climbed down and stood there looking at each other blankly in the florid light of the big spotlight that was rigged over the door of the building. They looked like men poorly made up for a minstrel show; their eyes flashed whitely, all white in their black faces; the uncolored space around their mouths gave them each the same, impersonal, wide, clowny grin.

The pumper and the tank truck sat there surrounded by idle men until daylight. With the first, faint light there came a stirring damp breath from the northeast, from the thrice-burned-over hills.

Allen got stiffly down from the driver's seat and stood looking blindly around him.

"Well," he told the Harbor men—so grimy now it was hard to tell them from the Frenchville crew—"I guess you can go home, boys. Thanks. I hope we won't need you again. I think this'll quiet him down," he said numbly.

"That wind's the wrong way for him. Leave the pumper right here; but all but three or four of you go home and get some rest. If it blows southwest again, we'll need you fast. I think."

At daybreak Emmy Tilton was sitting at the square table in the middle of the bare shed looking idly at her hands. It was funny how dead skin looked under the combination of early, thin, gray daylight and the weakening yellow glow from the lamp.

She had been getting Powder's meals on time for two days now and, when he didn't come for them, had scraped each one carefully away as if it were as important to remove all evidence of them as it had been to get them.

She was nearly through clearing the last one when Powder came home. Hearing him come and looking out the window at the trees bowing from the northeast, Emmy

257

found herself humming a jointless, untuneful little noise through teeth clenched with nervousness.

"They fooled me," he said wearily, weariness as honest in him as it was in his enemies. "I didn't think they could keep it up; but by the gods they did! Well, now I know what I'm up against. I'll get 'em now. It's all right. They can't win, you see, Emmy. The Lord's on my side and He just wasn't ready to finish them off. This is just another dry easterly. The wind'll shift again by tomorrow."

Emmy didn't turn.

"Emmy," Powder said, "what've you got to sing about? You must be happy, Emmy! Don't you hear what I'm telling you? They beat me this time. It's kind of hard, one against so many."

He said: "This damned wind! It's come off the wrong way. I can't do much in an easterly. Has to be southwest. That's best to give it a good run, a good start."

Emmy ground her teeth together viciously; but she could not stop that irritating little hum. Sickness and terror welled up in the great, empty hollow where her heart and lungs and stomach had once been.

"Emmy!" Powder said.

She turned and gave him a mild, sweet smile as if he had been talking about the weather merely for conversation's sake. Not as if he had been telling her the fine details of his madness.

Infuriated, his eyes narrowing, he reached for her; but she slipped by him like water and out into the bare, trodden yard. She paced the empty length of ground to the lumber pile and back again, looking around her at the peaceful, gray-feather sky, at the denuded hills, at the empty cellar. Still smiling, still humming. The hum was almost something she recognized and she searched her mind closely for the words that were nearly there. Just another minute and she

258

would have it. If only he didn't say anything to break into her concentration. It was aggravating, like having a familiar word or a well-known name on the tip of your tongue and not being able to make your vocal cords take on the necessary shape to give it sound.

Powder was standing in the open door watching her, scowling, curious.

"Emmy," he said. "What're you going to do?"

She looked at him and saw that she had scared him a little. Of course she couldn't stop to speak to him right then. She had to remember what the song was. She shook her head at him and kept on pacing, her hands beginning a cold, unreasonable twining together.

The beat was there, she had the rhythm of it. As soon as she recognized that, she had the words, too. She began to sing softly, keeping step with the sound of her own voice:

Mine eyes have seen the glory of the coming of the Lord.
He is trampling out the vintage where the grapes of wrath are
     stored.
He hath loosed the fitful lightning of his terrible swift sword.
His faith is marching on.

Powder's mouth dropped open and when she started in on the chorus, he shook his head and turned away. She was crazy! No doubt about it. But he was too tired to stand there and watch her. He had to have sleep. She was harmless enough.

He lay down on the bunk and, as he was drifting off, he could hear her still going it out in the yard. Her thin, monotonous voice came to him through veils of sleep:

> *Glory, glory, hallelulia,*
> *His truth is marching on.*

Under a lowering sky, gray as the breast of a Canada goose, so low it looked as if it touched the spiky tops of the hills in the east, Mike came home that morning. As he walked up the path to the door, moving like a marionette, and as tired as he was, every nerve in his body was alive to the false promise of that light easterly wind. It was northeast and that wasn't too good; but in any other year he would have sworn it was going to rain.

Rain!

Deliberately he set up each letter in his mind like a child's blocks and stepped back to look at the result. It would have to do more than rain! They would have to have the second deluge before he'd sleep easy in his bed at night.

And too often since last July he had looked at this same promising sky, felt this same northeast wind blowing, and thought it would rain. All his knowledge of weather signs had proved false. All summer long the weather station report on the radio had been right.

"Increasing cloudiness. Increasing northeasterly winds, backing to northwest late in the day. Tomorrow, onshore winds fifteen to twenty miles an hour. Fair."

In his sleep he could hear that voice, calmly singing the monotonous prelude to fair weather.

But there was something a little different today and for a minute he was too tired to think what it was. Then he realized that there was dampness in that east wind. As he stood facing the wind, he could feel the parched, tight skin on his face coming to life, feel the harsh pull of it slacken across his cheek bones. Thank the Lord for small blessings. Maybe it would never rain again; but a day like this would cool off the hot spots, give them a chance to relax.

"You can't fool me," he said aloud to the inimical, promising, retreating sky, and went into the house.

Tiz wasn't home yet and the quiet, warm desertion of the kitchen curled around him like a blanket. He almost sat down at the table and went to sleep.

Satan came screeching out of the front room, prepared to do drastic battle for the honor of his home. Seeing Mike, he looked embarrassed for a moment and then asked loudly to be fed.

When Mike bent over to fill the cat's milk bowl, he knew he wasn't going to straighten up again unless he did it fast. He splashed the bowl half full, set the milk bottle on what he thought was the sideboard, and turned toward the stairs. With his foot on the first tread, he heard the crash behind him; but he couldn't even look to see what had happened.

"Must have put it too near the edge," he mumbled. The only thing in the world that mattered was sleep and he couldn't stop to wash or eat before he did it. He simply turned in at the first bedroom door, lay down on the neatly made white bed under the open south window and fell asleep with violent abruptness.

No boats left the Harbor that morning. At five o'clock when the ebbing tide started to chuckle under their sturdy, white sterns, they were all pointing to the northeast, like sheep all staring in the same direction. By the time the tide had reached the halfway mark on the pilings under the sardine factory wharf, leaving the barnacles to click and suck in the dampness, the boats were nosing more into the east itself, swinging around with the wind. The air grew increasingly raw and did so with an authority that had been lacking from it all fall. By eight o'clock the wind had moved again and was blowing from a few points south of southeast.

At nine o'clock the tide turned and began flooding darkly back up the Harbor before the quartering wind. The clear, green, acrid water poured back into the tidepools that had lain coldly waiting under the gray sky. It edged slowly up the clam flats, raising a little cloud of mud to obscure its advance. With it came the first hard-driven, reluctant spatters of rain.

When Tiz walked up the path a minute or two before nine, she felt the first drops against the back of her neck, sharp as tiny pellets of lead. She took one look at the sky, dived through the door, and snapped on the radio. She didn't have to wait until the news was over for the weather forecast. It was second in importance only to the commercial. Even that calm, regulated announcer's voice had a shade of the personal about it this morning: Tiz hung over the brown box, gulping in every word as if she herself had been without water to drink for days and had found it at last.

"The best news we have this morning is rain. All over New England. Drenching rain began in Boston early this morning and is rapidly spreading north over the entire area. It is expected to last well into tomorrow morning. It has already reached as far north as Washington County and will give immeasurable relief to the fire fighters still battling stubborn blazes through the parched woodlands."

That was all she'd wanted to hear; but after she turned the radio off, she still couldn't believe she had heard it. She went over to the window, reluctant to look out for fear it would all turn out to be a colossal joke the Lord had chosen to play on them. She looked first at the trunk of the Northern Spy and it was already wet and gleaming in the steely light. The roof of the woodshed was so wet she could no longer see the separate dark spots where the individual drops fell. As she stood there stiffly, from the cellar beneath the kitchen came a sound she hadn't heard for so long that she scarcely recognized it—the first, reluctant, musical drip of water running into the cistern from the roof gutter.

Afterward she thought she must have waited there for nearly an hour, dazed and skeptical, expecting it to stop. She saw the gray curtain coming down over the far hills, hiding their porcupine backs. The nearer woods grew faint and blurred out. Before she turned away from the window, water was sluicing so thickly over the glass that she could see the Spy tree only with difficulty.

"Mike!" she said loudly and, turning, made for the stairs.

She could hear him snoring when she reached the top. Following the sound, she found him sprawled on the bed in the spare room, his face and hair running with water pouring in on him through the unguarded window. Even that had failed to bring him up out of his dungeons of sleep.

"Mike!" she said from the door.

He didn't move. She went quickly over to the bed and laid ungentle hands on his shoulders, shaking violently.

"Mike! Mike, wake up! I don't care how tired you are, you *can't* sleep through this! Wake up!"

He opened his eyes a slit and looked at her logily.

"Wha?"

"Look out the window! Feel—on your face! Mike, it's raining!"

"I don't believe it." He groaned and started to roll over. Taking full advantage of his motion, Tiz grabbed the edge of the mattress and turned him off onto the floor. Mike landed on his hands and knees and looked up to receive the full deluge from the window in his sleep-sodden face.

"My God!" he said. "It *is!*"

"Wake up," Tiz shouted. "I can't stand it alone."

"How long?" Mike, still on his knees, turned his sooty face on her and its expression tied her stomach into knots of laughter, near hysterical with relief. Mike gulped hard against the sudden lump in his throat. Tiz wasn't sure whether it was rain alone that was streaking the soot on his face.

"An hour. For an hour, anyway. The news said it'd last till tomorrow."

"Where's the wind? I don't believe it. It can't."

"Wind's southeast. Backed around about eight o'clock."

Mike didn't get up. He just sat there letting the rain blow in upon him, his face widened foolishly into a grin.

"My Lord, that feels good!"

"I couldn't believe it was going to keep on," Tiz said exultantly as if she alone were personally responsible for the rain. "I didn't wake you until I was sure. I—"

She stopped short, her breath cut off in her throat, her eyes hauled irresistibly to the window through which she could see nothing. The fire whistle was blowing furiously.

"What—" Mike said. And then she was standing alone in the room listening to the pound of his feet on the stairs. A moment later the door slammed and his car screamed out of the yard and up the road.

At nine-thirty, the steady drumming on the tarpaper roof just over his head brought Powder wide awake out of his uneasy sleep. He had been dreaming that it was raining hard and when he first woke up he thought he was still dreaming.

When his numbed brain took in the fact that this was no longer dream but actuality, he sat up on the edge of the bunk with dismay clutching at his empty stomach and listened deadly to the unremittant, heavy-footed stride of the water on the roof. He couldn't bring himself to look out the window; but against his cotton-shirted shoulders, he could feel the difference in the quality of the cold that came around the thin, flawed glass.

"I let them wait too long," he said dully.

When the door opened he thought it was Emmy coming in out of the rain; but when he looked up, it was not Emmy at all.

Jay Stone's face had a worn, angular, bony look and Powder had never seen anyone look so tired. For a moment he felt real pity; and then, when he met Jay's eyes, accusing and dangerous, the pity melted before the heat of fear.

"Powder," Jay said smoothly. "I haven't seen you around the last day or so. Where you been?"

"Where everyone else's been," Powder said sullenly. He looked away from Jay because he could feel his own fear so strongly he was sure it must show in his face.

Jay stood doubtfully watching him. His own careful mind told him he hadn't seen Powder, but he was too tired to to be sure he was right. He was unwilling to take his own conclusion for anything more than suspicion.

"Are you accusing me—*me*—of setting those fires?" Powder said sharply.

"I'm not," Jay told him. The whole structure of his conclusion looked pretty flimsy to him as he stood watching Powder's face, as worn and tired as any he'd seen. Heavily he turned away. "I just wanted you to know what I was thinking, Powder."

"Where you going? What you going to do?"

265

"I'm going to do a little checking on those fingerprints now," he said and went on carefully, trying to reassure himself, feeling it was only fair to let Powder know how he was reasoning. "The way I figure it, your prints ought to be on only one of those cans, Powder, and I've found three cans altogether. Yours ought to be on the one Tiz found that night. If anyone's are on all three, they've got some explaining to do. Far as I can follow it, mine are the only fingerprints there'd be any excuse for being on all of them."

He went over to the water pail and stood looking at the thick glass tumbler that stood beside it.

"That your glass?"

Powder said: "Yes. No!"

Completely aware that he had no right to be doing what he was doing, Jay wrapped the glass carefully in a dish towel.

"Of course," he said stolidly, "if there are only three sets of prints on that can you and Tiz found, Powder, they'll be hers and yours and mine and I won't need this glass."

When he went out, he left a frightened and dangerous man behind him.

For a few minutes Powder sat there, his head in his hands, before he straightened abruptly and glanced carefully around the shoddy, little building. He was alone. Emmy was still somewhere out there in the rain.

He had let them suffer too long. He saw now that he had misunderstood. His moment had come again and again, and he had failed to recognize it. The Lord had not intended revenge to take the form he, Powder, had let it take.

He shook his fist at that maddening, solid roar of rain. He felt as if he were drowning in the noise of the water, going under, pounded down.

He crossed to the stove and looking in found only a bed

266

of glowing, hardwood coals, Thoughtfully he shook them down through the grate into the ashpan. He took that out, went back to his bunk, and poured a good half of the coals into the gray coil of worn blankets. With careful intent he heaped the rest in a little pile of heat against the wall and laid a few sticks of kindling across the pile. Then he sat down beside the table to wait. It didn't take long. The acrid smell of the blankets burning had already filled the room, strong enough to make his eyes water, when the kindling took crackling life from the coals and sent the first red tongue of flame up along the punky, wide, old boards. Fortunately Emmy's feeble attempt at insulation was highly inflammable and that caught next and the smoke from the corrugated cardboard was even worse than that from the blankets.

Powder sat there as long as he could. When he finally staggered over to the door, the small room was dark and obscured. Ruddy flames were lighting the murky corners and they had a deep sound, like the change in the voice of a big cat when his diet shifts from milk to meat.

He snatched the door open and went out into the downpour, leaving it open behind him so there'd be a good draft. Smoke issued from every fold of his clothing and stinging tears mixed with the clean, heavy rain on his face. He saw Emmy immediately. She was huddled on the board pile, clutching her short jacket around her, her shoulders hunched against the wind and the water.

"It's all right, Emmy," he told her firmly. "It's all over now."

He wondered momentarily where she had been when Jay came up to the shed. She couldn't have been sitting there like that.

Against the red rectangle, he looked thin and wild and

unkempt. Inside the shack there was a sudden roar and a billow of smoke burst out the door. The glass in the window above his bunk made a sucking, reluctant sound and vanished like skim ice melting.

Powder took a final look, nooded his head, and started slowly toward her. When he was abreast of her, Emmy saw that his eyes were drawn inward, centered on some idea he had deep in his mind. He went past her as if she were a bump on a log and she sat, as cautious and self-effacing as a rabbit hoping it won't be seen, watching him. She knew when he reached the edge of the duck pond because he hesitated infinitesimally and she held her breath. He went on, moving more slowly with the water clutching at and weighing down the legs of his overalls.

He waded slowly out from the shore and she made no move to stop him. She sat there watching as coldly as if this had all been worked through to its inevitable conclusion long ago and anything she said or did would not have the slightest effect.

He went down like a figure of sand crumbling, and she could no longer see him at all, what with the rain and the smoke and a blurring behind her own eyes.

Far away and out of another existence, she heard the sound of the siren, the sound long dreaded and long anticipated and blowing now for her.

Oh God, she prayed, don't let them get here too soon. Not before he finishes what he's doing.

That pond was the only possible source of water and they'd be sure to think of it first thing.

When the red truck turned moaning into the yard, she was waiting for it down by the road. She flung herself, a screaming, demented fury, before it, her single idea to keep them away from the pond as long as she possibly could.

She had been right. They thought of it immediately; but the two men who went to put the suction hose into the water saw nothing but the water they needed.

Twenty minutes later the pumper was pouring a mixture of mud and water into the heap of smoking cinders that was all that was left of the woodshed. Only then did any of the drenched, angry men think of Powder.

"Where's Powder?" Mike came over to stand before the shrunken, tiny figure and stare down at her accusingly. His thin shirt and pants, soaked through, clung stickily to his skin. His face was streaked and shining with soot and water. "For God sake, where is he? He wasn't inside there, was he?"

Emmy shook her head numbly, incapable for a moment of answering him with an actual sound. From over by the duck pond somebody yelled, a quick, surprised bark of half-scared sound.

"They found him," she said, looking Mike squarely in the eyes. "That's Powder they've found now."

"What did he—?" Mike began harshly.

Emmy shook her head again helplessly.

Tiz, who had been standing beside her, put an arm around her shoulders, thinking: Another lame duck! And then she was ashamed of that, recognizing the need of one human being for another. It was hard for anybody to be alone and her own need was here, too—to be needed.

"You better come along with me, Emmy. You're wet through. Come over to the house and let the men take care of it. They'll do everything that's necessary."

Mike stood watching them go, blankly, trying not to think. When he turned toward the pond he was shivering uncontrollably with the cold and the end of excitement.

Dressed in clean, dry, warm clothes again, Mike sat in

269

the middle of the kitchen floor with his feet in a tub of hot water, shaking his head.

"I never had *any* idea in the world," he said firmly.

"Well." Amory tilted his chair back and looked thoughtfully at his big hands holding his cap. "The guy must've been crazy."

"He was." Tiz's voice was unequivocal. "He certainly was, judging from what she told me." She brought the teakettle and poured boiling water carefully into the tub. Mike let out a roar which degenerated into a surprised sneeze.

"Oh, dammit!" he said.

"Tiz, you got to let me talk to her," Amory protested halfheartedly.

"Not one word," Tiz said firmly. "She's asleep. You'll just have to wait until she wakes up because I don't intend to let you wake her."

"You certainly go to great lengths to be sure of my company," Amory grumbled. "I suppose I ought to be flattered."

"Be anything you want to," Tiz said cheerfully, taking the sting out of her words with a smile. She went to answer the shrilling telephone before it had a chance to ring again.

"Hello. Who? Yes, he's right here."

Amory half rose, but she shook her head and held the receiver out to Mike.

Sure that he knew who it was, Mike made a lunge for the phone and tipped over the tub. He didn't even hear Amory's exclamation or Tiz's sharp protest.

"Hello, Ginny," he said loudly. There was a dead silence at the other end of the line. "I know it's you," Mike said. He sneezed again and again said: "Oh, dammit! Where are you?"

"Er—Mike, have you got pneumonia?" The raucous,

masculine voice made Mike jerk the receiver from his ear and look at it unbelievingly.

"Who *is* it?" A little subdued, he replaced the receiver.

"Well, I'm sorry. It's me, Al."

"Oh."

"But she's down here," Al said quickly. "I'm looking right at her. By was here with her and he just went off out looking like a thundercloud. I didn't know but if you got down here fast— *You* know. I didn't know but this might be the time."

"Tell her—" Mike began. "No. Don't tell her anything. *I'll* tell her. But you hogtie her if she tries to leave. If she's not there by the time I get there, I'll kill you."

He heard Al say, "That's gratitude," in a hurt voice before he slammed the receiver on the hook and ran for the door, not even seeing the two, astonished faces watching him. He nearly forgot that he didn't have any shoes on, remembered at the last minute, and came back to thrust his wet, bare feet into the black shoes that stood beside the stove. He didn't wait for anything else, and was out of the house before either Tiz or Amory could say a word.

"Mike, you'll get your death of cold," Tiz called uselessly after him through the sheeting rain.

"No," Amory said thoughtfully. "Nobody who feels like that is going to catch cold, Tiz. Take my word for it."

She shut the door and came slowly back toward the stove, her face blank with amazement.

"I will be condemned!" she said.

"My Lord, the young ones certainly make love different now than they did when *I* was his age. I wonder—" Amory's voice faded musically. "Maybe I better change my style. Would that make any difference, Tiz?"

"I don't know," Tiz said. She was keeping her back to

him and Amory, smiling slightly, waited for the inevitable moment when she would turn to face him. When she did she had the coffeepot in her hand.

"Tiz," Amory said. He got up and came over to her. "Will you put that damned coffeepot down. Every time I get anywhere near you, what happens? That thing's in the way."

"Where—" Tiz said—"where'll I put it?"

Masterfully Amory took the coffeepot out of her loose grip and set it down with a crash on the stove.

"Leave it right there," he said. "For just five minutes."

The knock on the office door made Byron jump a little. Jay straightened up. He had been leaning over By's shoulder looking with weary realization through the valuation book and he welcomed the interruption.

"Come in," he said loudly.

A familiar figure eased through the door and shut it softly to stand there grinning at them.

"Well, well," Jay said. "I've missed you, Arthur."

Arthur Pederson gave him an unabashed grin, revealing that there were no teeth on his upper jaw between the canines.

"Thought you might have," he agreed. "Didn't want to let matters go out of your mind altogether."

"You haven't had an order for two weeks. I didn't know but what you might have got a job." Jay tried his best to look forbidding.

"Judast, Mr. Stone, I ain't been able to eat a bite for two weeks. Had the indigestion something fierce. But I'm getting kind of hungry now. I haven't got a thing in the house to eat. My wife and the kids've been living on baked-up flour and water for the last three days—" Without a break in his voice, Arthur went into his spiel.

"When you going to get pride enough to go to work, not come begging to the town?"

Jay sat down at the typewriter and fed a slip of yellow paper into the rollers. "What d'you need?"

"Everything." Arthur shook his head. "I'm real low on everything."

"Why didn't you help out this last week?" Jay's fingers were busy hunting out the letters for a grocery list. "Everyone else's been working twenty-four hours a day, fighting fire."

"I been working, too," Arthur said brightly. "Twenty-*five* hours a day. Feeling the way I did, I didn't even take time out for lunch."

"You'll get paid for that time." Jay stooped dead in the middle of the list and stared accusingly at Arthur.

"I know," Arthur pointed out reasonably. "But I got to eat till I *do* get paid."

After he had gone triumphantly out with his grocery list, Byron said angrily:

"What do you bother to argue with him for? He's nothing but a deadhead and always will be. You know darn well you've got to give him that list if he asks you for it."

Jay got up to go over to the window and make sure Arthur went to the Red Front and not the quality grocery around the corner.

"I know it," he agreed amicably. "But he likes to feel he's talked me out of something. He hasn't got much to be proud of, By. He likes to feel he can talk me down."

"Pete sake!" Byron said, disgustedly. Jay gave him a quick, curious glance. Byron didn't sound like himself. He sounded like a man looking for trouble and that wasn't like him. Well, Jay shrugged, he was so glad to see rain, he felt too good to fight with By. He looked out the window in

273

time to see Arthur disappear obediently through the door of the Red Front across the street. Glancing a little to the left, Jay saw a thing that nobody had seen on Main Street for ten years or more.

Jonesy Dawes' mother, swathed in a large yellow slicker, black umbrella spread full, market basket over her arm, came tottering briskly up the road and followed Arthur into the store.

Jay gasped and was about to call By's attention to this shattering event when something else happened and took it completely out of his mind. Mike Arey's car rounded the corner on two wheels and screeched to an imperative stop in front of the café. Mike shot out of the car just as Ginny Hanscom came out the big door. They met in the middle of the sidewalk. Fascinated, open mouthed, Jay watched.

"My Lord!" he said. "There's more going on on Main Street than I've seen in years. Wouldn't old Jasper have a conniption fit if he could see that!"

"What?" By snapped. As he came over to the window, Jay remembered something and thought he knew why Byron had been as hard to get along with as a poison pup all morning. Jay had never before been standing beside an angry man who was watching the girl he was supposedly going to marry get treated like that right on a public street. It was an uncomfortable situation. By's face looked like a thunderhead coming up in the north. Jay cleared his throat.

"Ain't you— Well, ain't you going to *do* anything? Ain't you going down there and—?"

"*Ah, shut up!*"

Discreet as always, Jay looked away from By with an effort. But he simply could not pull himself from that window.

"My *Lord!*" he said a minute later. "I don't know as that's quite decent. Maybe *I* ought to do something."

In spite of the rain, Mike and Ginny were beginning to gather an audience, of which they seemed to be oblivious.

Al Cairns thrust his long face, a little redder than usual, out the big door.

"Mike!" he whispered hoarsely. "Hey, *Mike!*"

"Hmmm?" Mike didn't let her go; he simply loosened his arms enough to look past her shoulder.

"You charge twenty-five cents a head," Al said, "you'd get enough out of it to buy a ring."

Mike cast a blank, startled glare at his audience and dived into the car, pulling Ginny after him.

Watching the old Chevy careen off down the street, Al shook his head admiringly.

"First time in my life I was ever right about a woman," he told the world. "I thought it was just the right time, and by the judast, it *was.*"